Kr
stay fabu

# FABULOUS FILTHY FRIEND

## THE FURY FAMILY SERIES
### BOOK 2

## GWYN MCNAMEE

Fabulous Filthy Friend
by
Gwyn McNamee © 2020, © 2023

**Cover Design: Tiffany Black and TE Black Designs**
**Cover Model: Forest Harrison**
**Photographer: Wander Aguiar**
**Editor: Stephie Walls**

# 1

**FLYNN**

S*hit.*

*My dick might have looked better at that other angle.*

The harsh glow from the computer screen and the dim lighting in the bedroom cast strange shadows the way it is now. And the last thing I want is for the main attraction to look anything less than absolutely stellar.

After all, it's what everyone is here for.

The main attraction.

My God-given gift.

That needs to look *perfect.*

I lean forward to reset my laptop back to its original placement. From this position, my cock can really shine in all its glory. The real *star* of HRD4U's website. I initiate the video, stroke my hard length, and comments spring to life on the bottom of the screen, drawing a grin across my lips even though no one watching can see it.

There we go.

That's what I've been looking for.

About time HRD4U.

I feel like we've been waiting for hours.

Have you considered my offer to come take care of that for you?

"Sorry to keep you waiting, ladies...and gentlemen. I had another commitment before I could get online tonight."

A string of hearts and smiley faces appear along the screen—the viewers' responses to my apology. I really do hate to be late for my performance, but Rachel needed me, and I'm a sucker where Rach is concerned.

She needs something...I come running, without a second thought, no matter what I'm in the middle of or what I have scheduled. That's what best friends do. And tonight, she needed her best friend's shoulder to cry on. It didn't matter that it was painful to watch her breakdown over another guy who didn't deserve her anyway; I would never leave her if she needs me—in *any* way.

*Ever.*

But now, it's time to forget her dating woes and to make some other people very happy.

"So, what would you like to see tonight?"

I casually stroke my dick and slide my palm over the head, sending a zing of pleasure straight to my balls. A flurry of comments appears, and I try to read them and keep up while still focusing on the job at hand—or in hand, as it might be.

Of course, this would feel a hell of a lot better if a certain woman's smooth, soft fingers were wrapped around me, if *she* were the one bringing me the ultimate pleasure. Whispering in my ear. Touching me so intimately. Making me come apart.

But that's out of the question.

Not when we've been best friends for so long, and she only sees me like a brother. The good girl from next door can never be anything but that. No matter how much I might wish for it. And fantasize about it.

She will never see this side of me, never know how agonizing it is to see her every day and know I can't have her.

These people who watch are the only ones who will see what happens when I think about being with Rachel. How completely even imagining it overpowers my entire body.

And one part in particular...

> We want to see you come.
>
> Don't tease us, HRD4U.
>
> I want to see more.
>
> I want to see your face. Tilt the camera up.

*Nope.*

That's *never* going to happen.

In the almost year since I started doing the webcam thing, I haven't shown my face or used my unaltered voice, and I don't plan to anytime soon. Likely, never. The anonymity of being HRD4U allows me the freedom to do this and make some extra cash while still being able to show my face at church and Mom's house.

It also gives me an outlet for all the pent-up sexual frustration I have from being around Rach every day and not being able to act on my feelings for her. The truth has sat on the tip of my tongue for so long, it's permanently burned itself there, but each time I've been tempted to tell her I want more, I've swallowed the words down like a lead weight that sits in my gut and leaches poison to my heart.

It's miserable, a constantly, dull ache in the center of my chest that reminds me that even *I* would never be good enough for her. And I won't risk our friendship just because I have a crush.

*Fuck.*

*Who am I kidding?*

It's more than a crush.

I love her.

And I have since the day I looked out my bedroom window and saw her moving into the house next door almost five years ago. Struggling with the boxes from the back of her car, her hair pulled on top of her head in a messy bun. In cut-off jean shorts and a stained pale blue tank top.

She was the most beautiful thing I'd ever seen then.

Still is.

It was the kind of instant attraction reserved for fairy tales and romance novels.

The kind that never happens in real life.

But it became something so much more.

Something deeper.

Something that eats away at my heart and soul every damn day.

Five years of being the "friend." Of going on "dates" that aren't dates. Of listening to her cry and complain about her shitty "boyfriends" when I know I'm the one who understands her and truly *loves* her.

All of her.

And that's precisely what's kept me from pursuing her.

Because she doesn't want a guy like me—who watches porn, who likes rough, filthy sex, who lets strangers watch him walk around naked, and who jerks off to make money.

She'd be sickened if she knew.

My sweet Rachel Fury would never be able to look me in the eye again, let alone want to date me.

So, it's *this* instead of being buried inside the woman I love.

My hand and an internet full of women—and men—who are willing to pay to watch me stroke myself.

It's a fantasy world I've created out of necessity.

Freedom from the financial, personal, and spiritual pressures crushing me every day.

When I'm like this, I am HRD4U—naked hunk with a magnificent cock. I can't be Flynn McAllister, mild-mannered stockbroker and financial consultant, and do these things. Flynn would think about what he's doing too much. Flynn would dwell on it. Flynn would let the Catholic guilt that's been driven into him since birth eat away at him until he gave himself ulcers.

Which is why I'm HRD4U and try to push all of Flynn to the background during my shows—except his best friend. I can't get her out of my head for *any* amount of time, and certainly not when I'm hard and need inspiration for my shows.

I stroke my dick harder and faster, twisting my wrist with each upward movement to create the perfect friction along my length. "You beautiful people want to see me come?"

A stampede of smiley faces, thumbs-ups, high-fives, and hearts hit the screen.

> Yes HRD4U!
>
> Give it to us!
>
> We want to see it!
>
> I wish I was there!

I relax back across my bed, close my eyes, and conjure a vision of Rachel leaning over me, her cascade of caramel hair creating a curtain around my face as her lips find mine and she lowers herself onto my dick. Hot and wet. She engulfs my entire length, and her tongue slips into my mouth so I can taste her for the first time.

*Fuck.*

The sweet glide of our sweat-slickened skin against each other. The lash of our tongues tangling. The moans and pants. The whispered "I love yous" breathed out into the room.

"Fuck! Yes! Ride my cock, baby." My breath catches as the slow tingle starts at the base of my spine. "Take me hard. Make me come in your sweet cunt."

The dirty talk always does it for me...and the viewers. It's become a staple of my performances as much as it has been in my bedroom since I fucked my high school girlfriend and the words just slipped out.

Another reason Rach and I can never happen. As soon as I open my mouth, she'll go running for the hills. It isn't the kind of stuff you say to a kindergarten teacher while buried inside her...

The woman of my fantasies rolls her hips, grinding down on me, and mine bow up to meet hers.

"Fuck, yes. Squeeze me with your pussy. I want to feel you come for me, baby."

Dream Rachel clamps down on me, and rides me even harder, seeking her own pleasure as mine finally builds until I can't contain it any longer.

My orgasm slams into me—a tsunami of pleasure and pent-up emotion after spending hours with her earlier. Surrounded by her scent. Enticed by her soft, light touches. Tortured by the tight embraces. Seduced by the easy laughs. Angered by the tears over yet another douchebag.

I shoot my load up across my abs and chest then lie panting for a few moments, trying to blink away the spots dancing across my vision and regain my breath before I look at the computer screen.

> Jesus Christ!
>
> That was hot!
>
> HRD4U THANK YOU!
>
> Oh my God my ovaries just exploded.
>
> SO FUCKING HOT!
>
> What I wouldn't give to have that big thick cock inside me right now. Are you single? I can be over there in five minutes.

I chuckle lightly and lean forward, giving the viewers a show of my cum, spread out and glistening across my skin.

"I *am* single, but I don't get involved with any of my viewers." Which is why I rarely even bother to read the private messages sent to me through the site. After a quick glance, they all end up in the trash bin. One can only reply *no* to so many propositions before it becomes a tedious, annoying time suck. They'll have to settle for me in virtual form. "I'm thinking about making pancakes in the morning. Check back in with me or sign up for alerts for when I go live if you want to watch. Have a good night."

Mine is about to end with me passing the fuck out.

I click off the recording and drop back down onto the mattress with a groan. That floaty, post-orgasmic haze still envelops me, and I linger in it for a few moments because I know it won't last.

It never does.

I should probably feel like a whore for selling my body like this, letting people watch me jerk off, letting them ogle

7

me walk around my house doing things naked with a hard-on.

But I don't.

At least, not when I'm HRD4U. When I'm Flynn, when I log off the site, when the real world encroaches on the persona I've created, *that's* when things get a lot more complicated for me.

Which is why I'll stay like this a few more minutes. Until the evidence of what I just did chills. I'll remind myself of why what I'm doing is okay.

It's a bodily function, something we've all done. And for me, it's a way to make up for the money I lost in the market crash. It's just a part of life. So is suffering with the knowledge that I'll never have Rachel as my own.

They're realities I have to do and learn to live with. But things could be worse. I could still be struggling to pay my mortgage, and Rach could have moved in to some other house all those years ago instead of twenty feet away from my front door in Redondo Beach.

Having her so close might be torture, but losing her would be worse.

Such is my daily agony.

One I'll start all over again tomorrow.

———

**RACHEL**

My phone buzzes on the nightstand, drawing my attention away from the display on my computer screen. The *very* graphic, *very* hot display from the *very* interesting website I just discovered while scouring the internet for some good material...and immediately subscribed to.

*Who could be calling at this hour?*

8

I reach over, check it, and accept the call because if I don't she's liable to run across the street to make sure I didn't fall down the stairs and break my neck. "Hey, what's up?"

Such crappy timing...right when I discovered HRD4U.com and had a mind-blowing orgasm while watching him work himself over.

Alicia fumbles her phone slightly. "Nothing, what are you doing?"

My eyes drift over to my screen, and I tug the comforter up and over me. "Nothing."

*At least, nothing I'm going to admit to.*

What I do in the privacy of my bedroom isn't any of Alicia's business, even though she thinks it is and I usually end up telling her about it, anyway.

That's the problem with best friends; they tend to know *everything* about you, whether you want them to or not. There's only one thing I've managed to keep secret from Alicia and Flynn, and it's *not* something I plan on revealing —ever.

Something crashes in the background behind Alicia, and she covers the phone. Muffled yelling—probably at Cade—follows, but she returns with an exasperated sigh. "Are you still wallowing?"

I scoff and roll my eyes, even though she can't see me. "I was never wallowing."

*Lie.*

She snickers, and Cade says something to her in the background, only the lilt of his Australian accent discernable. "Bullshit. At lunch today, you barely ate two bites, and you looked like you hadn't slept in days. He's not worth it. That dude was never going to be your happily ever after, and you knew it deep down. It was only two months. It's not like you were with the guy for two years."

"I know." Two months is nothing in the grand scheme of

9

things, and I shouldn't be so distressed by the breakup. But logically *shouldn't be* doesn't mean I'm *actually not.* "It still sucks, though."

Alicia offers a sympathetic sound. "Yeah, it does. Breakups *always* suck. But Cade agrees with me—you need to move on and not think about that d-bag. I assume you've been wallowing *all* day after I tried to cheer you up with nachos and beer?"

*Dammit.*

She knows me too well. And I hate that. But the truth is, I *would* have wallowed all day had I not called Flynn and asked him to come keep me company.

"No. Flynn came over when I got home from lunch."

Alicia releases a deep, exaggerated sigh, and I can picture her rolling her big blue eyes at me. "Of course, he did."

I clench my jaw and push myself up until I'm sitting against the headboard. "What's that supposed to mean?"

"You know exactly what it means. Rachel, you can't have a best friend who's a guy and expect the guys you're dating not to have an issue with it."

*Ugh.*

I do *not* want to have this argument with her again. For the one-millionth time. I guess it's not really an *argument,* per se, more like a disagreement over the realities of my situation. Alicia means well, and I always appreciate her blunt form of honesty in my life, but I'm sick of justifying it to her—amongst other people. "Flynn and I are just friends."

"That may just be what you tell yourself, or it may be true. Either way, Flynn is hot. Like, *really* fucking hot. And that's intimidating to any guy you're dating to know you spend that much time with the guy who lives right next door."

"She's right, Rach. Flynn is *really fucking hot!*" Cade's humor reaches me through the line.

I laugh despite my annoyance. It's hard to ever be mad at him. "Do you *have* to talk about stuff like this on the phone with him in the room?"

Alicia laughs. "No, we could come over and do it there instead in person."

"Ha. Ha. Very funny." Though, it's a threat they might actually fulfill if it weren't after ten and Connor and Brandy weren't asleep.

Sometimes becoming best friends with your neighbors has drawbacks. Like their ability to literally cross the street to harass you about imagined romances that don't exist. Or like having them state the obvious.

I don't need Alicia to tell me how gorgeous Flynn is. I would have to have been blind not to notice it the second he walked out of his front door and across the grass toward me the day I moved in. But I had just lost Mom and wasn't in any place to see anyone as anything other than a friend, and it was quickly apparent that Flynn is way too much of a Catholic school mama's boy to handle me.

If I told him I watch porn and masturbate almost daily, like to be spanked, and all that other stuff I fantasize about in the bedroom, he'd probably turn beet red and bolt for the confessional booth with a prayer for my soul coming from his lips.

Not that I don't appreciate his concern for the eternal well-being of my soul, but that kind of religious commitment isn't something I ever understood. Not with the way we grew up.

Dad was always on the road during the season, and he was mean and cold when he was home. Mom wasn't the type to find solace in organized religion the way Flynn does. His weekly Sunday morning trips to church with his mom only confirm what I've always known about Flynn—he's too much of a gentleman for it to ever work out in the end.

He may be beautiful, but all I'll ever do is admire him as a platonic friend and cry on his shoulder when yet another failed relationship breaks my heart. Because one thing Flynn is incredibly good at is taking my mind off the bad stuff in life.

Things are simple and easy with him.

That's the way I want it to stay.

Alicia may not know about my secret predilections, but I've made myself clear that Flynn is a close friend, nothing more. Though it seems she needs another reminder tonight.

"Nothing is happening between Flynn and me, Alicia. You know that."

"Whatever you say, girl. If you're not gonna go for that, can I set him up with someone?"

I bite back my first inclination to tell her to shut up.

He's not mine to claim.

I know that, logically.

Yet, the idea of him with other women still makes me...

*Jealous maybe?*

It's a feeling I hate and don't want to even consider. Flynn deserves to be happy, and if I thought Alicia could find that for him, I would agree to a set-up in a heartbeat—at least, that's what I tell myself. But for some reason, when I think of Alicia's friends who I've met since she and Cade moved in with the kids, no one measures up to what my bestie deserves.

Because he deserves the *world*.

Someone who will appreciate what a caring, giving, kind, and gentle soul he has. And I'll protect him from any woman getting her claws in him if she's not right for him. Kind of like he does for me with the men I date.

He warned me Sam wasn't good for me, but I didn't

listen. I fell for the charm and quick smile and ignored the warning signs. Things were good between us but never *great*. I never had that *need*...that draw to him I've always expected to have for the one I'm meant to spend the rest of my life with.

Maybe I was stupid to think that giving it longer, giving it a chance, would change that. That I would *develop* those feelings. It never happened, and Flynn saw from day one that it never would. Yet even though Flynn was right, he never brought out the "I told you so." Instead, he came over with a bag full of sugary theater snacks and hung out to watch a movie.

I cried a little more than I should have given the lack of connection I actually had with Sam. But then Flynn wrapped his arm around my shoulder, and any bad feelings I had lingering simply disappeared.

He always manages to make me feel better even in the shittiest of circumstances. And he wouldn't leave until I assured him I was okay, which I mostly was. But a little sexual release always makes things easier to deal with. Hence, the sexy display I've now almost totally missed because of Alicia's call.

"Hello? Rach? You still there?"

"What? Oh, yeah. Sorry. Here."

"So, can I set him up with someone?"

"How did we go from you calling to check on me to you setting up Flynn?"

She chuckles. "Is that a no?"

I chew on my bottom lip for a second. "If I can meet the girl first and screen her, then...maybe." It's time to stop being selfish with my BFF. There might be someone out there for Flynn who shares his values and won't scandalize him behind closed doors.

13

"Woot! I'll take that as a win. So, what are you doing now?"

"I already told you. Nothing."

*Another lie.*

With my B.O.B. between my legs on the bedspread and the internet browser open to HRD4U, I had been doing anything but nothing prior to her call. "I'm probably going to sleep soon."

"Why don't you come over and have a drink with Cade and me? The kids have been down for hours."

"Nah." It always seems a little strange to be hanging out, drinking with Alicia and Cade now that little Connor is in my kindergarten class. Kind of unprofessional and forbidden, though they've never seemed to care.

"But it's Saturday, and I spent the whole day with the kids. I need some adult time."

"I know what day it is, Alicia. I'm just not up for it tonight. Go have some *adult* time with Cade. I'm sure he won't say no to that."

"True. He won't." The smile is evident in her voice. "Well, don't wallow for too long. I don't want to have to use my key to come drag you out of that house. He's not worth your misery, Rach. You have to stop dating these guys you know are never going to last long."

*She's right.*

There are only so many times I can fake it through another boring round of sex with a guy and pretend I'm having a great time and that I came. All these nice guys, the ones Mom and Dad and Bash and Jameson would want me to be with, the guys I *should* want to be with, are precisely the ones who bore me to death in bed, which is why I'm not going to risk anything with Flynn.

No, my best friend, the handsome stockbroker from next door, will have to remain only those things, and I'll spend more time with my B.O.B. and HRD4U. I just wish he didn't use that damn voice distortion and hide his face.

The man is an Adonis.

I need to see more and hear that dirty mouth say those filthy words without the electronic interference...or my good friend talking in my ear.

"I gotta go, Alicia."

"Whatever, enjoy your date with B.O.B."

*Smartass.*

I drop my phone onto the nightstand and return my attention to the computer screen.

My wallowing days are over.

# 2

FLYNN

Water trickles down my chest and disappears beneath the towel wrapped around my waist. I didn't bother fully drying off after my shower —being wet is only an added benefit to my subscribers. One of the things that drives them absolutely wild, and I love knowing I'm making their days better.

I head toward the kitchen with my laptop in my left hand, prepared to fire up a new live as soon as I settle in. The viewers on the HRD4U site love watching me perform menial, everyday tasks like cooking or cleaning...as long as I do them naked with an erection.

Which isn't difficult.

I've never had a problem getting it up and keeping it there, not with as often as I think about Rachel.

Since I've continued the Sunday morning pre-church pancake tradition Mom and Dad started when I was a kid, I might as well combine the two and give my subscribers some early morning entertainment. Nothing like cracking eggs and whisking batter with a boner to get them worked up and totally make their day.

My foot barely crosses from the living room into the kitchen when the front door flies open and slams back against the stopper.

*Crap.*

"Oh, good! You're up." Rachel sails in with that caramel hair streaming behind her, a grin on her face, and her attention focused on the two massive coffee mugs balanced precariously in one hand while she slips the key into her pocket with the other. She kicks the door closed behind her with one foot. "I made you a latte. I still don't understand why you didn't get the machine that makes the specialty drinks. Seems like such a waste to have one that only makes *normal* coffee. Blech."

*So much for making naked pancakes today.*

Maybe giving Rach a key was a bad idea—especially since I apparently can't even hear her putting it in the lock.

*A little warning would be nice.*

She hasn't walked in on me doing one of my performances, but if she had come another minute or two later this morning, it would be a hard one to explain.

*Literally.*

The viewers will just have to wait for another show. Rach cock-blocked them without even knowing it. But seeing her instantly puts me in a better mood.

I grin, watching her struggle to keep the mugs level. "Because *you* have one. Why would I need to spend the money?"

Her green eyes dart up and land on me, and she freezes mid-step, coffee held out to me. Her gaze trails up and down my wet body, and I bite back a chuckle. At least it's good to know she appreciates how hard I work in the gym to keep this body, even if she'll never get to experience it.

I set the laptop onto the counter and take one of the mugs from her outstretched hand. "Thank you." I glance down at myself. Walking around the house almost naked is usually reserved for times I know I'll be alone...or with my online friends only. "Sorry, I wasn't expecting you so early."

Rachel isn't exactly a *morning* person. I don't know how she manages to make it to school by seven every morning to deal with all those kids. Seriously, kindergarten teachers are saints. And when she's not forced from under the covers at the ass-crack of dawn, she usually sleeps until at least nine on the weekends, so being up and going this early is definitely unusual.

And the way she's practically vibrating suggests she's already had at least one latte.

*What got her up so early?*

She shakes her head and seems to snap out of whatever trance she's in.

It's too bad I caught the flash of attraction there because if I hadn't, it might make it a little bit easier to accept the fact that I can never have her. I'm old and wise enough to know attraction isn't enough. And it's not worth the possible fallout.

I run my free hand back through my wet hair. "I was just going to make pancakes. Want some?"

She licks her plump, pink lips and nods slowly, her eyes glazing over slightly. "Yes, I definitely want some."

*Was that a reference to me or the pancakes?*

My body can't seem to tell, and something stirs between my legs that will make things very uncomfortable between us if she notices.

*Stop, Flynn.*

*She's talking about the pancakes.*

*Don't read into her comment.*

I narrow my eyes on her as I take a sip of the latte.

French Vanilla. My favorite. Of course, she knows that. She knows everything about me. Well...except for what I do online and that I'm a closeted freak in bed.

*Awkward.*

"I'm going to put on some clothes." It's the only way to remove myself from temptation and to keep the ever-growing hard-on I have from springing out from the towel to say good morning to her. "If you want to start mixing the batter, you know where everything is."

She winks at me and leans up to press a chaste kiss on my cheek. "I sure do."

I crane my neck and watch that beautiful ass sway on her walk over to the kitchen.

*Goddammit.*

Yoga pants should be illegal. They're one giant cocktease —especially on *that* woman.

She reaches up to grab a mixing bowl from the top shelf, but her fingers barely brush it. "Ugh, being short sucks. Why did Bash and Jameson get my dad's height and not me?"

"I'll help you with that." I set the mug onto the kitchen island on my way over and move to stand behind her.

The bowl that's just out of her reach is well within mine. My chest presses against her shoulders, and a barely audible whimper slips from her as I reach around her to set the bowl on the counter. "Here you go."

I step back, and she turns to face me with her bottom lip pulled between her teeth.

*Sweet holy hell...*

"Thanks, Flynn."

"I'm gonna go change now." I practically race down the hallway to my bedroom while pressing my cock down with one hand.

*Down, boy. Not her. Not ever.*

I tug on a pair of jeans because the gray sweatpants I normally wear around the house will only emphasize my massive dick and what she does to it. With any other girl, I might try to advertise what I'm packing, but with Rach, it just feels dirty.

Wrong.

Abhorrent.

So do all the things I want to do to and with her.

Maybe a hypnotist could do something to my brain to get me to be able to forget how I feel about her. God knows I've tried everything else. Even praying to the big man upstairs for help and guidance, a way to move on. One hasn't presented itself yet, though. Or if it has, I've been too busy looking at Rachel's ass in her tight spandex pants to notice it.

I tug a T-shirt on over my head and quickly run the towel over my hair one more time before I wander back out to the kitchen.

Powdered pancake mix floats through the air like dust and covers my counters. Smudges of the wet, sticky batter mar Rachel's perfect cheekbones and forehead.

The laugh that erupts from my chest booms around the room, making her jerk her head up to look at me. "How the hell did you make such a mess in two minutes?"

She lifts her slim shoulders and lets them fall while whisking the bowl in front of her. "The bag just exploded?"

"Exploded?" I walk over and find the bag of pancake mix ripped to shreds. "It looks like a chupacabra got this."

She tosses her head back with a ringing laugh that echoes in my ears and has my already-straining cock pushing against my zipper even more. "A chupacabra? I like that." She grins. "You know"—she elbows me playfully in the stomach—"you're funny when you want to be, McAllister."

And I always seem to want to be when I'm with her.

Mostly because that laugh is always like a jolt to my system. What I imagine a line of cocaine hitting my bloodstream would feel like. A rush of pure joy and adrenaline.

She's like a drug to me, only without the negative side effects. Except for the fact that I'm alone because I can't imagine being with anyone but her...and she's off-limits.

And the longer we live next to each other and the closer friends we've become, the harder it is to keep going on like everything is normal. When she first arrived, I was still able to date and have a good time with other women. But the more I got to know Rachel, the less enticing other women became until I had stopped actively pursuing anything.

It's pathetic.

It's wrong.

It's unhealthy.

I'm self-aware enough to know all these things, yet my heart won't let me open it to anyone else when I see the perfect woman almost every day.

And I need to break myself of this obsession before I say or do something that crosses a line with her and drives her away. She can't see how she affects me. That would be like a neon sign screaming *Flynn is in love with you! Flynn is in love with you!*

So instead of kissing that enticing smile from her lips, I force myself to grin at her and contemplate how to rescue the bowl before she causes even more of a disaster. "Yeah, I have my moments."

———

## RACHEL

He has more than his moments.

Flynn is hilarious, and he knows it. The self-deprecating humor is classic for him, though. He always leaves me smiling and laughing even when I feel like shit, which is exactly how we became such fast friends.

I needed that when I moved here, having just lost Mom, and I still do. Someone who can always make me happy even in my darkest times.

Her death left a gaping hole in my heart that may never heal, one that was ripped open again with Dad's recent death and dealing with Bash and Jameson's bullshit through it all. Though, having Flynn around has helped the edges of that hole scar up a little. I'm not sure I would have made it through the last few months without him. So much of what makes Flynn a great person is what his parents instilled in him—respect for others, faith in humanity, and a caring nature that oozes from every pore.

After my call with Alicia last night—and once I had finished watching HRD4U's performance and myself—I couldn't help wondering if the solace he finds in church is something I shouldn't be so quick to dismiss. Maybe there's something to it I've been ignoring without really experiencing it myself.

I stir the batter, sending more splashing over the rim. In all the years we've been friends, I've never actually gone to Mass with him and his mom, only met them for coffee and breakfast a few times after. But it could be time to try something different. "Are you heading to church later?"

He nods, leans in, and tugs the bowl from me. "You can't be trusted with this."

I drop open my jaw in mock annoyance.

He flashes me his patented grin, his grayish-blue eyes

glinting. The muscles on his bicep flex and pull against the fabric of his T-shirt as he whisks the batter. "Yeah, we're going to eleven o'clock Mass. Mom had something going on this morning beforehand."

"Is it okay if I come with you?"

The question surprises even me, despite having been thinking about it since last night. I can't remember the last time I was in a church, let alone willingly. Even for Mom's and Dad's funerals, we had simple viewings at the funeral home, nothing religious. But for some reason, it seems like the right place to be this morning. Probably more because of the company than the location.

He turns his head and examines me for a minute like he doesn't recognize who he's looking at. Then slowly, a grin pulls at his lips. "Of course. You know my mom loves you."

"And I her." That gaping hole might never completely go away, but Emily McAllister has sure helped ease some of the pain there as much as Flynn has.

I can see where Flynn gets it from—his kindness, his good heart, his sense of humor, even his good looks. Niall McAllister was nothing to sneeze at either based on the pictures I've seen of him, but Emily is drop-dead gorgeous— striking sandy-blond hair, a shade lighter than Flynn's and gray-blue eyes, he inherited from her. I wish I'd gotten a chance to meet his dad, but he died when Flynn was young. That's part of why he simply *got it* when I told him I had recently lost Mom. He understood the loss, the anguish, the desire to hide away and forget the world. But he didn't let me. His forcing me to stay active, to go out with him, to do *something*, even if it was simply watching a movie, really helped me get through the worst. First, when I moved here, and then again, when Dad died.

Flynn's a mama's boy through and through. And that's a huge compliment.

He knows how to treat the women in his life, which is one reason I'm so protective of him when Alicia tries to set him up. He's a real catch. Any woman would be lucky to have him as a boyfriend or husband.

It's too bad mama's boys don't do it for me. I'll just have to continue the hunt for a guy with a heart of gold who's also filthy in the bedroom.

He watches me from the corner of his eye. "Don't take this the wrong way, Rach, you're more than welcome, but why do you want to come to church?"

It's a fair question. But I'm not sure the answer is so simple. "After our talk yesterday and then one I had with Alicia last night, I decided I wasn't going to wallow anymore. There have been too many bad things in my life recently. Things I let throw me off my game and get me off course. I'm ready to get back on a good one."

A tiny smile plays at his lips. "And this new course involves finding religion?"

I bark out a laugh. "Doubtful, but you always seem to really feel centered and calm after Sunday Mass and coffee with your mom. I just think maybe it would be nice to join. Kind of a fresh start."

He considers my answer for a moment. "I'm glad you're not letting that d-bag get to you anymore."

"Nope." I nod toward the stove behind us. "I got the griddle heating."

"Great, we should be all set." He turns away and sets the bowl next to the stove. "I assume you want chocolate chips?"

"Hell yeah!" My sweet tooth is aching for something.

He wanders over to the pantry and returns with a bag of chocolate chips while I climb up onto a stool at his island and let my eyes rake over my best friend.

I really don't know what I would've done if he hadn't lived next door. It was a horrible time. I was such a mess back then, trying to make it through the day, feeling like I had lost my best friend because Mom was just that. She was the one I ran to when I needed comfort and reassurance. The one who gave me the best advice. Then, she was just... gone. I had Bash and Jameson, but they had their own lives across the country, and my rocky relationship with Dad wasn't anything to lean on.

But Flynn saw my distress, the hole in my life, and he filled it.

*I should thank him for that someday.*

He would never expect a thank you. He's just being Flynn. But I owe him a huge one.

His long arm stretches up to grab plates from the cabinet next to the stove. Every movement sends the muscles under his thin T-shirt rippling and that beautiful hard ass of his flexing in his jeans.

Alicia definitely didn't need to remind me how hot he is. But now that she has, it's like it's been intensified by a hundred. Walking in on him wet and almost naked certainly didn't help.

*Why are the things that would be so wrong for you always the most attractive?*

It's like raccoons. They are so cute and cuddly looking... until they infect you with rabies. Not that I'm comparing Flynn to rabies but getting involved with someone I know can't fulfill my needs is almost as bad. Kind of. It would definitely kill our friendship.

Flynn glances at me over his shoulder. "Did you do anything last night after I left?"

A hot flush spreads up my neck and across my cheeks. There's no way he doesn't notice it, either. Flynn notices everything.

I vigorously shake my head. "Nope. Nothing."

*Just watched HRD4U jerk off while I had a date with B.O.B.*

But he doesn't need to know that.

He'd be appalled if he knew what I did, or how badly I want to know who HRD4U really is. The voice distortion he uses to conceal his identity and the fact that he never shows his face means that'll probably never happen, but a girl can dream.

And I did last night. About his filthy talking and his big cock and all the wonderful things we could do with some time together—all hypothetically, of course. I would never meet up with a porn star from the internet. I'm not that stupid, nor am I going to risk my job by getting involved with someone like that. I can't even imagine what Principal Klister would say if he ever got wind of it.

Flynn turns around and sets a plate with three pancakes piled high in front of me, then he spins to the fridge and returns with a stick of butter on a small tray.

I lick my lips, cut off a slice of butter, and slather it on my pancakes. "Maple syrup?"

His eyebrows shoot up. "Those things already have so much goddamn sugar in them; your body can't possibly process all that properly."

I chuckle and shrug. "Still want maple syrup."

He sighs and turns back to the fridge. When he returns, a bottle of Wisconsin's best natural maple syrup sits in his hand.

I grin and grab it from him. Growing up in Michigan, we always had this on hand. Mom insisted it was the best despite having access to local syrup. "Only the good shit, huh?"

He chuckles and turns back to the stove to start his pancakes. "You know me, only the good stuff, babe."

*Babe.*

I love it when he calls me *babe*. What should be a demeaning and masochistic term is so different coming

27

from Flynn's lips. My damn heart melts. It's endearing and adorable, and completely not meant in a negative way at all.

*Why can't I find someone as nice and as good-looking as Flynn but as filthy as dirt? Is that really so much to ask?*

It's really too bad Flynn's strict Catholic upbringing has made him so sexually repressed and shy. The man never discusses sex, like it's not even on his radar. And I can't even remember the last time Flynn went on a date or I saw a woman over here. It had to have been over a year ago.

*Such a damn waste.*

I pour the syrup all over my pancakes, grab the silverware, and dig in. A moan slips from my mouth at the first bite.

Flynn freezes at the stove and looks over his shoulder at me. "Good?"

"Impeccable."

Him *and* the pancakes.

# 3

FLYNN

Kneeling between Mom and Rachel, while staring up at Jesus on the crucifix, hanging over the altar, has a ten-thousand-pound rock of shame and regret sitting in my stomach and makes my skin crawl. I reach over and scratch at my arm like some sort of addict who needs a fix, but it does nothing to quell the feeling growing inside me.

His eyes seem to see right through me.

They watch me as I shift uncomfortably under his assessment.

It's like He knows what I do, what I did just last night.

It's like He can see the dirtiness marring my skin—the sin blackening my soul.

I always knew the Catholic guilt had been driven into me hard my entire life. Twelve years of Catholic school and Mass at least twice a week will do that. But until this moment, I didn't *really*, *truly* feel it.

Maybe because I've avoided thinking about what I do while I've been in this building. It has been easy to try to push it to the side when it's Mom and me. I focus on her. On praying for her to find happiness again. Praying for her health. Praying for her to have everything she ever wants or needs to live a fulfilling life. I rarely pray for myself. The only thing I need is the woman kneeling next to me, and there's nothing God can do to help me in that department. Even praying for help moving on hasn't done shit.

Having Mom on one side, Rachel on the other, her elbow brushing against mine every few minutes, her lyrical, beautiful voice singing along with the choir, has the guilt I've managed to keep at bay for so damn long clawing at me.

*I should be sitting in the confessional for the rest of my life.*

Father Lafayette says something that doesn't even register, and the congregation rises. I can't drag my eyes away from the crucifix, though. The cold, hard, brown, glossy painted eyes never leave mine. Judging me. Stripping me as bare as I was on screen last night.

*Stop looking at me like that.*

Now, I'm actually going crazy. Talking to a damn statue like it's a real person instead of an inanimate object designed to do exactly what it's doing to me.

Rach nudges my ribs, and I scramble to my feet while Father Lafayette drones on, his prayer nothing more than a senseless jumble. I focus on him, though, trying to pick out anything that sounds like recognizable syllables that might form actual words my brain can process.

Perhaps he has some wisdom to bestow on me. Something that will help me sort through the quagmire I'm suddenly drowning in here.

*I really messed this up.*

Having Rachel come with me was a bad idea. I should have anticipated this. Seen it coming. I should have known the weight of what I've been doing would eventually come crashing down on me. I just never suspected it would be because the two women I love are bracketing me in the house of God.

I can't possibly ever get clean again after everything I've done. And I can't come clean to the women in my life either. Rachel would be disgusted. Mom would disown me if she knew. She'd ask herself where she went wrong. Where her perfect, sweet, innocent son has gone. Why I would resort to something so abhorrent.

Mom won't understand. It's not only about the money. It's the freedom to be everything I want to be. The ability to be *someone* else. Someone who doesn't feel the guilt. Someone who doesn't love Rachel when he can't have her. HRD4U *has* Rachel every single time he performs.

But there's no way to erase what I've done. I can't go back.

*Can I? Is it possible?*

I mean, what I'm doing is natural, a part of life. I'm just letting people watch.

*What's so bad about that?*

The man on the cross stares down at me again as if to say, *"You've got to be fucking kidding me with that question."* My eyes meet his again, and I shudder.

*You know what's so bad, Flynn.*

People begin filing out of the pews. I hadn't even realized the service had ended.

*Thank you, God!*

The massive church suddenly feels like a damn coffin. Lid closed. Nails driven in. No oxygen. No light. No escape.

I push past Mom, rush down the aisle, and fly down the steps out into the crisp, fresh air. Gulping at it desperately, I shove my hands through my hair and tug at the ends, the sharp bite of pain to my scalp a welcome change from the agony ripping me apart inside.

A small hand finds my arm, and I jump and whirl around.

"Flynn, are you all right?" Rach's voice can't hide her concern. Neither can her soft, caring eyes peering up at me.

I shake off her touch, turn away, and scrub my hands over my face.

*Not at fucking all.*

But there's no way to explain it to her. Not that she'd understand. And if I say I'm not okay, she's going to poke and prod until I tell her *something*. Then, she'll see through the lie and dig and dig until I come clean. *So*, I suck in one last fortifying breath, steel my features, and turn to look at her. Hurt and bewilderment cross her lovely face.

*Shit.*

My heart aches, and that rock of guilt rolls in my stomach again, heavier now. I shouldn't have shoved her hand off like that. She was just trying to make sure I was all right. It's not her fault I'm a fucking mess.

Her bottom lip quivers slightly. "Are you okay?"

"I'm fine. Just got a little claustrophobic and hot in there. That's all."

She offers a slow nod and chews on her bottom lip—a sure sign she's not buying my story—but she lets my lie slide. "Your mom wants to go grab coffee. You up for it?"

"Sure."

*Not really, but I can't blow off Mom.*

Rachel steps forward and loops her arm through mine for the walk down the street to my car. "You sure you're okay?"

I thought I was getting good at covering my true feelings around Rachel, but she sees right through my shit as if she's inside my head. Every damn time. "Yeah, I'm really busy at work and dealing with some stuff there, and it all kinda caught up with me during Mass."

It isn't a total lie. Work is the main reason I became HRD4U in the first place. The market crash a year ago practically wiped me out, and it decimated several of my largest clients who fled with their tails tucked between their legs. For someone who works on commission, it was catastrophic.

That left me scrambling to cover my mortgage, car, and student loan payments, even though I never really thought I was living above my means. HRD4U was supposed to be a quick, easy way to get caught up. I had no idea it would become this huge or that I'd enjoy it so much. That it would become a release I needed almost as much as I need Rach in my life.

Her head drops against my shoulder as we walk. "Well, you know you can talk to me about anything that's bothering you, right?"

"Yeah, right."

*What about if what's been bothering me is my unrequited love for you?*

There have been so many times I've been tempted to say just that, to blurt out how I truly feel, but I've always managed to rein myself in. If those words ever left my lips, if she ever knew how I felt, and if I lost her because of it, I would *be* lost. And no amount of religion would ever help me be *found* again.

As much as I may want her in my bed, I need her in my life more.

But she means well, and the pain in her voice, probably thinking I don't feel like I can talk to her, makes that ache in my chest actually sting. "I know I can."

"Just like you listened to me whine and complain about my breakup, you can complain about whatever is bothering you."

I chuckle. Helping Rachel through her breakups has to

be my *least* favorite friend job. Listening to how those guys treated her, like she was expendable and low on their list of priorities, makes my blood boil, but I'll do it every damn time if she needs me there. Alicia does a lot for her, too, but when Rach needs a shoulder to cry on and someone to have a deep, emotional chat with, she always seems to end up on my doorstep.

My car comes into view, and I pat her arm. "I do appreciate it, really."

I stop next to my car, and she leans up to press a kiss to my cheek. My face tingles, and heat spreads through my body at the contact.

All I want is to drag her against me and turn my head to press my lips to hers, but instead, I suck in a deep breath and let her slide down and walk around to the passenger side.

She flashes me a smile and tugs open her door. "We better get going to meet your mom."

"Yeah, we better get going."

And I better look up the confession schedule.

———

RACHEL

"And then he whipped off his diaper full of poo and came running at me screaming, 'Poo-poo, poo-poo' while he flung it all over the room. His little wienie was dangling and flopping around. Oh, my God. I laughed so hard..." Emily laughs and shakes her head.

I practically choke on the coffee I just took a sip of and have to smack my chest to get it down my throat rather than spew it all across the table.

*Oh, my God!*

Once I manage to swallow my coffee, the laughter bubbles up, and I drop my head back against the top of the red-vinyl booth and let it flow so obnoxiously, the table next to us glares.

They can chill.

It's a loud diner on a Sunday after church, not a five-star restaurant on a Saturday night. Their kids are making more noise than I am. And this story deserves a full-on meltdown type laugh.

I shake my head and swipe at the laugh-tears forming in my eyes. "That's the most adorable thing I've ever heard."

Picturing little baby Flynn running around like that…so damn cute. I grab his arm and squeeze it, and he groans and sinks next to me on the bench of our booth. If he had a hat, he would probably tug the brim over his face to hide the red blush across his cheeks.

"Seriously, Mom, do we have to tell these poop stories?"

*Yes, yes, we do. We absolutely do.*

If Mom were here, she would probably be jumping in with similar embarrassing anecdotes about Bash, Jameson, and me, too. It's such a "mom" thing to do, and it makes me miss her even more. This entire line of conversation has totally made my day. I can't remember the last time I laughed this hard. And I really needed it.

As much as I want to insist on not wallowing, another breakup feels like another step back from finding the future I really want. And if I take any more in the wrong direction, I don't know if I'll ever regain the way forward. I'll spend the rest of my life being Alicia and Cade's third wheel and then Flynn's when he finally finds his perfect person.

Emily laughs and holds up her hands in surrender. "All right, all right. No more poop stories."

Flynn narrows his eyes at her. "No more stories. *Period.*

Right, Mom? Rachel has heard enough about my childhood for one day."

The strain in his voice has me smothering my laugh with my hand. I shouldn't be laughing so hard at his expense but come on...that's hilarious.

He turns his head to glare at me, his gray-blue eyes flashing with annoyance. Flynn's obvious distress sobers me quickly, though, and I remove my hand and take another sip of my coffee.

Kids really do the funniest things, and baby Flynn must have been precious. I definitely need to ask Emily to bring some pictures next time.

Flynn turns back to his mom and gives her a pointed look. "Mom, Rachel doesn't need to know this stuff. Really."

I elbow him in the ribs. "Maybe I don't *need* to, but that doesn't mean I don't *want* to."

The corner of his mouth tips up into a smile that he's definitely fighting. It's good to know he can still joke around and be playful even when he's annoyed with his mom and likely me for ganging up on him.

I wink at him. "It's always good to have blackmail material on your best friend."

His smile only grows, and he shrugs. "I guess I'm fucked, then."

Emily's eyes widen, and her mouth drops open. "Flynn Joseph McAllister! Language!"

He scoffs and holds up his hands as another laugh bursts from my chest. "Sorry, Mom."

She *tsks* under her breath, then leans forward to place her elbows on the table and rests her face in her palms. Her eyes—so similar to her son's—dart between us. "You two have been best friends for a long time."

Flynn shifts and glances out the window to his right, though there doesn't appear to be anything that interesting out there, just Sunday morning traffic winding lazily through town. "What's your point, Mom?"

"Well, are you ever going to be more than friends?"

He stiffens next to me. I'm glad he and I are on the same page with this so it doesn't get awkward. His eyes remain locked on something outside on the street. He doesn't even want to look at her.

This whole conversation is making him super uncomfortable. Emily brings it up almost every time we're all together, so he should be used to it by now. Maybe whatever happened back at Mass today has put him on edge.

I shake my head. "No, Emily, like we've told you a hundred times, we're just friends. Totally platonic."

She sighs and gets a dreamy, faraway look. "I know, but a mother can dream."

Tears burn my eyes. She just wants to see Flynn happy, like Mom would want to see *me* happy. And I'm sure seeing us together confuses Emily—like it confuses Alicia and according to her, any guy I date, too.

I don't understand why people can't grasp the concept of a platonic relationship between a guy and a girl. It *is* possible. We're proof of that. Five years going strong. I reach across the table, and Emily places one of her hands in mine.

"Emily, you know that no matter what happens, I will always be in Flynn's life. Even when he gets married and I hopefully eventually get married, and we finally find the loves of our lives, I'll always be his friend and yours." I glance over at him. "He's stuck with me for life."

She nods, and tears pool in her eyes. Her hand slips from mine, and she swipes at her cheeks. "I know. I just want so much for both of you to be happy and to have what I had with Niall."

From the stories they've both told me, it seems Emily and Niall had an idyllic marriage. The kind everyone dreams of and hopes for. A true happily ever after. Losing him so young brought that perfect life to a screeching halt.

A freak heart attack they never saw coming. That's the thing with life, though. You never know where the twists and turns will take you.

There are times I wish I had that kind of childhood, that kind of relationship to use as a model for my own marriage. But Mom and Dad were about as far from idyllic as possible.

The man had a lot of faults. Ones he was only able to recognize, admit, and apologize for at the end of his life. I could be bitter about it, the way Jameson still is and Bash was until Dad was literally on his death bed, but if things had been different, I probably wouldn't be so close with either of them.

Having a big brother to look out for me and a little one to protect, in turn, meant we formed a bond as siblings that Flynn never got a chance to have because of his father's death.

It's why I miss them so much and have felt so lost since Dad's death. They're the only family I have left, and we all see each other so rarely. It makes having friends like Flynn around even more important.

Flynn leans forward and grabs his mother's hand. "I know, Ma, and we both will be. Eventually…"

My heart aches at the sadness in Flynn's voice. There's a longing there. Almost as if there *is* someone. Someone he's interested in, maybe even in love with. Someone he can't have or is possibly hiding from his mom and me.

*So why doesn't he want to talk about it?*

*Is that what was really going on back there in church? Was it really about work?*

It's now my mission to find out.

That's what best friends do. They pry and poke and prod until you open up and reveal your deepest, darkest secrets, and they help you work through them. And while there are always things I'll never tell Flynn, I'm not going to let him get away with keeping whatever's eating him up from coming out.

That's just not a healthy way to live.

# 4

RACHEL

"Thanks for the coffee, Mom. I'll see you next week." Flynn hugs his mom, and she kisses him on the cheek and whispers something into his ear that makes him cringe and nod before she approaches me.

Emily throws her arms around my shoulders and squeezes tightly. "It was really good to see you, Rachel. Don't be a stranger. You don't have to be hanging out with this guy"—she motions over her shoulder with her thumb—"to give me a call if you need anything."

Her eyes search over me sympathetically, like she can see right through the brave face I put on sometimes and she truly understands what I'm going through. Losing both Mom and Dad in a five-year span has left me feeling lost and vulnerable, especially so far away from Bash and Jameson. The McAllisters have offered me a "found family" here, and I never want them to think I take it for granted.

"I appreciate that more than words can say." I squeeze her tightly. "Thank you, Emily."

"Figure out what's up my son's ass today."

I pull back and snicker. Leave it to Emily to call him out. Even she can see something is bothering him. Though, I don't know if I'll be able to get him to talk given the way he reacted outside the church. He's definitely on edge and defensive, which is so unlike the Flynn I know and love.

She winks at me and waves. "Bye, guys."

I follow Flynn to his car, and we climb in quietly. He starts it and takes off out of the diner parking lot without a word.

A strange tension hangs between us in the car—one I haven't ever felt with him before. I glance over at him. With his eyes focused on the road, it's hard to tell if he senses it, too, but I don't know how he couldn't. It's never like this for us. Things are always so...easy and comfortable. There are very few people in the world I can just *sit* with in silence without it getting awkward, and Flynn has always been one of them.

Even when we first met, it was like something clicked. I always attributed our fast friendship to the fact that I tend to get along better with men. Having two brothers turned me into a tomboy early in life, and I spent most of my time chasing after them with a hockey stick or baseball bat instead of playing dress-up with the girls in the neighborhood.

Flynn has always been like another brother to me since Bash and Jameson are so far away. So, having whatever is unsaid between us causing a rift is unacceptable.

I swallow thickly and clear my throat. "So...you want to tell me what's been bothering you today?"

He releases an annoyed-sounding sigh and glances over at me. "Didn't we already have this discussion after Mass?"

"Yes, but it seemed like you were holding something back at coffee with your mom." And this question is either going to get me an answer or push him further into whatever this attitude is. "Is this about a girl?"

He stiffens, and Alicia's words from the other night float back into my head. *Flynn is hot. Like, really fucking hot. And that's intimidating to any guy you're dating to know you spend that much time with the guy who lives right next door.*

Maybe Flynn is suffering from the same problem. Maybe whoever this girl is can't help but be jealous of how close we are. Maybe she doesn't want him seeing me anymore. Maybe he's been put in a crappy position and he doesn't know how to handle it without hurting her or me.

"Look, Flynn, I don't want our friendship to get in the way of you being with someone you really like. If there's a girl and she's not comfortable with us or how close we are, I would understand that. I mean, I hope we can always be such good friends, and I wouldn't ever want anything to come between us, but—"

"Just stop." His words come out guttural and low, not his usual soft, even tone.

"What?" I jerk my head over to look at him.

His hands tighten on the wheel until his knuckles whiten. "Please, just stop."

"Stop what? Trying to be your friend?"

His jaw tightens, and a muscle there tics.

I shake my head and fight the burn of impending tears. "I don't understand what's going on with you, Flynn. Everything was fine this morning before church, but then—"

"But then nothing. We don't always have to tell each other everything, Rachel. There are some things maybe sometimes we should want to keep private."

There isn't any malice is in his words—and he probably isn't even wrong—but they hurt all the same.

I recoil from him and blink away the tears starting to form. "Wow. Who are you, and what have you done with my best friend? Because you're certainly not acting like him today."

He doesn't respond, and we're almost home. He takes the turn onto our street, and our houses appear. This is my last chance to get a word in.

"You know what happens when you bottle stuff up and you don't talk about what's bothering you, Flynn? You become like my father and my brothers. They were all so emotionally repressed that sometimes it was like talking to a wall. My father ruined his relationship with my mother and all of us because he cut himself off from all of his emotions except anger. And Jameson couldn't even bring himself to come to Michigan to say goodbye to him. At least Bash finally got it through this thick skull and realized that he needed to clear the air before Dad died. If that hadn't happened, then Bash would have spent the rest of his life harboring all that anger, and who knows where it would've led. I still worry about Jameson and what not being there is going to do to him."

Flynn opens his mouth to respond, but I hold up my hand.

"No, just listen. You were there for me through all of that. I don't understand why you can't let me be there for you now—whatever is happening."

And the fact that he keeps pushing me away today feels worse than any breakup I've ever been through because I never loved any of them.

Not really.

Not the way I love Flynn.

He's my best friend for life, or so I thought.

Now, it feels like I'm losing him, and I have no idea why.

———

## FLYNN

The pain in my chest intensifies, like a knife has been shoved into my heart and twisted round and round, shredding every bit of it until there's nothing left but a bleeding mess that used to hold my soul.

That's what hurting Rachel does to me.

Seeing her tears.

Hearing the anguish in her shaking voice.

The concern for *me*.

The last thing I want to do is cause her any pain, but the more she keeps poking at me, the closer I get to coming out and saying what's really bothering me. And the conversation with Mom over coffee only made things worse. That woman knows me far too well and sees way too much. Every time she brings up Rachel and me getting together, it's like placing another nail in the coffin. Her whispered words before she left were like lowering me down six feet below.

*Tell her how you feel.*

Like it's that easy. Like everything will simply fall into place once I confess my undying love for her.

It couldn't be further from the truth.

I know Rach too well, and I am *not* what she wants.

And Rachel pushing me like this isn't going to help. All it does is force me to realize how much I need her. How much I need her *friendship*. How I won't be able to survive if anything comes between us. And my feelings for her already are. They're making me hurt her and push her away when all I want to do is draw her close and never let her go.

I need to quash them.

Pretend they never existed.

Move the fuck on so I never have to see this anguish on her beautiful face again.

Though, she's doing that for me by turning away and staring out the window.

She has every reason to be mad. I didn't mean to snap at her. I didn't mean to act like I don't appreciate her concern, but what do I do when the source of all my distress is the person trying to make it better?

The woman who holds my heart in her hands sighs, and the sound goes straight to my soul. "I don't know what's going on with you, Flynn, but even your mom noticed something was wrong. I wish you would just tell me what it is so I can fix it."

I pull into my driveway and slam on the brakes, throwing my car into park a little more aggressively than I intended. "What's wrong is that you won't leave it alone right now. What's wrong is that you keep asking and asking and asking, and I keep saying that I don't want to talk about it, but you keep pushing and it's only aggravating me. Sometimes, I just need to be alone with my thoughts and to breathe without you forcing me to talk."

Because if I talk...I'm going to say things I can't take back that will make you run away forever.

Her eyes widen, and tears slip down her cheeks. "Because I *care* about you, Flynn, because I want to help with whatever you're going through."

That's such a Rachel thing, too. Helping. Wanting to make things better. It makes it even harder not to grab her and kiss the hell out of her. The only way to keep myself from doing that is to do the opposite. To get away from her as fast as I can until I can control myself again.

"Right now, you're only making it worse, Rach. Please, just leave it alone." I throw open my door, climb from the car, and stalk away from my best friend, without a glance back. If I look and see the hurt I caused that I know is there, I might cave. I might tell her everything.

*And then where would I be?*

Alone, without the woman I love or my best friend. With the only people to keep me company being those who pay to watch me jerk off on the damn website.

It feels like I can't win anymore.

I unlock and push open the front door, then slam it shut behind me. Pressing my back against the hard wood, I squeeze my eyes closed and suck in several deep breaths that do nothing to ease the pain in my chest or the churning of my gut.

Walking away from her when she's so upset might break me. I smash my fists back against the door and shove away from it. Hard steps bring me down the hall to my room, and I fall onto the bed and bury my face into my pillow.

Bringing her with me to church was a bad idea. All it did was make things that had been building up spill over, and I have no idea how to put them back in that jar I had carefully placed them in.

The worst part is she's totally right about bottling things up inside. I saw the way she struggled with her dad's illness. And the fact that Jameson wouldn't see him one last time. Wouldn't clear the air or offer him forgiveness. Not that he needed to. You can't force someone to do that, but Rachel is so damn sweet, so caring that she didn't want her father to die without making amends. And while she was able to do that with Bash, Jameson is more stubborn, and she worries about how it will affect him in the future.

And now, she's worried about me, too. That whatever I'm holding back from her is going to eat away at me. She might be right. It probably will. It has since the day I realized I was in love with her, and it's only gotten worse watching her go on date after date with these guys who are all wrong.

But I have to accept the fact that I'm never going to be the guy who's right. If I don't do that and make some sort of decision to move on, I'm going to lose her anyway. I'm going to suffer the one thing that I fear the most.

So, I need to find a way to explain this to her. I need to find a way to tell her that whatever is bothering me is in the past. I need to suck it up and make an effort to get back into the dating pool. It's the only thing I can do.

It's time for me to move on with my life and help both of us find happiness, even if it can't be with each other.

# 5

## FLYNN

I crank on the water as hot as it will go. It's the only thing that might burn away the feeling of guilt after church and coffee today. Over what I've done...and for how I treated Rachel.

But she just wouldn't drop it the entire ride back to the house; it was unbearable. To be trapped in the car with her, smelling her perfume, seeing her lips tremble, hearing the hurt in her voice. And yet, she kept pushing until I broke—it was either tell her I love her or get her to stop talking.

No man is that strong.

*Or maybe a better man than I am would be...*

I slam my palm against the counter in the bathroom and fire up the laptop while I wait for the water to heat. My shoulders ache with the tension I've been carrying around since Mass, and I drop my head and squeeze my eyes shut.

*God, I was such a dick to her.*

As my fingers tightened on the steering wheel, I was so close to coming clean and telling her how I really feel. Closer than I've ever been.

*I could have let it slip.*

*I could have lost her.*

My gut churns, sending acid up my throat, and my chest aches. I shake my head.

*You didn't say anything. Everything is fine.*

Except I snapped at her. I told her to leave it alone—in a not-so-friendly way.

I've *never* talked to her like that before. I've never let myself get so worked up around her. I've always hidden how I feel and put our friendship first. But today, everything was just...too much to handle.

Rachel's almost walking in on me making naked pancakes. The way Christ seemed to judge me from the crucifix. Mom's comments at the diner. All of it built and built until I couldn't contain it anymore.

My mind won't stop spinning, going over everything Mom and Rachel said. And now, I can't stop seeing the shock and pain on Rach's face when I told her to drop it.

I'm the one who takes that look *off* her face, not the one who puts it there. I'm not one of those guys she dates, the ones she has zero chemistry with who use her and then dump her like she's nothing. That's not me. I would *never* hurt her, yet I let myself get so wound up, I did just that.

There's only one way to relieve the stress and tension.

And it's the thing I'm best at.

I'm good with numbers and managing portfolios, but when it comes right down to it, jerking off seems to be my true calling.

I make these people happy, and I get a release.

It's a win-win.

*As long as I don't think about what I'm doing.*

*As long as I'm HRD4U and not Flynn.*

I reach down and grasp my cock, letting it harden in my hand before I log on and hit the button that will send an alert to all those who have signed up to let them know I'm live.

Standing in front of the computer, my abs and dick fill the entire screen. Almost instantly, the little icon in the corner that shows the number of viewers ticks up.

Five.

Ten.

Thirty.

Eighty.

One hundred and twenty-two.

Three hundred.

Four hundred and twenty-one.

A good number for a Sunday night.

"Good evening, ladies. And gentlemen." I never want to leave out a big part of my viewers. "Tonight, I thought we'd take a nice long, hot shower to unwind after a tiring weekend."

Oh, my God.

You didn't reply to my PM. Did you see it?

Yes, get wet for us.

I would love to shower with you. Are you sure I can't come join?

How about a double-feature tonight?

At least I'm putting a smile on *someone's* face today. It's a minor consolation for the day I've had, but I'll still take it. It may be the only one I get for a while.

"I know all of you would love to have an opportunity to come experience this"—I grab my cock and shake it gently —"live, but unfortunately, you're going to have to settle for the show."

> Boo.

> That sucks.

> Don't leave us hanging.

I chuckle as I stroke myself with one hand and slide open the glass door to the shower with the other. "Have no fear, I would never leave anyone hanging. I'll make sure you get a good show tonight."

With the computer angled toward the shower, they won't miss a second.

The hot spray hits my skin, and I release a sigh. "Do you folks want to hear what I would do if you were here with me right now?"

Through the glass, I can still make out the responses.

> Yes!

> Oh, my God, dirty talk! Tell us!

> Tell us what's in that filthy head of yours.

Talking myself through it helps me visualize the real thing. The real thing I've been fantasizing about for so long, I can't even remember a time it wasn't in my head.

*Rachel.*

*Always her.*

"On your knees, babe. I want to see that filthy, hot, wet mouth of yours wrapped around my cock."

A vision of Rachel under the cascade of water fills my head. Rivulets flowing over her breasts. Down her stomach. Disappearing between her legs.

Her bright-green eyes shine up at me as she opens her mouth eagerly. I shove past her soft, pink lips and down her throat. She moans around my hard flesh, the vibration almost making me come on the spot.

I close my eyes and let out a strangled groan as I use my free hand to steady myself against the tile. "Fuck, yes! Make that noise again."

Long, hard strokes.

The continued sensation from her soft moans and the glide of her tongue along the underside of my dick.

The water surging over us.

Steam enveloping us, giving her an almost ethereal look even down on her knees.

A slow tingle starts at the base of my spine.

"Suck my cock, baby. Make me come. Take it."

Small, soft hands grip my ass and tug me toward her. She swallows me even deeper until the base of my dick presses against her lips and the head rubs against the back of her throat.

"Fuck. Fuck. Fuck. Oh, God. Yes, keep going. Deeper. Swallow my fucking cock."

She complies and swallows, her throat moving and rippling along my length. I withdraw, and she sucks in a deep breath. Her hand slips from my ass to grip the base of my erection and squeezes with every stroke while she sucks harder with her mouth. She works me higher and higher. Drags me closer and closer. Then she deep-throats me again.

*Jesus.*

"Yes, babe, I'm gonna come." My hips thrust forward aggressively, fucking her face, making her gag on my cock. "Swallow every fucking drop. Take it all."

*Take all of me. As if you don't already have it...*

A wave of ecstasy rolls through me, and I can practically feel the muscles of her throat contracting around my dick as I empty myself into her.

———

## RACHEL

My orgasm crashes over me like a tidal wave slamming into the beach only a few miles away. A massive explosion of pleasure coursing through my veins, settling in my limbs, shattering my body, and leaving me spasming.

*Holy hell.*

I lie back against my bed and force open my eyes to watch the aftermath of HRD4U's cataclysmic release perfectly timed with mine.

*God.*

His dirty talk is like throwing gasoline onto a raging fire. And I have had one burning for a long time. Hiding what I really want in a partner is more frustrating than I ever imagined it could be. All the nice guys I date can never measure up, and I was too afraid to ask them what I wanted for fear of losing the relationships I had.

But this guy...

My mouth salivates, thinking about being in the shower with him, having his cock rammed down my throat, tasting his cum as I swallow down every drop.

Salty.

Sweet.

Imagining his hard muscles rippling under my fingertips has them itching to touch him in real life.

My clit throbs, hyper-sensitive after my orgasm yet craving more.

I would touch and lick and kiss every inch of that man.

Again.

And again.

And again.

And something tells me he would do the same.

He's not just a taker. He's a giver. Something about the way he talks to the viewers—even with the electronically distorted voice—elicits a sense of calm, like he's everyone's best friend and an incredibly caring man.

Who would be the perfect lover.

*At least in my head.*

In real life, he probably has some major fault—they all do. Perfect men only exist in pornos and romance novels. They don't live in Redondo Beach, California.

*Is it really so much to ask?*

*Although, even if there were one here, how would I ever find him?*

I can't exactly advertise what I like. Not only would I be fired if the parents found out their kids' kindergarten teacher is a closet freak, but it would also invite sick weirdos into my life instead of sweet, decent guys who know how to talk dirty and have superb fucking abilities. The two co-existing is such a unicorn that I'm convinced it can't happen in real life.

One experience in college, one amazing night with a dirty-talking, spanking, hard-fucking guy from that frat, changed my life. Without that, I would never know what was missing now.

*Why did he have to be so damn good?*

I've been ruined for "ordinary" sex ever since. I might as well accept that I'll spend the rest of my life alone watching HRD4U with B.O.B. rather than coming on some perfect man's cock.

*Pathetic.*

But it's my life. And after the sort-of argument I had with Flynn today, I needed something to make me feel better.

He's never snapped at me like that. Never pushed me out and completely shut down. It was the first time in all our years of friendship when I've felt like he was hiding something from me, something that might be important.

Maybe he thinks I'll be jealous if he has a secret girlfriend, or that I'll be mad at him for not telling me about her right away.

I wouldn't be, though. Not really. Not if she makes him happy.

That's all I've ever wanted for him, and tonight I needed to forget about the argument. To forget the weirdness of today. To be *happy,* even for a few minutes.

HRD4U was the only one who came to mind who would do that.

*That's even more pathetic.*

Sitting home alone, watching internet porn...

*How did my life come to this?*

The comments on-screen come fast and furious, like he and I just did.

> HRD4U! That was so hot.

> Oh my God!

> I would suck your dick!

> Can I please come over? We can do this for real.

I read while I wait for my heart rate to return to normal. It continues to thunder against my ribcage staring at the mysterious man with the perfect six-pack and muscles so hard and tight they look like a Roman statue.

HRD4U slowly grabs a bottle of shampoo, and his hands disappear, presumably up to his hair. Not being able to see him from the collarbone up makes it difficult to know for sure, but every little movement sends his rock-hard muscles rippling. With the water cascading over his skin and the steam floating up around him, it's like a damn wet dream come to life.

*God, the man is well-built.*

Beautiful body.

Beautiful dick.

And he's so damn nice and down to Earth with the women who watch him. He treats them respectfully, doesn't make sleazy comments, or take any of them up on their offers of sex—at least, that's what he says.

He seems like a genuinely good guy, and he's single, too, according to the comments he's made.

I guess good guys—and girls—do finish last and have to pretend to be good *always*. At least if they want to keep up appearances and maintain their jobs. Both things that are, unfortunately, necessary for me, which doesn't leave me a lot of options. So, HRD4U is the plan for now, and for as long as it takes to find the perfect man.

My eyes follow every movement as he grabs a bar of soap, lathers it, and massages it over his body...slowly and deliberately.

Chiseled chest.

Bulging biceps.

Washboard abs.

That damn *V* thingy that makes my knees weak.

Then down over that magnificent dick that's already hardening again.

The man knows exactly what he's doing, and he's a master at it.

His hand wraps around his cock, now slick with soap, and he moans.

"Well, ladies, who's ready for round two?"

He strokes himself slowly from root to tip, rolling his palm against the head.

I grab my vibrator from where it fell between my legs and fire it back up. If he's going again, so will I. Maybe five or six times.

Just remembering how goddamn hot this all was will be enough to keep me going all night, even after he logs off.

But before I start up again, I reach over with one hand and type out the first comment I have ever made on any of HRD4U's videos.

Why don't men like you exist in real life? Why is it so hard to find a nice guy who can talk filthy and fuck dirty? If you know where to find one, I want one. So please, let me know. I'd appreciate any help I can get.

# 6

## FLYNN

I f I have to stare at this screen full of numbers much longer, I'm going to throw my computer off this damn desk. I pinch the bridge of my nose and rub at my tired, aching eyes.

*"Be a stockbroker," they said. "It'll be fun," they said.*

Well, it sure as hell isn't like it is in the movies. No lavish parties with overflowing champagne. No yachts with dozens of beautiful models throwing themselves at you. No mansion and expensive car.

I'm not rolling in the dough, and in this economy, neither are my clients. All the red on these portfolios gives me a migraine, and I squeeze my eyes shut against the distortion creeping into the edges of my vision.

Maybe if I don't look at it, then it won't be true. But when I open my eyes again, the same numbers taunt me like angry little assholes.

No one saw this coming. No one could have predicted the way the market tanked over the last year. I know I'm not the only one who lost money—their own or their clients'—

but it doesn't make me feel any better when I have to explain that this is a part of the deal if they're going to play the market.

It's a gamble. One that could make you millions or put you in the doghouse. My personal losses necessitated HRD4U in the first place, but my clients don't have the luxury of becoming someone else for a while to make extra cash. Most of them have businesses, important jobs, mortgages, wives, and kids...

Things that a lot of people lost when their portfolios ended up in the shitter. And it doesn't look much better now than they did six months ago. The only hope on the horizon is the rumor that the Federal Reserve may be making an interest rate cut soon. But with the government, we never know if it's all bullshit or if it will really happen.

It would mean a nice surge in a lot of portfolios, including my own. Not enough to make HRD4U unnecessary, but it would be something. And for clients with larger investments than my own, it could mean millions.

A knock on my door has me jerking out of my pity party. Dan leans against the jamb with a knowing grin and his sandy-blond hair a disheveled mass instead of slicked back in perfect placement like usual. He looks like he may be having the same type of day I have had. "Does your Monday suck as much as mine?"

I nod and shove my office chair away from my desk with a groan. "How could you tell?"

He chuckles and holds up his hands. "Lucky guess."

*Or I look as shitty as I feel.*

I glance at the clock on the far wall. It's only 4:30, but I can't stay for another hour. Not after the weekend I had. Not after my fight or non-fight whatever the hell it was with Rachel.

*My meltdown.*

That's probably the most accurate description.

Dan hitches his thumb over his shoulder. "You want to get out of here and grab a drink?"

*A drink or five...*

I wouldn't normally be going out for drinks on a Monday night, but a cold beer or nice whiskey or bourbon sounds pretty good right now. "Yeah. Actually, that sounds awesome."

With a heavy sigh, I push out of my chair and lean over my desk to shut down my computer, letting the numbers that have given me so much grief over the last few months vanish—at least until I get in tomorrow and have to deal with them again.

I follow Dan out to the hall, and we weave through the central secretarial cubicles on our way to the elevators.

"Mr. McAllister?"

I grimace at the sound of my name coming from Darlene's lips, but I turn back to her with a forced smile. "Yes?"

She waves a stack of pink message slips at me. "I know you didn't want to be disturbed earlier, but you have a few messages."

Not wholly unexpected, given the fact that I've been shut away in my office all day without taking any calls. Though I don't want to know the answer, I need to ask all the same. "Anything urgent?"

She bites her lip and glances toward Marty's office, but with his door shut, there's no way the boss can hear whatever she's about to tell me. "I wouldn't say it's urgent per se, but Dustin Kelly called again, right before lunch."

"Shit." I glance at Dan, who gives me a sympathetic look.

He's heard all about my issues with Mr. Kelly over the last few months, and I'm sure he doesn't want to hear about him again.

"Did he leave any specific message this time?"

Darlene shakes her head. "Just that he wants to talk to you."

I run a hand through my hair and groan. "I don't know what the hell he expects me to say?"

All he does is rant about how much money he lost like there's anything I can do about that. There are only so many times I can explain it to him and have it go in one ear and out the other. There are no guarantees in this business, and that was made clear.

Darlene twists her hands together and shifts uncomfortably. "I know, sir, that's why I didn't interrupt you with his call."

I pat her on the shoulder in an attempt to help assuage some of the dismay on her face. "Don't worry about it. I'll deal with him..."

*Eventually.*

But not today. I don't have it in me today. Hopefully, by the middle of the week, I'll have the energy to tolerate another tongue-lashing from Dustin Kelly.

Darlene glances between Dan and me. "Are you leaving?"

"Yeah." *Thank God.* "I'll see you in the morning."

I follow Dan to the elevators and lean against the back wall of the cab as we descend. The steady motion and slight rock of the elevator only makes me more tired. I drop my head back against the metal behind me and squeeze my eyes shut.

It does nothing to help quell the ache building in my head.

Dan leans next to me. "So, Kelly still giving you shit?"

"Yeah. And a few others." I open my eyes and glance at him. "I really wish people understood that when we warn them about high-risk stocks, we mean it."

He elbows me with a grin. "You and me both. But you know, with the way the market tanked, it wouldn't have mattered where his money was really."

"That's very true. But it doesn't stop the guy from blaming me."

The elevator dings, and he claps me on the shoulder. "We're all in the same boat. Try not to take it to heart so much."

That's funny coming from him because I know how much he genuinely cares. Dan's a good guy, a real genuine person who feels as bad and guilty as I do when we can't make things work for clients.

Letting down anyone sucks. But letting down someone who has entrusted their life savings to you is another. Though, it doesn't compare to letting down Rachel, which is exactly what I did this weekend. I've never told her how I felt about her for fear of losing her friendship, but by keeping it bottled up, I only pushed her away in the process.

I can't keep doing this. And like I've told myself a hundred times, I need to force myself to accept that we won't be together and move on with her as my best friend and nothing more. Yesterday proved to be the tipping point in that respect.

And tomorrow, I'll work on that.

Tonight, I'll have a drink and try to forget all the bullshit.

We step out of the elevator, and our shoes echo on the concrete as we make our way into the parking structure and toward our assigned parking spaces with our names affixed right above them.

Dan stops abruptly and grabs my arm. "Dude, you have a flat tire."

"What the hell?" I rush the last few feet to my used BMW. "Shit."

The rim sits against the concrete, all air long gone from the rear left tire. I crouch down to look at the black rubber.

Dan moves around me toward the hood. "Flynn, the front one is flat, too."

He walks around the car as I lean down to examine the bottom of the front tire.

*Two flats? What are the chances of that?*

I stand and release an annoyed sigh. "There's been a lot of construction lately on the road to the office. Maybe I just got a couple of nails in them."

Dan stands on the other side of the car and shakes his head. "I don't think this is from nails, Flynn. They're flat on this side, too."

"Fuck!"

There's no way I have four flat tires randomly. I squat again and take a closer look at the front tire, sticking my finger along a visible slit.

"Jesus." This puts it all into perspective. "It looks like someone slashed my tires."

———

**RACHEL**

It's like the Monday that never ends. Every hour has dragged, and every kid has acted like a total hellion today.

*I love my students. I love my students. I love my students.*

Sometimes, I need to remind myself.

Over and over again.

Like right now.

Wrangling twenty five-year-olds can be trying on a good day, and today wasn't a good day.

Not by a longshot.

There are definitely times when dealing with other

people's kids makes me question my desire for my own. Though not really. I love kids so damn much; it would be hard for me not to have a little brood. Still, some days all I want to do is go home and drink, and that is definitely today.

*Mondayest Monday ever!*

Though, my mood probably has a lot more to do with my fight or whatever it was with Flynn than anything. I haven't been able to get that look in his eyes out of my head —like he was drowning in something.

I didn't think he could surprise me anymore. But the way he snapped certainly surprised me...and not in a good way. This weird tension between us just feels so wrong, especially because I don't know why he reacted like that.

Maybe if I knew...

Maybe if I understood...

But that reaction wasn't Flynn at all.

He's the one who is always so even-keeled and composed. He doesn't lose his cool easily, and never with me.

It's left me unsettled in a way I haven't felt in a long time. In a way that I really hate. One that makes me want to jump on a plane to fly back home to Michigan. Only that isn't home anymore, and no one is there.

Dad's gone. House sold.

Bash is in Vegas, blissfully happy with Greer.

And Jameson is in New York, trying to build his restaurant empire after his win on *Prime Chef*.

This is the only home I have. And Flynn is such a huge part of it. Having things weird between us makes everything feel off.

*And hopefully I didn't take that out on the kids today.*

I pull into the driveway and pause to stare at his house. It's too early for him to be home, but I still look for lights in the windows. It's hard not knowing whether he even wants to see me or not.

My chest tightens, and I force myself to pull into my garage and climb from my car before I dwell on it too much and make my shitty mood even shittier.

*Give him space.*

*Don't breathe down his neck.*

My phone rings as I turn off the ignition.

*Please be Flynn.*

I didn't even realize how badly I want to talk to him until now, until I'm not sure if I can. I glance at the screen with hope blossoming and sigh.

*Jameson.*

"Hey, Jamo, what's up?" I climb from the car and grab my bag.

"Rach..." Something clanks in the background behind him, and his muffled yell tells me he's probably in the kitchen, like usual. "Do you have a minute?"

I chuckle, open my door, step inside, and drop my bag. "I do, but it sounds like you're busy as hell."

He laughs. "Yeah, but that's a good thing."

"How are the plans for the restaurant coming?"

He releases a heavy sigh. Baby brother was always the melodramatic one of the family, and that hasn't changed with age. I wander into the kitchen and pull out the half-bottle of wine from the fridge.

"It's going okay, I guess. Grant agreed to be my primary financial backer. But he wants fifty-one percent in exchange and wants input on location and some other things."

I pour a glass and take a sip. The cool, crisp pinot grigio gives me a moment of relief from the stress of the day. "You're willing to give over that type of control?"

It's not a very Fury trait. Especially not for Jameson. He

makes Bash look like he's easy to boss around—something any of his coaches would disagree with.

"I don't want to, but I don't know if I have a choice. I'm still pretty young, and restaurants are about the riskiest investment you can make. I'm lucky I have a friend with money willing to do this at all."

"That's very true." Though, I'm sure if he asked Bash for the money, he would give it to him. Even though they are like oil and water at times, they're still brothers, and deep down, they love each other. But Jameson would never go to Bash for help. It's just not in his nature.

He jostles the phone for a minute. "That's actually why I'm calling."

"What is?"

"Well, I was hoping I could talk to Flynn about something."

I freeze with my glass halfway to my mouth while my heart sinks into my stomach. "Why don't you just call him?"

"Why? Because I wanted to talk to you, and I figured you two would be together."

We probably would be if there weren't this weirdness. Mondays are usually Webflix, beer, and pizza to help ease our way into a new week.

I gulp some wine and set down the glass with a shaky hand. "No. He's working late tonight. I'm not sure when I'll see him next."

A beat of silence passes between us before Jameson clears his throat. "Is everything okay?"

I tighten my hand around the wine glass and fight back the sting of tears. "Yeah, why?"

"Because everything doesn't *sound* okay. Are you and Flynn fighting or something?"

*Or something.*

I sigh, grab my wine, and drop down onto the couch. My

eyes drift closed, and I press my head back against the soft, plush back. "That's just it. I don't know."

"What do you mean you don't know? Hold on, let me go outside so I can hear you better." Shuffling and a banging door follow. "Tell me what's going on."

Jameson usually isn't the one to be offering any kind of life advice, but with Greer so close to making it into the playoffs, Bash is a little preoccupied right now. "Tell me what's going on, Rach."

I sigh. "I don't know. He got weird with me this weekend."

"Weird how?"

Jameson could offer me some insight into the male psyche. Though being in Jamo's head isn't anywhere I'd ever really *want* to be.

"It's hard to explain. He was acting off at church—"

"Whoa. Whoa. Whoa. You went to church?"

I bite my lip and cringe. "Yeah. Why?"

*Stupid.*

I should not have said anything about it. Not to Jameson. Because now I've opened up a line of conversation I know he doesn't want to have, and I don't have the energy to go through with him. "Don't worry about it."

"I'm not worried; I'm just curious. Since when do you go to church?"

*Well, fuck it.*

I guess it's now or never.

"I've been thinking about a lot of things since Dad died." The cold silence that greets my statement is exactly what I expected. "Jamo, you still there?"

He clears his throat again, harder this time in his annoyance. "Yeah, I'm still here."

I knew as soon as I brought up Dad, he'd shut down. "I know you don't want to talk about it, but—"

68

"No *but*. I don't want to talk about it."

"Then just listen, please. Because I really do need your help." Something I never like to admit to anyone, let alone the Fury boys. "I've been feeling very...I don't know...lost since Dad died. Even though I have Flynn and Alicia and Cade, and my work friends here, I feel out of place. Maybe it was because I was home in Michigan for those last couple of weeks with Dad, or it could have been seeing Bash and him finally finding a way to forgive Dad for what he put us through. I don't know. I just...miss you guys. I miss my *family*."

I hadn't intended to word vomit like that, and Jameson's silence tells me that he's as uncomfortable with my statement as I am.

We haven't really been a real family for a long time. After Mom died, we lost our only real reason ever to get together. Bash went off to play in Chicago, and Jameson ran off to culinary school. I took the job in California. We have been on opposite sides of the country, which hasn't really bothered me much before, but it seems like Dad's death has sparked something I didn't even know was there. The need for family. The need for that connection. And the fight with Flynn only makes it even more prevalent. If I lose him, too, I will really have nothing here.

Jameson releases a deep sigh. "I'm sorry you're struggling, sis. And I miss you and Bash, too. But we all have our separate lives now. We are all tied up in whatever is going on, but it doesn't mean I don't still think about you and him. Maybe we just need to make a more concerted effort to get together more often."

A tear trickles down my cheek, and I brush it away as I nod, even though he can't see me. "Yeah. I'd like that."

"Why don't you come to New York?"

"When?"

"Whenever. We haven't chosen a location for the restaurant yet, but I could use a woman's touch picking out some of the décor. I know the vibe I want, but you know..."

I chuckle and sip at my wine. "Yeah, I know you have awful taste."

"Hey!" He releases a deep laugh. "I resent that comment."

"Well, your ex-girlfriends prove my point."

"Ouch." He chuckles. "Look, I'm serious, though. Come see me whenever you want, even if it's just for a long weekend. Or maybe for your spring break."

It does sound nice, getting away from here and spending time with Jameson. The last time we saw each other was at one of Bash's games when they played in New York and I flew in for it. "I'll think about it."

"You'll be all right, Rach. You always are. And tell Flynn to call me when you see him."

My chest tightens again. "I will. Whenever I see him..."

If he's still talking to me.

# 7

RACHEL

"Ms. Rachel, why are you spying on Mr. Flynn's house?"

I jerk away from the window, and the blinds I was holding open to peer out of snap shut violently. Connor stares up at me in his cute Captain America jammies with one dark eyebrow raised, looking just like his dad anytime he questions me about anything.

"I wasn't spying."

His brow furrows, and he shakes his head. "Then, what were you doing?"

"Oh, I..." I glance at my watch to avoid looking the five-year-old in the eye while I dodge his question. "It's almost 9:30. I thought your mom put you to bed."

His brow wrinkles further. "But I'm not tired."

I've already dealt with Connor's boundless energy at school today. I don't know how Alicia and Cade do it, especially with Brandy on top of it.

I squat down to his level. "I don't think your mom is

going to accept that excuse if she finds you down here talking to me."

At his age, if I had been found slipping out of bed to wander around the house for anything hours after I should have been asleep, there would have been hell to pay.

He heaves out a heavy, exaggerated sigh, and I bite back a chuckle. Five-year-olds can be so melodramatic.

I point toward the stairs. "Go back to bed before your mom catches you."

"Are you gonna tell her?"

I shake my head and pretend to turn a key against my lips. "My lips are sealed as long as I don't see you back down here again. I'll see you tomorrow in class, buddy."

He grins and glances behind him toward the kitchen to check for Alicia. "Thanks, Ms. Rachel."

Connor hustles back up the steps in the nick of time as Alicia rounds the corner carrying two glasses of wine.

She glances around the room. "Were you talking to someone out here?"

I shake my head, take the wine from her, and turn back to the window. With my free hand, I peek through the blinds again and stare at Flynn's house across the street. "Did he say anything when he asked Cade to come over?"

Alicia drops onto the chair next to where I'm standing and shakes her head. "No, just asked if he would come over after we put the kids to bed."

"Do you think they're talking about me?"

She giggles and takes a sip of her wine. "I'm *positive* they're talking about you."

I glower at her.

Completely ignoring my disdain, Alicia waves and points to the chair across from her. "Move away from the window. You look like a stalker. "

Letting the blinds snap shut again, I scowl and then lower myself into the chair. "I'm not a stalker. I just..."

"You're just staring out the window at his house like a fucking stalker. If anyone should know what a stalker looks like when she sees one"—she points to her own chest—"it's me."

I bark out a laugh and shake my head thinking about the way they met. A lot of people would look at the way he obsessed over her and made excuses to visit her at the law firm she worked at as pure stalker behavior, but seeing them together, it's clear the feelings went both ways.

One of her eyebrows rises. "What? It's true. I probably should've had Cade arrested."

"Yeah, but you married him instead."

She shrugs and grins at me. "Well, can you blame me? You *have* seen his ass."

I drop my head back and laugh. "No, I can't blame you."

Because I *have* seen his ass—though, not intentionally. That was the *last* time I ever let myself into their house without texting first or ringing the doorbell to announce my presence. I've never seen anyone duck into a room as fast as Cade did when I came around the corner looking for Alicia.

I shake my head, drink some wine, and drop my neck back to stare at the ceiling. "You're so lucky."

"Why do you say that?"

*Isn't it obvious?*

I sit upright again and meet her gaze. "Because you found your soulmate. You have the perfect life."

She waves a hand at me. "Oh, no. Don't even start with that. You know what it took for us to get here. Our love story is anything but perfect."

"Maybe not in the beginning." Cade didn't have a clue how to approach Alicia without being an overbearing ass, and she didn't want to concede that she wanted him as much as he did her. "But look where you ended up."

A beautiful house. Beautiful kids. A loving husband. It's everything I've ever wanted.

Alicia nods. "Very true. But still, don't make the mistake of believing anyone's life or relationship is perfect."

I hate feeling like this. Off my axis. Like the world is spinning around me and I have no idea how to catch up with it or stop it. "Maybe I should just go over there."

"Why? If he hasn't come to you and apologized, he's probably not ready to talk about whatever is bothering him. Men can be idiots sometimes and keep everything in. You just need to wait it out."

Logically, I know she's right. But it doesn't make it any easier. Tears burn my eyes, and I swipe them away.

Alicia leans forward. "Oh, my God, are you crying? Girl, it will be fine. You guys are best friends. It'll work out."

"It's not just that."

If it were only things with Flynn being off, that would be manageable. I could deal until they resolved, hopefully sooner rather than later. But it isn't just him.

"What's going on, Rach?"

I sigh and take a sip of my wine. "Things have just been...rough since I came back from Michigan."

"Oh, hon. I know. You miss your dad."

I shake my head. "No, it's not that. I came to peace with the fact that he never was and would never be a good father, and he was never really in my life that much, so it's *not* that. I think it was seeing Bash and not seeing Jameson while also being in the house that was so much my mom's place. It really made me miss the boys." More than I thought possible. "I guess I'm kind of homesick, only not for a location. For the people."

Alicia offers me a sympathetic look. "Girl, I get it. I

moved across the country and was out here totally alone. But I made it out on the other side. And I have Cade and the kids."

A vise wraps around my chest, stealing my breath. "What if I don't have Flynn anymore?"

"Stop it. Don't even think like that. It's just a little tiff. Have you never fought with a friend before?"

I narrow my eyes on her. "Of course, I have, just not with him."

"It'll be fine. I promise, and I swear if Cade comes back with anything you need to know, I'll tell you. Until then"— she raises her glass—"let's just drink."

"Sounds good to me."

Only not too much since I have to deal with twenty five-year-olds in the morning.

---

**FLYNN**

Cade eyes me while he pets Prince, who snores lightly where he's curled up on the couch next to him. "You really look like shit, mate."

His accent doesn't help soften the sting of his observation, even though women seem to find it charming and sexy.

I scrub a hand over my face and sigh. "Gee, thanks, asshole."

*How the hell does he look so good and well-rested when he has two kids and a mastiff running around his house?*

"What?" Cade raises his dark eyebrows at me and smirks. "You want me to lie to you? You picked the wrong person."

I chuckle and shake my head. "I just rather you didn't state the obvious."

It doesn't take a rocket scientist to see that I've barely slept and have a lot on my mind. And Cade knows me well enough by now to recognize this isn't normal. Even at the height of the market's crash, when my entire world and career felt like it was crumbling, it wasn't this bad. Because I had *her*. My best friend to lean on and to keep me from wallowing in self-pity and guilt. And then I had HRD4U as a way to relieve stress and become someone else, someone with no responsibilities or clients to answer to, someone with no problems.

Now neither of those things are stress-free anymore. My shower release last night felt *off*. And then someone slashed my tires, requiring me to sit at my office late to wait for AAA to come to bring replacement ones. Plus...I now have a mastiff that weighs almost as much as me on my couch.

I motion toward Cade's companion. "Did you have to bring Prince with you?"

He takes a swig of his beer and pats him on the head. "He didn't want me to leave. Kept making those annoying whining sounds at the door as soon as I closed it behind me. Alicia didn't want him to wake up the kids."

"Well, he better not chew on anything or shit on my couch."

Cade feigns offense and places his hand over his chest. "I'm hurt you would ever think poor Prince could partake in such awful behavior."

I laugh and drain half my beer. "I've heard the stories and seen the evidence all over your house. But nice try."

Cade takes a swig of his beer and glances at Prince. "He's a good boy, most of the time. And I promise he won't do anything to increase your stress level. You're a wreck as it is. Is all of this because of whatever's going on with Rachel?"

I walk to the window and peek through the blinds across the street to Cade and Alicia's house. "Yeah."

*Because of Rachel.*

At least, that's all I plan on telling him right now. It's not that I think Cade would judge me if I told him about HRD4U and the guilt that has suddenly popped up over doing it; I'm just not ready to open that can of worms at this moment. It's enough that my relationship with my best friend is on the rocks.

"What happened between you two, anyway? All I heard from Alicia was that something went down and you aren't talking, which we all know is not usual."

"I know." I squeeze my eyes shut and drop my forehead against the cool glass of the window. "I fucked up, though."

"Why? What happened?"

"She came to church with Mom and me on Sunday, and afterward, we went out for coffee. I had a lot on my mind and having Rachel there didn't make it any easier."

"Why? Because you're in love with her?"

I jerk my head around to look at him. A smug smile tilts his lips.

Coughing slightly, I shift under his assessment. "I never said that."

"You don't have to, mate. I've been friends with both of you for long enough to know what I see. And what I see when you look at her is love." He holds up a hand to stop me from interrupting. "And not the kind of love between friends."

*Shit. If it's that obvious to him, is it that obvious to Rachel, too?*

"I didn't realize I was so transparent."

He laughs and leans back on the couch. Prince shifts with him and drops his head onto Cade's lap. "I think you do a fairly good job of hiding it from her, but Alicia and I have definitely seen it. Why don't you make a move, man? Why not see if she feels the same way?"

"Because she doesn't. It's been five years. If she liked me as anything more than a friend, thought of me as anything more than another brother, I would know by now. Something would've happened between us. She would've said something..."

Cade drains his beer and sets the empty bottle on the side table. "Would she? Why haven't *you*?"

"Because I don't want to risk losing her friendship."

His shoulders rise and fall. "Maybe she's holding back for the same reason."

"No"—I shake my head—"she's looking for a certain kind of guy, and I'm not it."

He snorts and sighs. "What kind of guy do you think she's looking for? Because it seems like none of the guys she's dated recently meet her expectations."

*Rachel's perfect guy...*

It's not something I like to think about. Someone else with her. Someone else kissing her. Someone else holding her hand. Someone else touching her.

But I know what Rachel needs.

"She needs a nice guy with a firm head on his shoulders who will treat her like the queen she is and give her his world."

"And you can't be that?"

I shake my head. "No."

And I can't tell Cade *or* her why not. And I would never be able to keep it from her if we were in a relationship that was more than friendship. I couldn't hide HRD4U or pretend I'm something I'm not.

"So, I think you need to make a decision. You either go for it, or you let her go. Shit or get off the pot, mate. Or you're going to drive yourself insane."

I squeeze my eyes closed. "I know. I need to start being a better friend and forgetting that I want more."

"How do you plan on doing that?"

"I don't know yet."

I need some time to figure it out, so I don't inadvertently say something that will send her running scared and push her further away than she already is right now.

I've created my own worst nightmare—a life without her in it.

And I need to figure out a way to fix it.

Maybe that starts with clearing my head about some other things...

# 8

**FLYNN**

"Bless me, Father, for I have sinned. It has been... gosh...ten years since my last confession."

When I was a senior in high school and the nuns made us go weekly. Which means I have a decade worth of sins to get off my chest. But it's really only two that are weighing on me enough to get me up and out of bed early to make it here before going into work after days of not sleeping since the fight with Rach. Only two that kept me up all night after Cade finally left. Only two that brought me to face my fear of God's wrath.

"And what brings you here today, my son?"

*Shit.*

Mom. Rachel.

The woman who commented on my feed the other night about what a great guy I seemed like and asking where she could find a guy like me.

It's left me wondering...

*Am I really a great guy?*

*Doing this?*

*Snapping at Rachel like that?*

If "great guys" did things like I do as HRD4U, I wouldn't feel so guilty or be so afraid of Mom or Rachel finding out. People always say only God can judge you, but the risk of being judged by the women in my life is truly what worries me the most.

I couldn't even be concerned about the punks who slashed my tires last night because Rach's face wouldn't leave my damn head. My car means nothing compared to losing her.

I release a deep sigh that fills the tiny confines of the confessional booth. "Well, Father. I've been dealing with some feelings of guilt lately about some things I've been doing."

"I see, my son. Guilt is often the way our conscience tells us we should not be doing something. What is it you've been doing to cause such negative feelings and disquiet in your heart?"

*Disquiet in my heart.*

Those words resonate through me and settle deep in my chest, in the very place the priest so wisely referenced. I never thought about it in those terms, but *disquiet in my heart* is the perfect description for what I've been feeling lately.

I can only imagine what the old man behind the partition is picturing—theft, rape, murder—the worst of the seven cardinal sins they warn us about in Mass every Sunday.

What I've been doing is nothing compared to those things we're always told will send us straight to Hell, but I still can't shake the weight from my shoulders or the feeling of dirt on my skin.

Lust is a deadly sin for a reason.

It still stains your soul, even if it doesn't mean getting blood on your hands.

It was so easy when I could separate HRD4U from Flynn, but that's getting harder and harder, if not impossible.

"It's not anything illegal or criminal or anything like that."

The old priest—Father Lafayette if I'm not mistaken—chuckles. "That's good to know, my son. So, what is the problem?"

"Well…"

*Shit. How do I tell this guy what I've been doing?*

It's probably best to rip off the Band-Aid. Just tell him.

"Father, I have a webcam site."

Silence greets me.

He clears his throat. "I'm not sure I follow."

Of course, he doesn't. This guy is probably ninety years old and has no idea what a fucking webcam is.

"Uh, it's a camera system that allows people to go on the internet and see me."

*All of me. In my birthday suit. And then some…*

"Ah, I see, and where's the problem?"

I bury my face in my hands and release a sigh.

*Jesus, is he going to make me say it?*

"They watch me do…things." That should be enough for him to draw the right conclusions.

"What kinds of things?"

*Oh, God…*

This is my penance right here. Having to actually say the words. This is the Lord Almighty telling me it's wrong and making me pay.

I clear my throat. "Well…cooking, cleaning, showering—"

"Showering?"

"Yes, Father, and...you know...choking the chicken."

"Choking the chicken? I'm sorry, son, I don't understand."

*God, strike me down right now.*

*Take me before I have to say these words.*

*Was this guy never a teenager?*

*Do priests not have any sex drive?*

Surely, this guy *must* have masturbated at least once in his life.

There has to be another way to say this. Another way to get my point across. "You know...beating the meat? Stroking the pole? Polishing the banister?"

He sighs. "I'm sorry, son, but you're confusing me here."

*Christ...*

"Father, I jerk off. I masturbate, and they watch me."

The temperature in the confessional booth drops about ten degrees, almost as if a cold front has slipped through as the words hang in the air between us. Undoubtedly, Father Lafayette has heard some interesting things in this box over the years, but I highly doubt he's encountered this one before. If he were in L.A. or Vegas, it could be possible, but Redondo Beach isn't exactly a hotbed of illicit behavior.

He pauses briefly and clears his throat like he's searching for his words. "And you do this for money?"

"Yes, women, and sometimes men, pay to watch me do this."

Saying the words out loud has bile rising in my throat. I've never told *anyone* about HRD4U, let alone a sexually repressed celibate priest who probably believes even *thinking* about masturbation is a sin.

"This is how you support yourself?"

"I have a good job, but I needed additional income when the market went south, and I kind of fell into this work."

The joking in the locker room at the gym about what a

wet dream I must be for women because of my physique and big dick is what got this whole thing started. One simple comment about a webcam. Something said in jest by a guy I lift weights with. He never knew I took the idea and ran with it.

"My son, I can see why you're feeling guilty about this. First Corinthians 6:18 says, 'Flee from sexual immorality. All other sins a person commits are outside the body, but whoever sins sexually, sins against their own body.'"

The words hit me one by one, each a blow to my already fragile conscience. Yet, growing up reading the Bible and having it read to me, I always knew there were contradictions. And one comes to mind now.

"But Proverbs 3:27 says, 'Do not withhold good from those to whom it is due, when it is in your power to do it.' Isn't that what I'm doing? A service to others? And First Corinthians 6:20 says, 'You were bought at a price. Therefore, honor God with your bodies.' I'm sharing my body, sharing what God has given me in his own image with others."

"I don't think the Bible quite had this type of situation in mind."

*No, it most certainly did not.*

Father Lafayette continues, "Nor the sexualization of society that has occurred in recent years. Which is just as much at fault for this type of behavior as your own actions. It's the cardinal sin of lust working its way into our collective psyche. The work of the Devil himself that cannot be ignored so easily."

*Wait, what? Is this guy giving me a free pass?*

It's been a *long* time since I've sat in a confession booth, but I don't remember it going like this in the past. It was more fire and brimstone, hours of penance, and less understanding back then.

Maybe times have changed in the church.

He shifts on the other side of the metal mesh separating us. "Are you hurting anyone with this behavior?"

I shrug even though he can barely see me. "I don't know. I hope not."

But I can't really know that.

*How could I?*

I don't know those people's lives. Whether or not they're married or in a relationship. Whether their significant others are okay with them watching me. Whether or not they have the money to spend on their site subscription or whether they are taking food from their kids' mouths to pay for it. Whether or not it's some kind of porn addiction that's destroying them slowly.

All I know is the people who watch *want* to watch. I'm not forcing anything on anyone.

"It sounds like the only real issue here is your internal struggle with your behavior."

"Yes, and something one of my viewers said to me the other night."

"Which was what?"

"She asked why she couldn't find a good guy like me, a nice guy like me. It made me wonder if I really am a nice and good guy doing this."

The priest sighs again, and through the screen, I can make out his hand rising and falling, almost like he's issuing a blessing. "My son, even good people do bad things or things that are morally questionable. God forgives all. The first book of John 1:9—'If we confess our sins, He is faithful and just and will forgive us our sins and purify us from all unrighteousness."

"What if I keep doing it?"

"He will continue to forgive you. That's what God's love is all about."

He makes it sound so simple. It's great that I have God's love, but it doesn't get me anywhere near Rachel's or help relieve any of this guilt. Nor does it offer me any advice on how to deal with my feelings for her.

"There's more, Father."

"More?"

The tension in his question tightens my chest. After *that* reveal, he's probably expecting something *really bad.*

"Yes." I rub at my eyes and sigh. "I was pretty awful to my best friend the other day when she was only trying to help me because she cares."

"To what do you attribute the negative behavior?"

"Shit." I scrub a hand over my face. "Crap. I'm sorry, Father. I...I love her. As far more than a friend, and I'm having a hard time reconciling the fact that I can't be with her."

"Does she not feel the same way?"

"No, she doesn't. We're just friends, and even if she *did*, if she found out what I've been doing, I know I would lose her forever."

Another silence falls between us, and he shifts and leans toward the mesh screen. "Son, you need to do whatever you can to lighten the load on your soul."

"What does that even mean?"

"Whatever you think it does."

*Not helpful.*

He's worse than seeing a psychiatrist.

"Father, what's my penance?"

Maybe ten million Hail Marys or Our Fathers will help. But I doubt it.

———

## RACHEL

Four days. More than ninety damn agonizing hours since I left Flynn's car on Sunday. The longest we've gone without talking to each other in five years.

And I'm a wreck because of it.

I never realized how much I rely on him for normalcy and comfort. How much his friendship really means to me. I thought I knew, but this has brought my true dependency on him to the forefront. The longer this goes on, the more I miss hearing his voice or him making me laugh.

Even when I had to go back to Michigan to take care of Dad during his final weeks, we spoke or at least texted every day. He was my rock, then, and despite my desire to go apologize and end whatever this is...I'm not sure I can.

*How can I apologize for something when I don't even know what I did?*

I can't.

Trying to find out what upset him so much wasn't wrong. He was just irritated. Alicia said he needs time to deal with whatever was going on that made him so...not Flynn.

So that means another night sitting here wondering what went wrong.

He's keeping something from me. That much is clear. There's something going on he doesn't want to discuss, and the only logical explanation is a woman. He's been so great about supporting me through this recent breakup, and all the others before, so if he *is* seeing someone, he might feel guilty about finally finding someone when I'm so single and miserable.

It would certainly explain things. Though definitely not excuse them. There isn't anything we can't talk about. Or at least, that's what I thought until Sunday.

But the longer this goes on, the worse I feel. It needs to end soon, for my own sanity.

Though, I can search for a way to pass the time until Flynn comes to his senses. At least HRD4U gives me a bit of a distraction. He's helped me make it through this crappy couple of days with sick kids, teacher conferences, no romantic prospects on the horizon, and the weirdness with Flynn.

His performances are fun and naughty and everything I need to relieve the stress I feel at the end of the day. So as long as I continue to come home alone every night, I'll be coming home to see if HRD4U is online from now on. A little release does everyone some good, and tonight, another lonely night without my best friend beside me on the couch or anyone to warm my bed, definitely calls for one.

I grab my computer and flip off the living room lights. A faint light in Flynn's window, visible through the partially raised blinds, gives me pause. He's home. I could go over there. I could demand he tell me what the hell his problem is and make him come clean. But that's not the kind of relationship we've had—angry and confrontational—and if I press him to talk before he's ready, I may end up only making things worse.

So, it's time to see what's happening with my favorite webcam star instead. I slip into my silky pajama pants and a tank top and settle onto my bed, even though it's only eight o'clock. It might as well be midnight with as emotionally exhausted as I feel.

My fingers fly over the keyboard to load the site.

But the knock on the front door has me jerking my laptop closed. Sitting here, waiting for HRD4U to come online is pretty damn lame. And desperate. And I don't want to become the wallower Alicia accused me of being only a few days ago.

I climb from my bed and slowly approach the front door. Only a handful of people would be on my porch at this time of night. And one of them isn't talking to me. I tug open the door, and Flynn stands holding a bouquet of wild daisies.

My favorite.

"Peace offering." It still isn't an apology for the other day in the car. The way he snapped at me. He hasn't offered any explanation, but it could be coming.

I shouldn't let him off the hook so easily.

He has to know how fucked up that was.

I narrow my eyes at him and put on my best scowl. His other hand appears from behind his back with a bottle of tequila.

*Well, hell...*

*How can I stay mad when he brought tequila?*

"Tequila?" I raise an eyebrow at him. "You know how you react to this stuff."

The man can drink brown liquor with no problem, but give him a little tequila, and he's sloshed within a few minutes with a wicked hangover the next day.

He chuckles and shakes the bottle, taunting me with it. "So, the fact that *this* is what I'm bringing you should tell you something."

I reach out and snatch it. "Come on in."

He follows me into the kitchen and sets the flowers onto the counter next to the bottle I put there. "I'm sorry. I didn't mean to snap at you. I was just...frustrated with some things. I shouldn't have taken it out on you when you were only trying to help."

*Amen.*

At least he's managed to come around to this realization on his own. Most men these days would think what he did was totally fine, not the least bit inappropriate. But Flynn isn't most men.

He's the best of the best.

The tops.

Even when he momentarily acts like a jackass.

After growing up with Bash and Jameson, I should have anticipated the occasional dickish move, and I can't hold a grudge against him when he's standing here apologizing.

"No. You shouldn't have." I grab a vase and two tumblers and set them on the counter next to the tequila and flowers. "But since you brought these humble offerings, I'm willing to forgive you."

A grin splits his face, and he reaches for the bottle. He pours us each a shot and pushes one over to me. "I appreciate that. Not talking to you has been weird. I should have come over sooner, but I thought you were still pissed and maybe needed some time to cool off."

*Time to cool off.*

More like time to heat up. With HRD4U.

I missed Flynn. I missed us talking and joking. I missed us just being...us. But HRD4U's feed at least gave me something to do and a way to ease some of that pain. Far more than I should have let it, honestly.

"I was pissed, but I'm over it. Let's never fight again." I hold up my glass, and he clinks his against it. "Please."

"Agreed. You're stuck with me for life."

This tequila is too good to do as a shot, so we each take a sip and laugh as both of our faces pucker slightly.

Flynn coughs and sets his glass back on the counter. "Whoa. That stuff has some burn."

"Sure does. I love it." I take another sip then grab the flowers and unwrap them before sticking them into the vase. "So, I forgive you, but..."

One of his dark eyebrows rises. "But what? Are you going to make me get on my knees and beg? Are you going to demand a lobster dinner in penance?"

"All great ideas but no." I cross my arms over my chest and examine him.

He looks exhausted, dark circles under his eyes and lines I haven't noticed before marring his face. "Whatever has been bothering you seems serious. I wish you would talk to me about it."

Flynn shoves a hand through his hair and sighs. "I know you do, but really, I'm okay. I'm just...figuring some things out. Nothing you have to be worried about. I promise."

His promise doesn't ease the tense ball of concern in my gut. "You promise you're okay?"

His hand flies over his chest and head in the sign of the cross. "Swear to *God*."

"Well, if you say so. Just remember I'm here if you need me."

"I'll always need you, Rach."

The pain lacing his words makes tears prick my eyes. "You, too." I take another sip of tequila and wave toward the couch. "You have plans tonight? Want to binge-watch something on Webflix and get drunk?"

He sighs and takes another sip as he stares at the flowers. "I wish I could, but I have a massive project due at work tomorrow. I'll be working most of the night. But let's do something tomorrow night."

"My choice?"

"Yep." He bobs his head. "Your choice, since I was the asshole."

"Oh, hell, yes!" I jump up and down and clap my hands. "Mini-golf. You owe me a rematch."

More like a chance to regain some of my pride. He decimated me the last time we played—and every other time, actually—but I can't let that walloping go unanswered. Flynn already has an ego, and he doesn't need it stroked. Though I have yet to beat him at really anything, let alone mini-golf, I have a feeling about this round. Like I'm going to win something big.

A sly smile spreads across his face, and he holds up his glass. "You're on."

Tonight, hopefully, a new live feed from HRD4U.

Tomorrow, a rousing game of mini-golf with Flynn.

It's shaping up to be a great end to a crappy week.

**FLYNN**

Rachel bends over in front of me and wiggles her ass from side to side before she takes her shot. I bite back a groan and lean against the bench next to hole number eight.

The miniature golf course is crawling with kids at this time on a Friday night, but I never mind coming to play. Seeing Rachel's competitive side always makes for incredible comedy.

It must run in the family because given what she's told me about Bash and Jameson, it seems they're all a little overly driven to win. Probably comes from their father.

She knows she'll never beat me, but she insists on coming back for rematches anyway. Then she gets all worked up when she loses, or she tries to cheat and thinks she can get away with it.

I deal with numbers all day, so there's no way she's sneaking something like a dropped stroke or altered score-card past me. I've called her out on her shenanigans more times than I can count over the years, yet she still tries. And I still laugh.

Every. Single. Time.

Because she's just so damn adorable doing it.

This is making the whole "get over her and move on with my life" thing even more difficult. I spent this week trying to get my head on straight about the entire situation. To get myself to a place where I could look her in the eye and tell her I'm not in love with her, if it came to that. But if she asked now, or pushed, I would crumble faster than a weak foundation.

Her ball whizzes through the alligator mouth, past the hole, bounces off the rear bumper, and comes all the way back to us. I lose it and dissolve into an uncontrolled fit of laughter while she stomps her foot and shakes her club at the ball.

"What the heck was that? I had that lined up perfectly!"

I snicker as I shoulder her out of the way to take my shot. "What's your definition of *perfectly*?"

She glowers at me. "Okay, *Tiger*, let's see what you got."

I grin as I line up my shot and swing the shitty little putter the course provided. My ball shoots forward perfectly straight through the alligator's mouth and into the hole with a satisfying *plunk*. "You mean like that?"

*Perfection.*

Which means Rach is going to be *pissed.* She hates losing. At anything. Especially to me. I turn back to her in time to see her scowl again and stomp her foot like the kindergarteners she teaches.

"That's not fair! You grew up playing golf."

I walk over to her, wrap my arm around her shoulder, and squeeze her gently. "True, but it's not like I've played much since high school."

Other than a few rounds with clients, I barely have time

to relax, let alone play on a regular basis. That fact doesn't seem to appease Rachel, though.

"Still, hardly a fair matchup. You played varsity golf, and I learned to putt on a course like this with a damn clown laughing at me trying to get a ball in his mouth." She slides out from under my arm and goes over to hit her ball again. This time, it heads straight for the hole and drops in. She jumps up and down and pumps her fist in the air. "Killed it this time. That's two for me and one for you."

We walk up toward the hole—around the fiberglass alligator and "water hazard"—which is currently inundated with the noise of screaming kids at the surrounding greens and lit by glaring overhead spotlights.

She reaches down to grab both of the balls. Her jeans stretch taut across her ass, and I have to look away.

*Too late.*

My dick swells, and I surreptitiously reach down and adjust it to a less conspicuous position. Hopefully, no one saw that; otherwise, I'll have the cops swooping down on me in minutes, accusing me of touching myself around kids like some sick pervert.

I may be a pervert, but I'm not *that* kind of pervert.

These are the types of things that can't be happening anymore if I'm going to move on and keep things from ever getting weird between us again. Maybe there's some pill I can take to kill my reaction around Rachel the way some men use them to keep it up, only I need to keep it down.

She rises, giving me and my straining cock a break.

I release a deep breath. "Where does that put the score?"

She shrugs and hands me my ball. "I think I have a few more strokes."

"A few more?" I raise an eyebrow at her.

There's no way it's only a *few* more. Rachel sucks. There's no delicate way to put it. She just does. Even after

97

five years of my trying to help, attempting to show her how to putt properly and how to time her shots with the crazy hazards set up on the holes, she hasn't improved a lick. I've seen five-year-olds putt better. Even little Connor can beat her when Alicia and Cade bring the kids along with us.

Still, watching her try is fun, and after all the weirdness between us this week, it's good to be back to our normal easy, laidback state.

"I'm not sure exactly." She bumps me with her hip playfully as we make our way to the next hole.

*Not sure, my ass.*

It's a stall tactic. One Rachel uses regularly.

Still, I can't fight a grin. "Well, let me see the scorecard."

She rolls her eyes, pulls it out of her back pocket, and hands it to me with a scowl.

I scan the card and fight to suppress a chuckle. "You have a dozen strokes on me...in just the last four holes." I burst out laughing.

She smacks me on the shoulder. "Rude much?"

The parents of the family currently playing hole nine turn and glare at us. Apparently, our witty banter isn't appreciated, yet they are letting their six kids run around like little demons, completely unchecked.

I lean in to her, so the judgey parents won't hear me. "I can't believe you wanted to come miniature golfing when you knew there would be screaming kids and you've already been around them all day, and all week."

She watches them with a smile. "Yeah, they can be a bit much, but honestly, I don't mind. They're happy and having a good time. Let them do it."

My heart aches at how damn sweet she is. How good. How goddamn wholesome. It takes a really special person to deal with other people's children all day, to teach them when all they want to do at that age is run around like wild animals.

"You want a brood like that eventually?" I nod toward the kids, and her lips droop into a frown.

She considers my question for a moment. Just long enough that an uneasy feeling crawls over my skin.

"I definitely want kids"—Rachel releases a sigh and nods toward the group on hole nine—"but I don't know about six. That's two-thirds of a baseball team. It can't happen without a guy, anyway, and we both know I haven't had a lot of luck in that department."

It's true; she hasn't. It's not that any of the guys she's dated have really been assholes or openly treated her like dirt. If they had, I would have fucking killed them. It's more that she chooses guys who have no passion for her, for them as a couple. The men she's been with never treated her like the most important thing in their lives and their relationships fizzle out quickly for one or both of them, leaving her heartbroken and single more often than not.

Rachel is far too amazing a woman to be single. She's total wife material, but she needs a guy who will see her for the queen she is and not take her for granted. One who is as passionate about her as she is about him. She needs a *good* guy, one who understands her kind heart and romantic nature. They just don't seem to be the ones she finds.

But maybe I can remedy that. Even though it fucking kills me to even make the suggestion.

————

**RACHEL**

We were having such a good time—laughing, joking around, and ribbing each other like we always do. Then he had to go and bring up the whole *do you want a bunch of kids* thing.

Of course, I do. And he knows that.

I wouldn't be a kindergarten teacher if I didn't love kids and want some. Eventually. But now I'm back to thinking about how pathetic my love life is instead of enjoying myself. Hearing the tick, tick, tick of my biological clock moving closer and closer to that time when it will be too late...

*Shut up.*

The non-existent sound ringing in my ears makes me shudder slightly, but I shake it off and avoid looking at Flynn, so he doesn't see how much his statement affected me.

We move silently onto the next tee and wait for the rambunctious family to vacate the other end where the windmill swings in front of the hole.

Flynn clears his throat. "So, I know you hate being set up..."

I turn and look at him, the annoyance already tensing my shoulders. "Oh, here we go..."

All my friends are constantly trying to set up dates with people they think I'll "mesh" with, and absolutely zero percent of them have panned out to anything more than an awkward dinner. Giant wastes of time. And not something I want to do again.

*I can't even believe he's attempting this.*

Flynn should know by now that I want nothing to do with set-ups. I've never crossed that line and tried to set *him* up—though Alicia's suggestion did get me thinking the other day. After his strange behavior, I wouldn't risk bringing it up now.

He shifts awkwardly. "And you know I've never tried to set you up with anyone, right."

I nod. He really hasn't. Which is always appreciated.

*Who knows what it would do to our friendship if I dated one of his buddies and it ended badly?*

I'd like to hope he would choose me over any male friend, but we all know someone always ends up getting the cold shoulder after those situations. Bros before hos and all that. And the last week has taught me that I can't handle anything coming between us.

Despite the fact that I'm glaring at him and trying to be pretty blatant about my lack of desire to be set up, Flynn pushes on with his spiel, like if he keeps going, I might change my mind.

"Well, this guy I work with—Dan. Super nice guy who's not afraid of commitment."

Red flags fly up, waving in my vision, warning me to beware. Anything that sounds too good to be true usually is. That isn't something you lead with, nor that you would normally tell a co-worker.

"Not afraid of commitment?" I raise an eyebrow at him. "How would *you* know that?"

He looks suddenly pained and rubs the back of his neck. "Well, he was married."

I throw up my hands and roll my eyes. "Oh, great."

That's the last thing I need—to get involved with some emotionally unavailable guy who is reeling from the loss of a marriage. No one wants to be a rebound.

Flynn chuckles and shakes his head. "No, no, no, not like that. He married his high school sweetheart. They never had any kids, and they just grew apart. It wasn't a bad breakup or anything like that. They're still on cordial terms. And they've been divorced for eighteen months, so it's not like this is a fresh wound or anything." He pauses and sucks in a deep breath. "Anyway, I actually think you guys would get along really well, and like I said, he's a super nice guy. The kind of guy you *should* be with."

*Super nice guy.*

Translates into boring mama's boy.

I can already tell where this is going. Nowhere fast. The kind of guy Flynn thinks I should be with is the kind of guys I've *been* dating since I moved out here and we became friends—solid job, kind, complimentary, opening doors, and bringing me flowers. There's nothing inherently *bad* about them. Dozens of women would probably fall over each other to snag men like I've dated, but they weren't perfect. None of them ever seemed to want to spend the kind of time with me that they should and there was never that *spark.*

And I can't exactly advertise what it is I *do* want without being ridiculed and potentially even worse. But if I say no, it's going to look like I don't want to even try and that I don't trust Flynn's judgment in this, and I actually do. He has never tried to set me up before, and he knows I'm still a little salty over the recent breakup, so I doubt he'd even suggest it if he weren't confident we'll have some sort of spark.

So, maybe I'm wrong. Maybe I need to give this guy a chance. He might surprise me...

The family in front of us moves on to the next hole, and we step up onto the fake grass.

He nudges me out of the way with a shoulder. "I won the last hole, which means I have the honors of going first."

"Asshole." I muttered under my breath, but his mouth drops open along with his eyes.

"Did you just call me an asshole?"

I slap my hand over my mouth. I almost never curse—at least not the bad ones—even in front of Flynn. Habit. I'm afraid if I get used to cursing in my everyday life, I'll also let things slip out in class, and nothing else sets parents off more than their kid's teacher dropping an F-bomb in the middle of story time.

He narrows his eyes at me and *tsks* the way Mom used to.

"What can I say? You annoyed me so much, I managed to let one slip out."

His laughter floats through the night air as he takes his shot. This one buzzes right next to the hole and ricochets back, stopping an inch away. I shove him out of the way and then bend to set my ball in place.

He leans on his club and grins. "Well, well, well, look whose competitive side has come out full force."

I sneer at him. "Watch and learn, buddy. Watch and learn."

He steps back and holds up his hands. "Show me how it's done, oh, wise golf master."

*Damn right, I will.*

I shoot a wink at him and send my ball rolling down the green artificial turf toward the spinning windmill. The sad thing is, I have a better chance at making this shot than I do at finding a guy I click with who will fulfill all my needs.

Mom always said to never settle. That when the time was right, the *one* would present himself, and it would be like the heavens opening and angels singing. I don't know where she got that crap. I never saw anything between her and Dad that suggested they ever had that kind of connection, but maybe by the time I was old enough to look for it, they'd been jaded by life and the luster had worn off.

I always remembered Dad as angry and violent with all of us. He never showed any of us, even Mom, and affection, but he must have had his moments if Mom stayed with him for so long.

The fact that Mom still believed in love enough to tell

me that gives me hope. That there *is* someone out there. Hiding apparently very well.

And who better to set me up than my best friend? The person who knows me better than I know myself sometimes.

# 10

RACHEL

My pink, glittery ball rolls down the lane and slams into the front pin perfectly, sending all ten flying.

"Yes!" I jump up and down and pump my fist in celebration as I make my way back toward where Dan sits, waiting for his turn.

He flashes me a grin and shakes his head. "I never would've brought you bowling if I knew you were a ringer."

I prop my hands on my hips and feign offense. "I am *not* a ringer."

He glances up at the digital scorecard and points to it. "Well, your score seems to suggest otherwise."

If you compare my score to *his*, maybe, but I'm not about to insult my date and ruin what's been a really fun night.

I wave him off. "Really, I'm not that good."

His eyebrows fly up. "So, I just really suck, then?"

I laugh and smack him on the shoulder. "You don't suck. You're just…"

One of his sandy-blond eyebrows rises again. "Bowling challenged?"

"Exactly. That's a great way to put it."

And he really does have a great sense of humor about it. Most men getting their ass handed to them on a first date would probably be annoyed.

He rises from his seat, grabs his ball, and glances at me over his shoulder. "I have a good feeling about this one." He winks at me, then lines up in completely the wrong position, and lets his ball go. It glides down the right-hand side of the lane and into the gutter, barely brushing the ten pin. It wobbles and eventually falls. He turns around and fist pumps. "At least I got one."

I can't help but laugh at his self-deprecating humor.

Flynn was right. Dan's a great guy. A really great guy.

And we totally get along. And have a lot in common. And seem to click. At least on a base-level. It's not like bowling is exactly the place or time to have any deep, meaningful conversations about anything.

The ball return spits out his ball, and he grabs it, lines up again, and manages to take out three pins this time.

I grab my beer and take a swig as he works his way back to me.

He snags his beer and leans against the computer console. "Where did you learn to bowl like this, anyway?"

I glance around the bowling alley and take in all the familiar sights and sounds. The crash of pins. The raucous laughter of teenagers. The smiles and celebrations. The cringes of disappointment. It all brings me back to a much simpler time. One when Mom was still alive and we were still a family—even without Dad there.

"My older brother played a lot of hockey when I was growing up, and the rink was right next to a bowling alley. My mom used to bring me and my little brother over to

daughter relationship we had volatile, at best. He was a shit father and an even worse role model as a husband. The only good to come from it was that I knew what I *didn't* want in a partner. Even though he came around in the end and tried to make amends before his death, it still stings when I think about him and his role in my life as a child.

Dan shrugs slightly. "That doesn't make it any less hard. He was still your father, right?"

I nod again. "Exactly."

A fact Jameson can't seem to come to terms with. He's still in deep denial that Dad's death can have any effect on him at all, and I'm not sure what it will take to get through to him. He's an emotional lockbox, always putting on a brave front and refusing to acknowledge anything can hurt him.

Meanwhile, here I am, getting upset because my date used a nickname.

*Let it go, Rach. Enjoy the night for what it is. And know what it isn't.*

This isn't the kind of attraction I expect with someone I'm going to have red-hot sex with.

It's nice. It's comfortable. I'm having a good time and definitely think Dan is attractive. That's been enough in the past. I'm just not so sure it's enough now.

I down the rest of my beer and grab my ball. Part of me wants to take it easy on him. It has to be tough watching your date decimate you. But my competitive side won't let me lose if I have the potential to win. That's a Fury trait I haven't been able to shake over the years. And Dan seems to be taking the beating like a champ.

"Get the strike!"

His encouragement spreads a grin across my face. I line up and send the ball spinning down the lane. It collides with the front pin, and the rest explode, but the seven pin stands, mocking me.

Dan claps behind me. "You got this, Rach. Go for the spare."

"Oh, I will." I flash him a grin before I send the ball straight for the final pin. It ricochets around the back and drops before I turn to him.

"You make that look too easy."

I wave off his comment and sit next to him. "But it's not. Years of practice."

"Well"—he leans into me slightly, his intent clear—"I would really appreciate it if you give me a rematch."

It's the least I can do. A second date. To see if things spark. And sometimes, the best way to see if that happens is to make that final move. I close the distance between us and press my lips against his.

———

FLYNN

I peek through the blinds for the hundredth time, but Rachel's house doesn't look any different than it did twenty minutes ago. The porch light still glares. All the interior lights are still off. No visible movement or signs of life.

She's still not home from her date, and it's almost one.

*Fuck.*

It likely means they're having a great time. Hitting it off. Doing exactly what *should* be happening on a date with someone who—at least on paper—should be your perfect match.

That shouldn't bother me so much.

Shouldn't, but it does.

It *really* fucking *does.*

Since I stood in this same spot hours ago and watched Dan ring her doorbell on that same porch, my entire body has been twisted up in knots. My shoulders tense. My hands clenched. My stomach churning. My blood rushing loudly in my ears.

I've always been a little jealous of the other men who took her out—*okay, a LOT jealous*—especially the ones who brought her home and got invited in. I couldn't even *think* about what was likely happening inside without getting physically ill.

But this feels different somehow.

*Worse.*

This is pure *envy*—another of the deadly sins I've apparently become so intimate with. All consuming. A violent storm of wanting what I can never have which feels even more powerful tonight.

Maybe because I arranged it as the ultimate proof to myself that I can move on and be a good *friend*, if nothing more. Instead, it's only become a form of personal torture I hadn't expected. Or maybe I did.

I might be a masochist and never knew it until this very moment.

Cade was right the other night when he said I needed to make a decision, and I thought I had. I thought I had chosen what was best for both of us. To make a concerted effort to move on—get her dating someone *good*, someone I can trust will treat her right, and start doing it myself if the opportunity presents itself.

I *thought* I was okay with this.

*Then why does it hurt so damn much?*

Dad's death was the worst pain I've ever experienced, but this comes close. Between our recent fight and her maybe out on a date with the man of her dreams...who I set her up with...it feels like death by a thousand cuts.

I take a deep breath and have to physically force my legs to move me back to my room. If I stay in the living room any longer, I'll be tempted to keep getting up and checking. And I don't stop wondering what's happening on their date. If they're clicking. If they're kissing or—

*Stop.*

It's stupid. It's petty and juvenile. It's *selfish.*

Yet...I can't stop myself from doing it.

I flop down onto the bed and stare at my ceiling. This is unhealthy. I need to get my mind off the fact that she's out on a date with somebody who's absolutely perfect for her. Someone I set her up with.

I grab my computer from the nightstand and flip it open. This other world, this other persona has become my refuge, and yet again, I'm turning to it as the lesser of two evils. Either spend the night pining for what I'll never have or spend it being someone else who might or might not be slowly blackening my soul beyond redemption.

The site loads, and I tug off my T-shirt and relax on the bed. Once the views pick up to close to a hundred, I flip on the camera and point it at my bare abs and hardening cock straining against my gray sweatpants.

"Happy Saturday night, friends."

The flurry of hearts and hellos scroll across the screen. I guess I shouldn't feel too bad about being alone tonight since so many other people are at home, too. But then again, they're probably not torturing themselves over someone they can never have.

"I'm having a bit of a rough night, folks. I thought perhaps chatting with you would help cheer me up."

Another string of responses floats to me.

I can come cheer you up.

> What is it you need, HRD4U? I can provide.

> I sent you another PM. Reply and I can take care of that!

I rub my hand over my erection. "I have just what I need right here."

*At least, I can convince myself I do for the time being.*

Sometimes physical pleasure is the only cure for emotional pain—a lesson I've learned well over the last few years.

I roll my hips and thrust my package toward the screen. Wearing gray sweatpants alone is like porn to my viewers. I could come in them without ever exposing myself and they'd be happy. But they've come to expect more than a tease.

And the way I'm feeling tonight...this needs to be a hard, fast orgasm. No toying around. Get the release I need, then I'm going to pass out before I can wonder about Rachel and Dan's date anymore.

I try to visualize a beautiful woman rubbing in place of my own hand, but despite every attempt to conjure up a blonde or redhead, a certain brunette keeps popping into my head.

Rachel's face.

Her lips.

Her hands.

Her tiny little moans of pleasure.

*Goddammit.*

With a groan, I shove down my sweatpants to free my cock, leaving the waistband just below the base. There isn't any need to look at the screen because I know how the viewers are reacting.

Even though they enjoy my longer, more detailed shows, they also love when it's like this. No drawn-out exhibition.

No detailed description of what I would do to anyone here with me.

These enthusiastic shorts show unrestrained passion—something everyone seems to be searching for. But despite my best efforts to keep my thoughts away from her, when I'm touching myself, it always becomes my fantasies with Rachel. What I would do to her. How I would worship every inch of her body. Make her come so many times she can't even walk. Lose myself completely in here. And I can't bear to voice that again. Not when she's out with someone else.

Instead, I stroke faster and grit my teeth against the urge to say her name. It hovers on the tip of my tongue like it has every single time I've done this since becoming HRD4U.

The orgasm builds rapidly, and I shoot my load up across my abs with a grunt. Hot spurts hitting my skin and cooling almost instantly, the same way my moment of bliss disappears in the blink of an eye.

I lie panting on the bed for a moment before I force myself up and glance at my laptop. As expected, the usual comments, hearts, and flower emojis fill my screen. I lean forward and scroll through them until I reach the bottom and freeze.

*INEEDSOMED is back.*

The one who had me thinking hard enough that I needed to go to confession and traumatize Father Lafayette with my filthy side-hustle.

INEEDSOMED

Thanks for the show tonight, HRD4U. I don't know what has you so down tonight, but I suspect it may be a special someone. I'm telling you, any woman who doesn't jump on the opportunity to be with you is a moron.

# 11

**FLYNN**

Another Sunday morning, another church service. At least this time, I don't have Rachel brushing up against me and her scent wrapping around me while I lock eyes with the man on the cross.

I'm not sure I could take that today.

Not after her date with Dan last night.

Even doing a live feed and relieving the tension didn't help with the pain of knowing what she might be doing with him.

Her porch light was off by the time I finished my feed and walked back to check the window—even though I promised myself I wouldn't. So, I knew she got home okay, but I couldn't stop wondering if she was alone or not...

*No.*

Even if that damn statue wasn't staring right down at me, those aren't the thoughts I want in my head. Not at home. Certainly not here. I close my eyes and shake my head to try to clear the mental images.

*Don't think about it.*

*It's not your business.*

I set them up because I thought they had a lot in common. It was the act of a good *friend.* One who should be happy if they like each other, not jealous. Something I've been reminding myself of since the moment I watched him walk up to her porch to pick her up last night. Something I will have to *keep* reminding myself of since her late return suggests things went well. If it hadn't, she would have been home well before I resorted to the sin of lust to try to forget about what she was out doing.

*Be happy for them.*

*Smile.*

*Breathe.*

I force my eyes open as Father Lafayette rises to his feet and motions for the congregation to do the same.

*Thank God it's almost over.*

This entire Mass has been unbearable.

Father's eyes keep drifting my way—especially during the sermon on lust that seemed very pointed and rather timely planned. And there was a look...almost like he knows it was me in the confessional and chose that particular topic today specifically for me.

It's supposed to be anonymous—a place to seek forgiveness without judgment. Yet, the conviction in his gaze now leaves no question—he knows what I do every night. As if it's not bad enough that the big man upstairs and his son are judging me, now I've got Father Lafayette doing it, too.

*So much for anonymity in the confessional booth.*

The words of the final prayer ring out, and as soon as the choir starts the closing hymn, I lean down to Mom. "I'll meet you at the diner for coffee."

Her hand shoots out and grabs my wrist. "You're not darting out of here again. We're going to mingle and say hello to everyone before we leave. They were all asking about you last week when you disappeared after the service."

*Dammit.*

I should've known it wouldn't be so easy to sneak away. It means a lot to her to be friendly with the congregation, and on a normal week, it might take anywhere from twenty minutes to an hour to finally make it down the back steps and out to our cars.

Sneaking away last week wasn't my best moment.

It was rude and selfish.

And it wasn't fair to Mom.

I force a smile, trying to ready myself for the onslaught of her friends and their relentless questions. "Okay, Mom."

She releases my wrist, and I remain in the pew for the recessional hymn. Voices of the congregation and the choir fill the air and settle over me like a heavy blanket of condemnation.

> *"And when I think of God, His Son not sparing*
> *Sent Him to die, I scarce can take it in*
> *That on the Cross, my burden gladly bearing*
> *He bled and died to take away my sin."*

I shift under the pressure and look down at the hymnal as Father Lafayette and the processional leave the front of the church and make their way down the aisle toward the back.

*Don't make eye-contact.*

If I don't look at him, he can't judge me.

*Why is it so easy to shut this out when I'm on camera and so damn hard here?*

Hundreds of eyes watch me on their screens every time I login, but I never question what I'm doing in those moments. Yet I take one step into this building, and it feels like I want to crawl out of my own skin.

Slowly, each row of parishioners files out, and I follow Mom down the aisle toward the back doors and the stairs leading outside. She pauses to greet friends and neighbors, and I shake the hands of faceless people and make pleasant conversation about the weather and families I don't know and whatever other mindless things people chatter about.

A few ask the dreaded "why aren't you married yet" questions, which I laugh off as visions of Rachel walking down the same aisle I just flick through my head, driving a knife into my chest again.

When we finally reach the rear of the church, Father Lafayette stands at the top of the steps, greeting parishioners as they move past him. His eyes light up, and he smiles as Mom approaches him. He takes her hand and clasps it between his. "Emily, it's always so nice to see you."

Mom smiles at him. "It was a lovely service, Father. Thank you."

He nods and smiles at her, and she moves down the steps, waving to someone below. His head turns, and his old, pale-blue eyes connect with mine. Any humor drains from his face.

*Shit. What do I do?*

Instinctively, I extend my hand.

He looks down at it.

It hangs there awkwardly.

For five seconds...

Ten...

Twenty...

Sweat forms on my palms, and I wipe the one not sitting out unaccepted awkwardly on my pants. This man knows what that hand has done. What that hand did just last night on camera...again.

He knows he will be touching the vehicle of my sin.

My skin heats the longer he doesn't take it. Bile rises up my throat. The world spins around me slightly. I sway on my unsteady feet.

Mom glances over her shoulder back at me.

*Crap.*

Someone is going to notice.

Slowly, Father LaFayette reaches out and clasps my hand. His grip tightens, and he shakes. "Flynn, always nice to see one of our younger members of the congregation. I do hope you've been behaving yourself."

I cringe internally but try not to react externally to his statement.

He knows. There's no question about it at this point. It was a not-so-subtle question about whether I've been continuing with the site since confession.

I squeeze his hand back and nod. "As much as I can, Father."

He frowns slightly, but I'm saved from any further awkwardness by the approach of the Jacobson family and their three kids from behind.

*Thank you, God!*

I release Father Lafayette's hand and book it down the steps toward Mom without a look back.

*Holy awkward.*

No way I can deal with this every week, knowing what he knows. I may have to convince Mom to switch to a different parish.

———

## RACHEL

Harsh, bright light streams in from the window and hits my face.

"What the hell?" I bury my head under the pillow. "Who opened my curtains?"

I throw off the pillow and reluctantly open my eyes to find the culprit heartless enough to do this to me.

Alicia stands in front of the window, holding two ceramic mugs from my kitchen. "You do realize that it's almost eleven o'clock?"

The smell of coffee hits my nose, and I groan. "I knew I'd eventually regret giving you a key. Why didn't you let me sleep?"

She chuckles. "Because you would sleep your entire day away if I let you."

*Not wrong.*

*But still...*

*Rude.*

The blinding-light thing is a little bit harsh. There's no way I'll get back to sleep now. I groan and sit up against the headboard. Alicia hands me a mug, climbs up next to me, and leans back.

She nudges my shoulder. "Drink your coffee and lose your attitude."

Alicia may be a bit harsh and direct at times—I think that's the litigator in her—but she's the kind of friend everyone needs at least one of. The one who will tell me the dress makes my butt look big or that I should never have done something. She's the real and honest one. The one I can always count on, even though she may tell me things I don't want to hear.

I take a sip of the steaming-hot latte.

*At least she made my drink right.*

She waggles her eyebrows. "So...how was the date last night? You must've been out pretty late because this is sleeping in, even for you."

I play with my mug. "Yeah, I didn't get home until almost one."

Her eyebrows rise. "Wow. That's the latest you've been out with anyone in a long time." She grins. "So, Flynn's friend wasn't a total dud?"

Laughter bubbles up in my throat, and I take another drink to give myself time to figure out how to answer that. "Definitely not a dud. He was actually pretty great. Like Flynn told me, he divorced his high school sweetheart over a year ago, but they're still on good terms and see each other because they share custody of their dog."

She drops her head back and booms out a laugh. "They share custody of a dog?"

I grin and nod. "It was actually rather adorable the way he talked about Simon, their German Shepherd."

"Gosh, could you imagine if Cade and I ever separated? The kids would be fine, but poor Prince would be a mess."

Our shared laughter fills the room. That poor dog is such a hassle, but the stories alone make keeping him around worth it.

Alicia sighs and shifts. "So, it wasn't weird dating a divorced guy?"

"Not really. The split was amicable, and other than the sharing custody of the dog thing, it seems like they both moved on. They haven't had any issues. He doesn't seem to have any baggage from that relationship."

"Well, that's good. Other than that, how was he?"

"Handsome. Intelligent. Funny. All the same things anyone could ever want in a date, but..."

"But?"

*It just wasn't* there!

"I don't know." I shrug and take another sip of my latte while contemplating the best way to explain it without telling her I came home after the date and immediately logged on to watch HRD4U.

Alicia frowns. "There was no spark?"

I shake my head. "No, actually, there was definitely a spark. It's more like there was a spark but no flame..."

She considers my response for a minute and then shakes her head. "Honey, you can't expect there to be a flame on the first date. You barely know the guy."

I glance over at her. "This from the woman who met her husband when he came into her office as a *client* and basically *stalked* her."

Her jaw drops in mock indignation. "Ouch. Totally true, but *ouch*." She shifts to face me and cradles her mug in her hands. "So, maybe don't use me as your guide here, since my story probably ends badly for anyone else, but my point is still valid. A spark is a good start. A spark can *start* a flame. Sometimes you need to get to know someone better before things fall into place and you fall in love."

*Fall in love.*

I probably wouldn't even recognize it if I *were* in love. It's nothing I've ever experienced. Attraction—sure. Lust—yes. Really, really liking someone—absolutely. But love? The all-consuming, need them to breathe kind of thing that Alicia and Cade share—I can't say that's anything I've ever had in my life.

Though it's probably the single thing that I've wanted most.

Maybe because I never saw it with Mom and Dad, and once Mom was gone, I needed something to cling to. Or I could just be a desperate, hopeless romantic.

I squeeze my hands around my mug until my fingers

whiten. "What if I can't find love? What if I'm not meant for it?"

She throws her hand into the air. "Well, you'll have great sex for a while, or in your case, mediocre sex..."

I chuckle. She has no idea the true extent of how unfulfilling my sex life has been. I can't even tell Alicia the truth about what I really want. All she knows is I haven't been getting it. And if she knew I have been fulfilling my fantasies lately by watching some random stud perform on the internet, I'd never hear the end of it.

"I hope I don't have mediocre sex for the rest of my life."

"So, go on another date with Dan, the guy you have a spark with, and maybe it will become a raging inferno of lust that will spill into the bedroom and wake up your dusty, yawning lady parts."

I almost choke on my coffee and sputter. "Jesus, you can't say stuff like that."

She raises an eyebrow at me. "Why not?"

"Because..."

"Because I'm a mom? Doesn't mean I can't enjoy good sex. And let me tell you, Cade—"

I throw up a hand. "I don't want to hear it. I still have to look him in the eye, you know."

She chuckles and climbs from the bed. "Are you awake enough to get out of bed and come to brunch with me?"

"Don't you have the kids?"

"Nah. Let them have some time with Daddy so we can have a mimosa or two."

As much as I'd love to stay in bed all day, a mimosa does sound good. My stomach rumbles. And some pancakes and hash browns wouldn't be bad, either.

I toss off the covers, set my mug onto the nightstand, and slide from bed. "Give me five minutes to change."

She leans against the wall with her mug. "So, are you going to give Dan another chance to stoke a flame?"

I grab a pair of jeans and tug them on. "We'll see what happens."

When Dan dropped me off last night, he didn't even attempt to make a move. We parted with a short, almost chaste kiss that left me craving more...but not necessarily from him. Hence my late-night log-on to the HRD4U site.

*Could Dan really cut it? Could there really ever be a flame there?*

*Or will the spark just fizzle out like all the other ones?*

# 12

## FLYNN

Our waitress returns and refills my coffee for the third time. The steam rising up from it gives me something to look at besides Mom. After my run-in with Father Lafayette, I can't even seem to look at her without my stomach turning slightly.

When you can't even look your own mother in the eye, you know it's bad.

*Shit.*

This might be the end of my career as HRD4U. He has been such a good thing for me, and he never got in the way of my relationship with Mom...until now.

And I don't want anything between us.

Leaving him behind would solve a lot of problems, but that doesn't feel right, either. Even if I didn't need the money, I still enjoy doing it. Or at least, I did, before the guilt showed up and became overwhelming.

It makes other people happy. I like doing that. And it gives me something else to keep me occupied instead of dwelling on my unrequited love for Rachel. I don't want to give it up, which means I need to figure out a way to get over whatever this is, just like I'm figuring out a way to get over my feelings for Rachel. Slowly. And maybe not well. But I'm trying.

"Earth to Flynn."

"What?" I meet Mom's eyes and can't miss the concern in them.

Moms never stop worrying about their kids, even when they're adults. I've done my best to keep from doing anything that would cause her to have to be concerned for my well-being, but it appears I've failed miserably.

She chuckles. "Where did you go just now?"

I shrug and take a sip of the hot coffee. "I'm here."

*Sort of.*

She laughs again, but it sounds forced. The apprehension lingering behind it makes her smile falter. "If you say so."

Twisting her mug between her hands, she stares me down, her mouth set in a firm line that's always meant she has something to say.

"What, Ma? What's that look for?"

The corner of her mouth tips up. It may have been a mistake to open that door. "Are we ever going to discuss the huge elephant in the room, or should I say, huge elephant who was sitting next to you on that bench last weekend?"

I drop my head back and chuckle. "Did you just call Rachel a huge elephant? Oh, she's going to love that."

Mom scowls. "You know that's not what I meant."

"I know, but still, I would avoid referring to women as elephants if I were you."

She nods at me with a grin. "Duly noted. But, seriously, Flynn, I think we should talk about you and Rachel."

The acidic, *really bad* coffee churns in my stomach. If Mom didn't love this place so much, I would insist we go

126

somewhere else after Mass each week, but I don't have the heart to bring it up when this was her and Dad's place for so long. It's a sentimental thing and has nothing to do with the quality of the coffee or food.

I push my mug away and instead reach for my water glass. Something cold might help chill the heat rising up my spine. "There's nothing to talk about."

My words come out sharp and a little harsher than I had intended, and Mom offers me a scowl.

"Your reaction just proves my point. I'm not blind, Flynn. You're in love with that girl."

I groan and rub my temples. "Even if I am"—I hold up a hand—"and I'm *not* saying I am—it doesn't matter. We could never be together."

"Why not?" Her question is so simple, and she says it like the answer should be, too.

*Far from it.*

If things were that easy, I wouldn't have spent the last five years with my heart belonging to someone who will never claim it.

"Because she's my best friend. If something were to happen and we broke up..." *Like perhaps she found out I jerk off for total strangers on the internet.* "I wouldn't be able to live with myself, knowing I had ruined the closest friendship I've ever had."

Mom *tsks* and shakes her head. "You're looking at this all wrong, Flynn."

"How so?"

She stares down at her coffee for a minute, and when she looks up, her eyes shimmer with unshed tears. "Yes, there's a risk that if things go badly, you could damage your friendship, but the potential reward far outweighs that. Look at your father and me. We were best friends before we got married. That old saying that you should marry your best friend is an old saying for a reason, kiddo." She swallows thickly. "Somebody you're friends with before you get romantically involved with usually already knows you pretty well. They know your deepest, darkest secrets. They know you in and out—likes and dislikes, the adorable little quirks that make you *you*, and you haven't scared them away yet. That's what makes them perfect for you. That's what makes you and Rachel perfect for each other."

If only she knew the truth. She wouldn't be talking like this is some fairy tale or cheesy romance novel. This is real life—where we have secrets we keep even from our best friends.

"I wish that were true, Ma, but it's just not."

Rachel doesn't know my deepest darkest secrets. She doesn't know everything that makes me tick. She's blind to a huge part of my life. Everyone is. And it's the way it has to be.

Mom means well, and what she said about her and Dad is true. They had the perfect relationship, the ideal marriage. They were always laughing and touching each other and kissing. As a kid, it grossed me out to know my parents were still so into each other, but now, as an adult, I can see how healthy the relationship was and how everyone should strive to find it.

What she said might be true for other people, it just isn't for Rachel and me.

I reach across the table and grab her hand. "Ma, I appreciate it. I really do, but there are things you don't know. Things you can't understand, and things I'm not really at liberty to discuss."

She narrows her eyes at me. "At liberty to discuss?"

That may have been the wrong phrase to use, but I hope she won't question me any further.

"I *can't* discuss."

"Are you all right, Flynn? You haven't really been yourself lately."

No, I'm not. And I know I haven't been acting like myself. Between Rachel and our argument, HRD4U and his adoring fans, work and unhappy clients, and Father Lafayette and his judgment, it feels like an avalanche sweeping me under it.

"I'm trying. I have some things I need to sort through and get over, move on from before I can really take the next step in my life."

She squeezes my hand and nods. "Just make sure that the next step is in the right direction. And if that direction happens to be toward Rachel"—she shrugs—"so be it."

A smile tugs at the corner of her lips, and I can't help but return it. She sees far too much and knows me far too well. She only wants what's best for me. But what's best for me and what I can have are two completely different things.

*Why does Rachel have to be so selfless and angelic and perfect?*

They're just some of the reasons I love her, but also the things that make anything between us impossible. Someone that sweet and innocent would be horrified by me, by my demands.

She's a kindergarten teacher, for Christ's sake...the last thing she wants is a man smacking her ass and plowing into her while talking about how hot and tight her cunt is. Mom may have faith that things will eventually bring us together, but I lost that faith a long time ago.

It's time I start broadening my horizons and stop being so focused on Rachel. She'll be my best friend until the day I die, but at some point, I need to stop pushing away every opportunity that's presented to me.

Rach had a shitty breakup and got back on the horse

and let me set her up with Dan. The least I can do is keep my eyes...and heart...open.

———

**RACHEL**

"You did what?" Alicia practically screeches the words at me.

I wince slightly where I sit across the table from her on the outdoor patio at our favorite brunch spot. Telling her about what happened last night after I got home from my date with Dan was a bad idea. The judgment and shock on her face are enough to have regret clawing away at my chest already, but all her talk of sparks becoming flames wouldn't get out of my head. When I think of flames, I think of someone like HRD4U, not someone like Dan.

"You heard me."

Her mouth gapes open. "Yeah, I heard you say you've been watching some dude jerk off online."

I glance around us, at the full tables of people enjoying their brunches, but it appears no one heard her comment.

*Thank God.*

When she says it like that, it sounds creepy. And like she thinks I'm desperate. But men watch porn all the time.

*So why, when a woman does it, does it become perverted or weird?*

I scowl at her. "Yeah, I have, but I'm not desperate. I was watching some porn, and, well, a pop-up suggested his website, so I thought I'd go take a look. And I discovered this guy, and he's not creepy at all and seems really nice and cool."

Alicia rolls her eyes and takes a sip of her mimosa. "Girl, I never said you were desperate. Everyone watches porn, and if they say they don't, they're probably lying, so you're not desperate, but you may be a tad delusional. Any guy who jerks off online and lets people watch is a perverted weirdo. There has to be something wrong with the man. He can't do that and be *normal* and 'nice and cool.'"

*Can't he?*

One of the very big reasons I've never told her about my proclivities before was the fear she might judge me for them and suddenly be uncomfortable with my teaching Connor, but now the need to defend myself—and other *perverted weirdos*—rises with my blood pressure.

"I fully admit I'm a pervert for watching it. And I don't think it's a bad thing."

One of her eyebrows rises, and she smirks. "I never said it was a bad thing. I loved my pervert enough to have married him, but he doesn't jerk off online for rando strangers."

"True"—I point at her—"but he did bang you in a supply closet. Not much better."

She collapses into laughter loud enough that it draws the attention of the tables around us. "Sorry!" She holds up a hand to them in apology before turning back to me. "I just don't want you ignoring the very real guy in front of you for an imaginary one online."

I bite my lip and peek at the other tables to make sure there aren't any prying ears before I lean forward slightly. If I'm going to come clean, now is the time to unload all of it. "That's been part of the problem with these guys I've been dating in the first place. They're all so boring and vanilla. If I told them I liked watching porn and using my vibrator, they would've been intimidated and scared and likely run for the hills."

"So, what? Are you saying you want a guy who will watch porn with you?"

"Hell yeah! And maybe use my vibrator and some other toys on me. And definitely dirty talk during sex. I *need* the dirty talk."

Alicia's jaw drops. "How the hell did I never know this about you? You fucking perv." A grin spreads her lips. "I love it. And there are plenty of men like that out there in the world. Sounds like what you need *is* a pervert."

"No, not a pervert." That makes it sound so illicit. "Just a *nice* guy who knows how to have some fun and get dirty in private."

"You mean a nice guy like Flynn?" She raises an eyebrow.

*Why does she have to keep bringing up Flynn like that's ever going to happen?*

She can't accept we are only friends and always will be. I had hoped explaining what I'm looking for would help her understand once and for all why we will never be more than friends.

"Yes, like Flynn, only dirty. Why can't there be a dirty version of Flynn?"

She chuckles. "Maybe you can make him dirty? Dirty him up?"

I shake my head and enjoy my mimosa as I contemplate a dirty Flynn.

It only makes me laugh uncontrollably.

I just can't. He's too nice. Too clean. Too wholesome. I mean, he attended Catholic school his whole life and still goes to church with his mom. He volunteers for overtime at work so that other people can have holidays off. He opens the door for people and always finds ways to cheer me up with something innocent like kicking my ass at mini golf. There isn't a dirty bone in his body.

Nice guys like *that* don't talk dirty or fuck girls brainless.

They're sweet and "make love" all the time. That certainly has its place and time, but not *all* the time.

"That will never happen." I wave a hand at her. "Anyway, I messaged the guy last night."

She freezes. "You what?"

"I mean, I didn't message him directly, but I commented on his video."

"Did he reply to your comment?"

"I don't know. I haven't logged back on. But I doubt it. I commented one other time and never noticed a response."

She scrambles to set her glass on the table and grabs my phone from next to my plate. "Let's check. What's the website?"

"H-R-D, the number four, and U, then dot com."

A laugh bubbles out of her mouth. "Hard for you? Really?"

"Just open it."

She giggles and leans forward across the table so I can see as the familiar site pops up. Her eyes widen at the very prominent picture on the cover page of his hard cock and torso. "Jesus, you're right. This guy's hot, and what a damn package!"

"I know." A warm flush floods my cheeks.

"And he does live feeds and also posts things on the site?"

I nod. "Yeah, he's got pictures of his dick, pictures of himself doing things in the nude, and then he does live video streams, and occasionally, he'll post them to the site, but it's mostly just for subscribers to see the lives."

"Well, shit. I don't see anything from last night." She scrolls on the screen for a second. Then her eyes drift up to the corner where my screen name is displayed. "Wait, is this your name? INEEDSOMED?"

I slip my hand over my face that's likely as red as a tomato right now. "It's all I could come up with."

"Jesus, girl"—she laughs—"you need help."

"I know."

I really, really do. The question is, what kind of help? Mental? Physical? Both?

*Probably both.*

A good, hard fucking with a little therapy thrown in for good measure might be just the ticket to finding sanity.

Alicia's brow creases. "What's this little red number one icon over your name on the top corner?"

I lunge toward her and grab the phone. "Holy shit! It's a private message."

"From who?"

"I don't know. I've never gotten one on the site."

She rises, rounds the table, and drops into the seat next to me. "Well, don't just stare at it. Open it."

I click on the icon. "Oh, my God. It's from HRD4U."

HRD4U

> I saw your comment on my live video last night and the one from the earlier feed. I know it can be difficult to find what you're looking for. I, myself, have been struggling to find someone. Though, honestly, I haven't really been looking, and like I said in the video, I wouldn't ever date one of my viewers.

*Crap. Did he think I was asking about us getting together?*

I wasn't.

*Well...I mean...*

If we had met under more "normal" circumstances and hit it off in other ways besides sexually. But that isn't the case. This is an online porn star and I'm a kindergarten teacher. I definitely wasn't suggesting we get together, and it would be a bad, bad idea.

Alicia slaps me on the arm. "Write him back!"

"Oh, my God, I have no idea what to say. For real, what should I say to him?"

She squeezes my arm and practically squeals with delight. "Just be honest."

"No." I shake my head and close my phone. "No, I'm not writing him back."

*What the hell would I say? Really?*

"You really should. It might be fun to chat with a hot online porn star."

I turn toward her. "Weren't you the one just telling me to give Dan a chance?"

She returns to her chair across from me. "Well, yeah. But why can't you do both?"

*Just be honest.*

*Easier said than done, isn't it?*

Especially when honesty means admitting my deepest, darkest secrets, the ones I just told my close friend only now. Then again, I don't know him, and he doesn't know me.

*So, what's the worst that could happen?*

# 13

FLYNN

The front door flies open, and Rachel flutters in with a giant pizza box balanced on her hand. "Hey, have you eaten yet? I come bearing pizza."

My stomach gurgles, and I drag myself up into a sitting position from where I've been reclining on the couch and motion toward the seat next to me. "Grab a seat. I was just trying to find something to watch."

*For the last three hours.*

It's been impossible to concentrate on anything. I've flipped aimlessly from cooking shows to reality home buying to 90s comedies. Nothing can hold my attention. Which seems par for the course lately.

Rachel plops down next to me, and her soft, sweet scent wafts across the narrow space between us, overpowering even the smell of the pizza and making my cock twitch.

*So much for getting over her.*

My conversation with Mom this morning didn't help anything. I can't get what she said out of my head. *You should marry your best friend.* I glance at Rachel out of the corner of my eye. She flips open the box, and I lean over to grab a slice of pizza.

I scowl at it and scrunch up my nose. "Really? Veggie lover's?"

Her shoulder rises and falls. "It's good." Her words are barely discernable around a glob of pizza, yet even talking with her mouthful, she's cute as fuck.

I grin at her. "You know, if it had meat on it and zero vegetables, it would be good. It's called a meat lover's pizza."

This argument never gets old or less funny. Even after five years of disagreement over pizza toppings, neither of us will ever change what we like, and we'll both suffer through eating each other's favorites whenever a piece is offered.

She laughs around her second bite. "If you don't like it"—she shrugs and sits back against the couch—"don't have any more."

"I'll eat it." I point a finger at her and try to restrain my smile. "Reluctantly."

She nods and waves her hand. "Yeah, yeah, whatever. I knew you would. When have you ever turned down pizza, or any food, for that matter?"

It's true. I never turn down a meal. Especially with her.

"You don't need to remind me how chubby I'm getting."

Her laugh floats over to me. "Yeah, right, Mr. Abs. So chubby."

The woman has no idea what it takes to stay in this shape and still eat the way I do. My early morning runs and daily workouts before she's even out of bed are worth it, though, to be able to enjoy a couple of greasy slices—even if they are covered with vegetables instead of delicious meats—and still be able to appear in prime shape as HRD4U.

She points toward the television. "What did you put on?"

"Nothing yet."

138

"Why don't we watch that movie on Webflix. That one everyone's been talking about with the zombies."

I arch an eyebrow at her. "Really? You want to watch a zombie movie?"

Typically, she's trying to talk me into some chick flick while I'm trying to convince her an action flick would be better.

She smiles and nods. "Yeah, blood and guts and the undead sound perfect for a Sunday evening."

"*Okay.*" Not exactly my idea of good entertainment, but if it's what she wants, I have a hard time saying no to Rachel about anything. "Whatever you want."

I find the movie on Webflix, select start, and reach for a slice of pizza. Rachel grabs for the same slice, and our fingers brush. A little jolt shoots up my arm, and I freeze. But she doesn't seem to feel it.

She brushes my hand away with a laugh. "Hands off. That's my slice."

I grab a different one, sit back, and peek over at her— seemingly unaffected by the slight contact the way I was. Maybe because she hasn't spent the entire day obsessing over me the way I have been her.

*How do I bring this up casually?*

It's been plaguing me since the moment I opened my eyes this morning. The question I can't figure out how to voice. The potential answer I might not want to know.

I swallow my bite and try to keep my eyes focused on the innocent woman who will clearly be a zombie victim on the screen so I don't have to watch Rachel's response. But my eyes drift over to her again anyway. "So? You had your date with Dan last night, right?"

She freezes with the pizza halfway up to her mouth, coughs, and nods slowly. "Yeah, I did."

"What's with that reaction?"

Her eyes flick over to mine. "What reaction?"

"Oh, don't start playing that game. Like I don't know you well enough to have noticed that. What's wrong? You mad at me because you didn't have a good time?"

She averts her eyes back to the television. "I never said that." A moment passes while she chews and pretends to watch the movie while I can see the wheels churning in her head. "I actually had a really good time. You were right. We have a lot in common."

"But..."

*There's definitely a but.*

I can always tell when she's holding back, and she's definitely holding *something* back from me about Dan.

She shrugs. "There doesn't have to be a but, does there?"

I shake my head and take a bite of pizza. "No. There doesn't always have to be a but. It just seems like there always is." Especially with the guys she's been dating lately. And if she really did like Dan, I would think she would have come over here raving about him and thanking me for setting them up. Her apathy speaks volumes. "Are you gonna see him again?"

The words burn leaving my mouth, and my throat tries to close around them. As if one date isn't bad enough. A second one would probably kill me.

She shakes her head. "I don't know. He asked if he could call me, and I said, yeah, but I haven't heard from him today."

"You probably won't."

*Shit. That sounded harsh.*

Her head whips around, and she narrows her eyes on me. "Why? Did he say something? Did you talk to him?"

I shake my head. "No. Just a guy-code observation." I shove another bite of my piece of pizza into my mouth and finish chewing. "He's gonna wait to talk to me at work tomorrow to see if you said anything about him first. He doesn't want to appear overly anxious or desperate or anything like that."

She laughs and covers her mouth, half-full of pizza. A second later, she swallows and her eyes flicker with amusement as she examines me. "Really? Aren't we a little old to be playing these *what did he say about me/what did she say about me* games?"

I point my half-eaten piece at her. "You're the one who just asked me if I talked to him and if he said anything, so it seems like you're both acting like children."

She presses her perfect-bow lips together in a firm line. "Touché." Her focus returns to the movie. "Hey!" She waves at the TV. "Start the movie over again. We missed the beginning."

I grab the remote and rewind it to the beginning.

She finishes the last two bites of her pizza, shifts closer to me, and drops her head against my shoulder, leaning her small body into me. That flowery light scent I will always associate with her invades each breath. I try my best not to stiffen—my body or my cock—at the contact and breath through my mouth so I don't inadvertently bury my face in her hair to take a whiff.

I switch my pizza into my left hand, wrap my arm around her shoulders, and tug her closer. The first zombie appears, and she yelps and jumps, snuggling even tighter into me.

Tonight is going to be torture.

*AGAIN.*

———

## RACHEL

I shouldn't be contacting him, but I haven't been able to get his message out of my head since brunch this morning. Even though Alicia goaded me and tried to get me to reply while she sat there, looking over my shoulder, I just couldn't do it. At least not with her that close. I needed time to think about whether I wanted to reply at all.

When I commented on his feeds, I never thought he'd respond in the thread, let alone in a private way. Lots of viewers make comments—hundreds every single time he does a feed. And he's never given any indication that he has replied to any of them.

*What was it about mine that made him feel like he needed to reply? And why the hell can't I stop myself from typing a response to his now, hours and hours later?*

Probably because I can't sleep after watching that horror movie with Flynn.

I thought some blood, guts, and gore might take my mind off everything—my homesickness for Bash and Jameson, my loneliness and desire to find love, my unwise attraction toward the mystery man on the screen—but I was so wrong.

Being snuggled up against Flynn felt so *good*.

Too damn good.

Good in a way it shouldn't and hasn't before.

Good in a way that it can't be because of what I want out of a partner.

What he can never provide.

I attribute it to the weird sexual charge I've felt since getting HRD4U's message this morning. One I apparently need to do something about, because my fingers fly over the keyboard to write a response to him before I can even second guess it.

> Wow! I wasn't expecting to get a message from you. I hope you didn't think I was trying to hit on you with my comments. I really wasn't. I was being serious. I have such a hard time finding men in this city who aren't mama's boys and aren't anemic in bed. I know you won't ever get involved with a viewer, and I swear I wasn't suggesting it, but maybe you know where I would find a guy like you in SoCal?

I hit send before I can stop myself. It was probably a stupid thing to do. I should have let it be and gone back to being a gawker, not a talker.

A few minutes later, the message icon blinks.

*He wrote me back!*

HRD4U

> You're brutally honest and direct. I like that. Any woman who can say exactly what she wants is a good thing. The chances of unspoken things becoming hang-ups are slim. But in terms of finding a guy, I don't know. I actually live in SoCal, too, but I don't exactly talk like this to my friends or other guys, so I don't really know what they're like inside the bedroom.

I freeze, staring at his words.

*He lives* here?

INEEDSOMED

> Wow. It's definitely a small world. And I kind of figured you wouldn't be able to send me in the right direction. A guy like you is one in a million and almost too good to be true.

HRD4U

> Am I? It doesn't always feel that way.

His self-doubt tugs at something deep inside me—the very same feeling I've been dealing with. It's hard to think you're worth it all when no one treats you that way. And it always seems I open my heart to people who won't—except Flynn, of course.

INEEDSOMED

> Everything I've ever seen tells me you are. But maybe I'm just jaded because of the lack of good men.

HRD4U

> Keep looking. The small world has lots of people in it. I have faith your prince will come eventually.

It's nice that someone has that faith because I'm not so sure I have it anymore.

INEEDSOMED

> ha ha ha :-) It's not a prince I want. That's the problem.

HRD4U

> Most girls want the fairytale ending and a prince on a white horse in shining armor. It's so...refreshing to chat with someone so honest. Most of the women who view my feeds would immediately jump on the chance to send me nudes and beg me for something—internet sex or a real meet up. I delete hundreds of PMs every day doing just that. It's been nice talking with you. Hope you enjoy my show tonight.

INEEDSOMED

> ;) Don't worry. I will.

With a huff, I fall back against the headboard and release a heavy sigh.

Tomorrow starts another long week, and with my regular teacher's aide gone, I'm going to have to deal with a sub. The kids can really act up when Michaela isn't with me, so I'm already anticipating the worst. And I'm not sure I can emotionally stomach it right now.

Everything has felt so off since Dad died, in a way that can't so easily be fixed. Heading to New York to see Jameson or Vegas to see Bash and Greer is starting to look better and better. If I wouldn't lose my job by taking a bunch of sick time on short notice, I would be tempted to book a flight and leave in the morning.

I grab my phone and dial Bash instead.

It rings twice before he answers. "Hey, favorite sister, what's up?"

The familiar greeting brings a smile to my lips. "Not much, favorite brother. I just haven't talked with you in a while."

"Is everything okay?" Concern laces his question.

"I'm all right, I guess."

"You guess?"

I sigh and close my eyes. "I talked with Jameson the other day."

"Really? Is there something wrong with him? I mean, besides the usual?"

I snort and chuckle. "He's fine. Busy, as always." I twist my fingers in my comforter. "We talked about Dad for a second."

Bash's silence speaks volumes.

"Well, I mostly talked. Jameson didn't want to hear it."

The eldest Fury sighs. "I'm not exactly surprised."

"Me, either. But I was trying to explain that I'm feeling a bit...lost lately."

"Come see me." The words come fast and sure, like he knows exactly what I need without me even saying it.

"Bash, I can't. I have—"

"You have vacation time."

I shake my head. "I took off too much time to take care of Dad. If I tried again, I'd probably be fired."

"Then I'll come to you."

That's an offer he never could have made even six months ago, but so much has changed—his life, his career. He gave up everything for Greer but somehow is happier than ever. I guess that's what finding the love of your life can do for you.

"You don't need to do that, Bash. I just wanted to hear your voice and check-in."

"Are you sure there's nothing you want to talk about?"

There are a dozen things I want to talk about, but I can't. Not with my big brother. Not with anyone—except maybe HRD4U.

*Why is it that telling things to a stranger is so much easier than telling my best friends or my brothers?*

"Really, Bash, I'll be fine. It's just been rough the last couple of weeks."

"Well, you know where to find me. And if you need me there, all you have to do is ask."

"I know, and I love you. Goodnight."

"Goodnight."

I hang up and open my computer again. The loneliness I've felt since Dad's passing threatens to overwhelm me and drag me down under a tide of despair at times like this. But knowing HRD4U will be going live tonight gives me something to look forward to.

Mom always said to be thankful for small—or in his case, very large—blessings.

# 14

FLYNN

The knock on my office door has my head jerking up.

Dan leans against the jamb of my door casually. "You got time to join me for lunch?"

I glance down at the papers spread out across my desk—a jumble of numbers and figures. They haven't been making much sense in my head for the last twenty minutes, anyway. After movie night with Rachel, the refreshing chat with INEEDSOMED, and my late-night solo session, I was utterly exhausted when my alarm blared this morning. My brain can't seem to get into gear.

*Fucking Monday...*

I stretch back in my chair, my back and neck popping. "Yeah. I could eat."

And actually, it isn't all doom and gloom.

Work-wise, things are finally starting to look up. A bunch of my clients' portfolios skyrocketed this morning after the Fed announced the reduction in the interest rate, making them very happy. Happy clients make me happy and make my days a hell of a lot easier than dealing with angry, disgruntled ones.

I can't seem to muster up any joy about it, though. Not when I know that Dan's going to want to talk about his date with Rachel. I've been dreading this moment since Saturday.

Setting them up was a bad idea. I hadn't contemplated what it would be like hearing how great things are from both sides. At least when she's dating someone I don't know, I'm not the one in the middle of them. And her reaction last night definitely showed she cares what Dan thought about their date. There was something there. Something I had seen even before they ever met.

Sometimes, I hate being right.

"Let's get out of here." He motions for me to follow him.

"Give me a minute to organize this shit, or I'll come back and get stressed out again right away."

He chuckles, steps into my office, then glances out the door before turning back to face me. "So, I went out with Rachel on Saturday."

I nod as my gut tightens. Lunch suddenly doesn't sound so appealing. "I know. She told me that last night."

His eyes widen. "You saw her?"

"She lives next door, Dan. She's my best friend. I see her all the time."

*Shit.*

That sounded rude and like I'm annoyed. It's not Dan's fault I set them up and they clicked. I need to dial it back a bit.

Thankfully, he doesn't seem to have noticed my tone. He chuckles and drops into the chair across from me. "Right, right. Isn't that weird? Having a best friend who's a girl, not to mention a *hot* girl?"

I open my mouth to answer, but I can't quite form any

response that doesn't sound jealous. So instead of looking at him, I stack the various piles on my desk back into order.

My silence doesn't seem to deter Dan, though.

"I mean, Rachel is *smoking* hot." He gives me a questioning look. "I can't believe you're not interested in her."

It appears I'm a better actor than I thought if he never picked up on anything. I busy myself with organizing my desk and try to avoid answering the question. "Did you have a nice time?"

He grins and nods. "Yeah, it was actually pretty great. One of the best first dates I've had in a long time. Did she say anything about me?"

I chuckle as our conversation from last night returns. It's like being back in middle school. "Not much."

"Is that good or bad?"

I shrug. This is the problem with setting up friends— you end up being stuck between them, whether good or bad. "I don't know. You'll have to ask her."

He chews on his nail and watches me for a minute. "You think I should call her and ask her out again?"

I clench my jaw and bite back the *no I don't want you to fucking touch her* response that tries to work its way up my throat. "Do whatever you want, Dan. I don't really know or have any control over what Rachel does with her dating life."

"Fair enough." He holds up his hands. "You want to stay out of it in case things go south."

"Sure, that's it." At least he offered me an out of this super awkward conversation.

He nods. "I get it; setting up friends is always risky. I promise I won't do anything to get her mad at you." He grabs his phone from his pocket. "I'm going to text her now before we head out."

*Of course, he is.*

I rise from my chair and slowly make my way around my desk as his fingers tap away at his phone screen. My eyes automatically drift to the time. Rach will be on her lunch hour. The only time she looks at or responds to messages during her workday.

*She'll probably be excited.*

And isn't that a kick in the balls.

The whole "moving on" thing seems a lot easier in theory than it is in actual practice. Even the little chat I had with INEEDSOMED last night can't keep away the pain of thinking Rachel may finally find someone who isn't me. What I said to that girl was true, at least, I've always thought it to be: the small world has lots of people in it. And I believe there's someone out there for everyone.

I just need my head to convince my heart that it's not Rachel.

My phone buzzes in my pocket, and I pull it out as I follow Dan out into the hallway.

RACH

Guess who just texted me?

I scowl at my phone.

Dan?

Her reply comes almost instantly.

:-). He says he wants to go out again.

Are you gonna go?

I told him yes.

My chest tightens. My arm tingles, and my phone falls from my hand onto the tile foyer in front of the elevators.

*Christ, is this what having a heart attack feels like?*

The pain radiates from my chest out my arms and up my neck to the back of my head.

*No, I'm too young and healthy for a heart attack.*

This is worse. This is hate and jealousy over a man I *like*, over a man I set up with Rachel, a man who is my *friend*.

Deep down, I hoped she would say no. I prayed I had misread both of them and the date totally sucked. I longed to have her say *no*.

"Rachel just said yes to going out again." Dan presses the down button and turns to look at me. "Hey, man, you okay?"

I suck in a deep breath. Two. Three.

"Yep." I bend down and grab my phone.

The elevator doors slide open, and I follow him inside. I force my fingers to type out a reply.

> Have a good time.

> :-) You gonna be around tonight? We can get Chinese?

I don't know if I can handle another night sitting next to Rachel on the couch and watching TV. Her arm brushing against mine. Or even worse, snuggling. Her laugh filling my ears. The chaste kiss on the cheek before she leaves for the night.

*No. Definitely not.*

I just need a little breather. A night off. Especially with this surge in the market, I'll be working late tonight as it is. When I do get home, I'll probably be too tired to do anything.

> Sorry. Working late.

> Okay. Talk to you later.

151

The elevator dings, announcing our arrival at the parking structure. I hadn't even noticed we were moving. I need to get out of my own head. None of this is healthy.

We step out, and I shove my phone back into my pocket.

Dan stops in front of me, and I bump into his back.

*What the hell?*

"Jesus, man!" He glances over his shoulder at me. "Who the hell did you piss off?"

I step around him and look over to my car.

All I see is red.

And not because I'm angry.

My breath catches in my throat as I stare at the red paint —or at least I *hope* it's paint—splattered across my windshield and hood.

Dan slowly approaches it. "Does that say *whore*?"

*Oh, God.*

I struggle to swallow back the bile threatening to make me gag. "Sure looks like it."

Somehow, I manage to keep my reply sounding calm when inside, my heart thunders against my ribs, my blood rushes in my ears, and my hands are shaking.

*This is bad.*

*This is so, so bad.*

He turns to me with a smirk. "You having hot sex that I don't know about?"

I move toward the car, slowly, as if delaying arriving there will make what I'm seeing disappear from my vision. But when I reach the hood, the offending word is still there.

A message.

One that, directed at me, can only refer to one thing.

I circle the car, checking for anything else, but the mock blood only appears on the front. "Not that I know of."

It's been two years since I dated anyone seriously, and that ended as amicably as possible. She said she felt my heart wasn't in it—probably because I was falling more in love with Rachel every day.

*But, oh, fuck.*

*What if one of my viewers found out who I really am...*

If they somehow figured out my real name, it wouldn't take much to find me. A simple Google search would bring up the firm's website and an entire profile on me. And our parking spaces down here are labeled with our names, so it wouldn't take any real planning to try to locate my vehicle.

The slashed tires could be written off as anything. A disgruntled former employee. A pissed-off client who lost money in the crash. Maybe even somebody who hates BMW owners because they think they're rich pricks. Which I definitely am not. If I were rich, I wouldn't need to be HRD4U.

I didn't worry too much about that because I *had* written it off as some weird fluke. Nothing like that had ever happened to me before, and there was no reason to think it was something to actually *worry* about. No real direct threat, at least.

But *this* is a very *specific* message. One directed at a very *particular* part of my life.

*Shit.*

I rub the back of my neck. As far as I know, no one else knows about what I do...except Father Lafayette, and I doubt he's coming all the way down here to my parking structure to desecrate my car in hopes that I'll reform my sinful ways.

"Kinda strange—first the tires and now this." Dan comes to stand beside me. "Any idea who did it?"

"Not a fucking clue."

All I do know is something is definitely up.

I reach out, run my fingers through the glossy red

marring my car, bring it to my nose, and sniff it. "At least it's paint and not blood."

Dan chuckles, but the humor doesn't reach his eyes. "I'm serious, man. What are you gonna do? Somebody seems pretty pissed at you."

I sigh and nod while rubbing the paint between my fingers. "Yeah. They do."

But it's not like I can report this to the cops. If I file a police report and tell them that I think it was one of my viewers, I'd be outing myself to the entire Redondo Beach Police Department—at best—and at worst, somebody else could get a hold of the police report and make it public. Considering what a small town and tight-knit community we are, this information would spread like wildfire once someone knows.

I can't risk that. "I'll check with building security to see if they have any cameras that caught anything suspicious." I turn and check our parking level. "I don't see any down here. I think they may just be at the entrance and exit."

Dan scans the area and nods. "And they did it early enough that no one coming out for lunch would catch them. Pretty smart, actually."

That's what worries me.

This isn't random.

And it's related to a part of my life that *must* stay private.

I need to be more careful and double-check all the safeguards I have in place for my identity—the company name and PO box tied to the website, the voice distortion software. And I have to review every live video I've ever done and every single photo I've ever posted to make sure nothing inadvertently ID'd me.

But I *know* there isn't. I'm meticulously careful about this.

Still, I need to check.

I pull my phone out of my pocket. But for right now, I need to find a detailing service that can come clean up my car.

Dan sighs and stares at the angry message. "So, I guess you're not going to lunch?"

I shake my head. "Sorry. Suddenly lost my appetite. And hey..."

He turns to me with an eyebrow raised.

"Please don't say anything about this to Rach if you talk to her. I don't want to worry her."

———

## RACHEL

The seven Chinese takeout containers lie open on my counter, and I stare down at my empty plate, smeared with various remnants of the deliciousness now sitting like lead in my stomach.

As always, I ordered way too much food.

Way. Way. Way. Too much.

But Flynn usually eats with me, and I've gotten used to having a little bit of everything—including the things I would never usually order for myself. So even though he's working late tonight, I ordered all his favorites, too.

If he stumbles home super late and didn't have anything to eat at the office, at least there will be something waiting for him here.

I climb from my stool at the counter with a groan and trudge over to the window to look out toward his still, dark house. Today was just as exhausting at work as I anticipated it being, and it's already almost nine o'clock. Unless I missed Flynn coming home, he's still at the office.

Unusual for him.

Even though he cleans up well and looks good in suits, they're definitely not his favorite attire. He'd much rather be home in a pair of sweatpants and a T-shirt than in a tie strangling his throat. If something kept him there late like he said, it must be important, or he would have just brought his work home with him and done it comfortably.

Which means he's likely miserable...and hungry.

I grab my phone and shoot him a text.

> Hey, are you home? I have extra Chinese. Your favorites.

The three little dots I normally see within a few seconds of contacting him don't appear. I stare at the screen for a few moments, but nothing.

*Strange.*

Unless he's in a meeting or talking to a client, Flynn usually responds almost immediately, and I doubt he has meetings or client calls this late.

*I hope everything is okay.*

Worry unsettles the massive amount of food sitting in my stomach. I press my hand against my abdomen to calm it and fire off another text.

> I'm gonna leave it in my fridge. Come on in and get it when you get home if you want to. I'm going to hit the sack early tonight.

Though, I'd probably sleep better if he came in to let me know he was home safely and had been fed.

*Why are you worrying, Rach?*

*He's an adult.*

But that doesn't prevent me from worrying about him the same way I do Bash and Jameson.

That innate "need to care for everyone" gene definitely passed from Mom to me. Even as a child, I was always mothering Jameson and trying to Bash despite him being older, stronger, and grumpy about it. Becoming a teacher for little ones just starting in school seemed so natural that I never even thought about doing anything else with my life. Now it's impossible to turn that off—even where Flynn is concerned, even though he's perfectly capable of taking care of himself.

I close all the containers and place them into the fridge, but my gaze darts to the window again.

More than likely, absolutely nothing is wrong. He's just at work. An unusually late night, but nothing to get into a tizzy about.

But my mental pep-talk doesn't stop me from sending another text, this one to Alicia.

> Have either of you heard from Flynn tonight?

Alicia replies almost instantly.

ALICIA

> No, why? Is he missing or something?

*Crap, now I'm worrying her for no reason.*

> No, he told me he was working late tonight. He just isn't replying to my text.

> Maybe he's on a date?

*Oh, God.*

That possibility hadn't even crossed my mind. But the weird way he acted during our little tiff coupled with this sudden late night "work session" suggest I might be right about there being a secret girl. Someone he can't or won't talk to me about.

> Don't you think he would tell me if he were on a date?

The thought that he might not makes me wish I hadn't eaten so much. It feels an awful lot like jealousy creeping up my esophagus—mixed with fried rice, crab Rangoon, sweet and sour chicken, and everything else I wolfed down.

But that can't be it.

I've never been jealous of Flynn dating, nor him I. Though it *has* been a while since he's seen anyone, jealousy just isn't our thing. We don't get green with envy or try to interfere with each other's lives. We're happy for each other when the other has someone in their life.

We don't *do* jealous or petty.

So, it can't be *that*.

It can't be why I suddenly feel like dropping to my knees in front of the toilet and unloading my stomach. The Chinese just isn't sitting well. That's the story I'm going with. The idea that I might actually *care* that Flynn is on a date and lied to me about it needs to go away—fast. It's too dangerous. Too complicated. Too much of the things Flynn and I have never been.

Before I can question it too much further, my phone rings in my hand, and Alicia's name flashes on the screen. I answer as I force myself to turn away from the window and staring at his house. "Hey."

"To answer your question, yes, I do think he would tell you if he were on a date. But I'm wondering why you're so worried he might not. Are you jealous...because you love him?"

She sounds so hopeful. Like she expects me to all of a sudden admit the deep, hidden feelings she thinks I have for him.

"Alicia, come on. Do I need to say it?" I sigh. "Of course, I love Flynn. He's my *best friend*. But now you *know* why it can never work. I would never risk our friendship to see if there's anything more there. Not when I know how he is. And I'm *not* jealous. I'm just worried because of how he's been acting lately."

"You're sure?" She doesn't bother to hide the skepticism from her voice. "Really sure?"

"Yes." Maybe that answer was a little too fast, but I am sure. No matter what, Flynn is my best friend and always will be. 'Til death do us part. Besties for life. Nothing more and never anything less. I won't let whatever weirdness happened between us the other day occur again. If he ever tries to shut me out or shut me down like that in the future, I'll start playing dirty.

"All right. Well, if we hear from him, I'll let you know. You do the same because now you have me wondering what the hell is going on."

"I will. Goodnight."

"Night."

She hangs up, and I pull the blinds aside again to check out his house for the umpteenth time. Still dark. And if I don't do something else besides wait around for Flynn to show up, I'll drive myself nuts.

I start to turn from the window when bright headlights move down the street toward me, and his car turns into the driveway.

*He's home.*

He parks on the driveway, then unlocks his front door, and the light in his living room flips on.

But still...no return text.

He must have been driving when I texted earlier, but he's home now. And I'm standing at the window like a total creeper watching his house.

*Again.*

*Connor was right the other night.*

This is what it must feel like to be a stalker. And it doesn't feel good.

Like I'm intruding on his personal life and space. Like I'm seeing things I shouldn't.

Flynn and I have always shared so much. Basically everything. But to keep tabs on his every move and obsess over something that I shouldn't be worried about crosses the line from "friend zone" to "stalker zone" for *sure*.

I close the blinds and force myself to head back to my bedroom to climb into bed. My laptop still sits on the nightstand where I left it last night before I finally fell off into a restless sleep.

The convo with HRD4U wasn't far from my mind today. It hurts as much as it gives me hope that guys like that are out there. I'm not sure I would have still said yes to Dan's second date request if it weren't for what HRD4U said. Coupled with Alicia's insistence to give it a chance, it felt like I was giving up too soon to say no just because we didn't throw ourselves at each other and tear off each other's clothes on the first date.

Sex on the first date isn't really my thing *anyway*, so I shouldn't so easily dismiss Dan because he was *respectful* and didn't *try*. It doesn't mean it won't be incredible when it *does* happen.

*Right?*

That question rattles around my head as I brush my teeth and climb under the covers. The key clicking to unlock the front door echoes down the hall and into my room, the quiet of the house making the sound even more noticeable. I stiffen on the bed for a moment before I relax.

*Flynn.*

He's the only one besides Alicia and Cade who has a key,

and there's absolutely *no* reason they would be here this late, especially after I just spoke with her.

The sound of the fridge opening and closing reaches me, and then his footsteps move down the hall toward my room. He appears in the doorway, still in his suit pants and what was once a crisp white button-down work shirt, the top two buttons open to expose his neck and top of his chest, but he appears to have ditched the tie long ago. His mussed dirty blond hair is even more disheveled than usual, and the dark circles under his eyes almost make it look like he's been punched, but it's clearly just sheer exhaustion.

He holds a take-out container in one hand and a fork in the other. "Hey. I figured you were still up since your text didn't come that long ago."

"Uh, yeah." I shift myself up until I'm sitting against the headboard. "Just got into bed, actually."

A loaded fork full of lo mein makes its way to his mouth, and he chews as he pushes off the jamb and walks over to the bed. He lowers himself next to me on the mattress and reclines against the headboard.

"This is good." He holds up another forkful. "I needed this after the day I had."

His exhaustion weighs heavily in his words, and I can't detect any hint that he was lying to me about where he was tonight. Maybe it is just work making him so touchy and moody lately.

I drop my head to the side and watch him eat. "You okay? I was a little worried when you didn't respond to my text."

He swallows and tilts his head to face me. "My phone died hours ago. Forgot to bring a charger to work. I plugged it into my car charger and saw your message when I got home."

"Ah."

A tiny smile tugs at the corner of his lips. "You don't need to worry about me, Mom."

I smack his chest. "Ha ha. Very funny."

The slow grin that lights up his face makes my chest warm. "It is nice you care enough to worry, though. I'm sure my mom appreciates you taking care of me since I stopped letting her a long time ago."

"You're welcome. Thank you for not getting pissy about me being a worry-wort."

"Never." His eyes darken for a split-second, perhaps remembering the way he snapped at me the other day for worrying and asking too many questions. "Thanks for dinner." He holds up the container. "As soon as I finish this, I'm crawling home to climb into bed myself."

"You look like you're about to pass out right here."

He grins at me. "I might."

It wouldn't be the first time we've shared a bed, but it has been a long time and none of those incidents were really on purpose. More like both of us passing out while watching a movie or TV and being too lazy or tired to move.

I wouldn't mind snuggling with Flynn most nights, but he looks like he needs a good night's sleep, and I need a hell of a lot more tonight after all the stress of the day.

I'll open my laptop once he leaves to see if I can get it somewhere else.

# 15

**FLYNN**

The lock clicks into place behind me after another Friday night out with Rach, and I trudge over to the couch and drop onto it with a sigh. I ate way too much tonight...and drank too much...

*Fucking tequila.*

I should've known better than to agree to go for Mexican with Rachel. She always insists on the bottomless pitcher of margaritas. And me and that much tequila *no es bueno*. Me and *any* tequila is bad—let alone copious amounts—but I still drink it for *her*. Because she loves it.

Which is why I couldn't say no when she wanted tacos tonight...and a rematch on the mini-golf course.

Long weeks require a release at the end, and this one was hell. The emotional aftermath of Rachel's date with Dan, the attack on my car that building security was zero help with, more late nights working now that the market is climbing...it all added up to utter exhaustion.

The only thing that would have gotten me out tonight

was Rach. But spending a night with her has its drawbacks —on top of the hangover I'm going to have tomorrow.

I unbutton my jeans and work my already hardening cock out. It can be a gift. The only time it becomes a curse is when I'm hanging out with Rachel, and she's bending over and wiggling that tight little ass at me all innocently.

Some people might think it's intentional, that she somehow senses what she's doing to me and enjoys playing with me, but it's one hundred percent innocent—like she is.

Rachel doesn't have any idea how badly she affects me. And if she did, she would probably end our friendship because she would never go there. She wouldn't want to risk sending me "mixed signals" if we kept hanging out so much.

It always gets so awkward when one friend develops these feelings for the other. Things are never the same. I've seen it happen to other people, and I won't let it happen to us when I know that door is closed.

Sitting on her bed with her the other night, eating Chinese only emphasized that fact. Her crack about passing out in her bed was just that...a joke. Because we have slept in the same bed together. Several times. But it was never sexual, even when I started realizing how in love with her I was.

Her comment wasn't an invitation or sexual innuendo. If it had been, she wouldn't have agreed to go out with Dan again only hours before. And the rest of this week has been a blur of meetings, telephone calls with happy clients, and avoiding angry ones who are now even *more* angry because they missed out on the huge market surge by pulling out.

I needed a night out. Really, I did.

I just could have done without all the cockteasing.

But at least it gives me a "little" something for my subscribers.

I reach forward on the coffee table and flip open my laptop. It takes a second to get the perfect camera angle of my hard-on. I snap a still pic and upload it to the site with a little message.

HRD4U

Hope you're having a nice Friday night, everyone. I'm exhausted and a little bit drunk, so no show tonight. I'll catch you soon. I promise to make it up to you.

Hearts, sad faces, and comments pop up within seconds in the comment section under the photo.

I don't know whether to be flattered or sad that viewers follow my site so closely that they see an upload so fast.

Damn HRD4U! I've been waiting all night.

Thanks for the "little" treat.

I'll save this for later.

Get some sleep HRD4U so you can give us a good show tomorrow.

Why are you ignoring my PMs?

HRD4U if I were there, I would keep you awake.

HRD4U, come on, you know you're gonna take care of that might as well do it live.

Normally, I would. But I'm not even in the mood. Thinking about Rachel being on another date with Dan next weekend when he's back in town has my stomach churning and my tacos threatening to make a reappearance. I lean forward to close the screen when the red personal message icon rolls over to 22.

*Ugh.*

I don't really want to deal with any of the PMs tonight. The angry ones. The horny ones. The begging ones.

*But what if it's INEEDSOMED?*

I wouldn't mind talking to her tonight. There hasn't been a single conversation with her that I haven't walked away from with a smile on my face. Even though the rest of this week has been little more than checking in with each other and saying hello, the fact that she isn't pushy and doesn't seem to want anything from me is incredibly refreshing.

The fact that she gets me thinking about a possible future with someone other than Rachel is both sickening and hopeful.

As much as I say it, I'm not sure I'm ready to move on from Rach. I'm not sure if I can. But this girl I've never seen, never met, never even talked to other than through messages, reminds me there are other people out there. Nice, friendly, really genuine women.

I click open my inbox. It *is* her.

INEEDSOMED

> Sounds like you had a rough night. I had one myself. A little too much tequila.

I chuckle as I type my response.

HRD4U

> Same. Is that why you're home alone at 10 o'clock on Friday night?

*God, that makes me sound really lame.*

Her reply pops up.

INEEDSOMED

> No. That's because I'm a loser.

I chuckle at the irony of her comment.

HRD4U

You're not a loser.

If she is, that makes me one, too.

INEEDSOMED

How could you possibly know that? You don't know me at all.

*True.*

But I have a feeling about her. Since she sent that first comment...

HRD4U

I can just tell.

INEEDSOMED

Oh really?

HRD4U

Really. I have loser radar, and it's not flashing right now.

INEEDSOMED

Ha ha ha. If I'm not a loser, then how come I'm sitting here, waiting for you to come online tonight?

I don't like for anyone who watches me to think of herself or himself as a loser for doing it. It's as bad as me considering myself some big sinner. Which logically, I know, isn't the case despite my ingrained Catholic upbringing making it difficult. Having it crammed down my throat for so long makes it all that harder to overcome. And I'm struggling. Massively.

Nothing wrong with wanting to have fun...

INEEDSOMED

But we're not having any fun. You said you're too tired and drunk.

HRD4U

I did say that.

But my still-hard cock throbs to remind me that it's there and could use some attention.

*I can't believe I'm going to say this.*

I lean forward and type the words.

HRD4U

I might be able to be convinced to have some private fun if you're up for it...

The longer the delay in her response, the tighter my gut gets. This was a fucking stupid idea. Really stupid.

*Did I actually just invite her to have webcam sex with me?*

It's one of the things I always swore I would never do. It crosses the line into actual hooker behavior as opposed to doing it myself. At least, it's how I've always rationalized that what I do on camera isn't prostitution. She's a paying customer...she has to be to view my live feeds. That means if she takes me up on my offer, she's effectively paying for sex...or a form of it. Only two people involved makes it sex in my book.

And my invitation seems to have stolen her words. But the request to open a video chat pops up on my screen before I can retract my statement.

*Holy hell. Well, I guess if she's okay with it...*

I double-check to make sure my face isn't visible—because the last thing I need after the two incidents with my car is another crazed viewer finding the *real* me—and click "yes."

The image on my screen makes my breath catch in my chest.

Perfect tits—high and round. Flat expanse of her stomach. And a pair of mile-long legs spread wide open to display a shaved and glistening pussy.

*Sweet mother of God.*

I'm going to need to go to confession again.

————

## RACHEL

I must be insane, or at the very least, really damn desperate.

*Why else would I be sitting online with a total stranger, buck naked, with my legs spread open, ready to rub one out?*

I've reached the lowest of lows, but honestly, I don't care. A girl's gotta do what a girl's gotta do, and right now, I have to do me.

Tequila always does this to me—turns me into a raging, horny sex machine. It would probably be wise to avoid drinking it until I have someone in my life who can satisfy this craving. It might prevent me from ending up like this.

Horny. Alone.

And apparently willing to do something *way* outside my comfort zone.

I can't believe I'm actually thinking it, but in this very second, I'd give anything to know where HRD4U lives so I could drive over and let him fuck me hard and whisper dirty things into my ear.

The man has a beautiful body, a beautiful dick, and a filthy mouth...

*What more could I ask for?*

Not much in this moment—except for it to be real and here.

A second after I send the video request, his stomach and hard cock appear on my screen. He reaches down and grasps his dick. "Jesus, you're fucking beautiful."

The voice distortion should be off-putting since it gives him an almost robotic sound, but right now, it's the last thing I'm thinking about, and since I have the same feature turned on, he's hearing me with the same alteration. Though I might be willing to have a little fun with my online friend, that doesn't mean I'm prepared to reveal my identity. It's one thing being INEEDSOMED, with the protection of anonymity. Being Rachel Fury isn't an option.

I laugh and run a finger down across my breast and over my erect nipple. "You think so?"

"I do."

Of course, he's going to say that; he's about to jerk off to me. Then again, if he didn't find me attractive, we probably wouldn't even be having this conversation because he wouldn't be hard or interested. He would have taken one look at the screen and lost his mojo. But that certainly hasn't happened.

His hand glides along his thick length. "Let me see you touch that beautiful cunt."

A shudder rolls through me at his words, and I slide a finger through the wetness between my legs. He growls low and strokes his dick.

*God, I'd give anything to have him right here, right now.*

Truly anything.

I can't remember the last time I was given a true and proper fucking. But watching this man, with the body of a god, stroke himself while watching me has me close to coming already.

The buzz grows between my legs, and I drag a finger

back and forth through my core and up over my throbbing clit.

"Fuck." I drop my head back as I swirl that tiny point of pleasure, but I don't want to miss anything.

I force my eyes open and back to the screen as my breathing picks up.

His big hand slides up and down his dick slowly. "Yeah, baby, do it. Rub your clit while I stroke my cock, thinking about you. Imagining being inside your dripping cunt. Thinking about having your sweet mouth wrapped around me and coming all over you, down your throat, and inside you. Fucking you so hard and so good that you won't walk tomorrow."

*Jesus, the man can talk a good game.*

The slow burn of my impending orgasm has me shifting on the bed to give myself a better angle. I shove two fingers inside me and work my clit with my thumb. He groans and redoubles his effort. His hand pumps faster and faster, up and down, sending his abs rippling and the muscles in his forearm and biceps bulging.

Heat spreads out from my center. "I-I'm gonna come."

Embarrassingly fast, too.

Like it's been so pent up, it's been sitting just below the surface, waiting to erupt at any second. It seems like that's where I've been hovering ever since I discovered HRD4U's site.

I let my head fall back, and wave after wave of pleasure courses through me, making it utterly impossible to see straight. Bright lights flash against my closed lids, and my breath catches in my throat as my orgasm fully consumes me, drawing me into that blissful state of hanging out in a hazy.

He growls then gasps. "Jesus! Fuck!"

There's barely time for me to open my eyes before his cum shoots from his cock and up across his washboard abs.

*Wow.*

My chest heaves in time with his, and he sags back with a heavy sigh.

Silence blossoms between us.

*What do you say after doing something like this with a total stranger?*

I've never done the one-night stand or random hook-up thing. That isn't really in my DNA. But I imagine this must be what it feels like right after.

*What's he thinking?*

*What a huge mistake this was?*

This is awkward.

*Should I log off?*

Finally, he shifts forward to grab something before settling back. He wipes his cum off with what looks like tissue and tosses it to the side. "Thank you. That was incredible. *You* were."

Warmth fills my chest at the simple compliment. Thank God he said something because I have no idea what I would have managed to come up with that wouldn't have made me sound totally lame. "It was."

The guilt I was expecting doesn't appear. Instead, a sense of relief fills me for the first time in a very long time. I got what I needed, what I've been looking for—something *dirty*—from a man I've never even met.

*I can't believe I'm going to say this...*

"Maybe we should do it again sometime?"

He pauses for a second, as if considering his options. "In person?"

*Holy shit.*

I hadn't meant that, but now that he's mentioned it,

would it really be that bad an idea? We live in the same area. We're both consenting adults.

*Why shouldn't we get together and enjoy ourselves a little?*

It doesn't mean we have to do anything. I'm not looking for a fuck buddy, but HRD4U seems like a genuine guy, and as long as we meet in public, I can always walk away if it's weird.

There would be no strings attached. No expectations. Just a meeting.

"Okay." My voice wavers a little. "We can do that. But I think we should meet somewhere public."

I need to be careful. He seems sweet and charming, but so did Ted Bundy. And Jeffrey Dahmer fooled a lot of people, including the cops, for a very long time. I need to protect myself and make sure I'm not arranging my own death.

That's a little morbid, but still.

"Good idea. Tomorrow night? At The Shed?"

The Shed is a good idea. Busy. Always lots of people. Very public. Plus, they have great drinks and food, and there are plenty of things to do—pool, darts, even board games at the tables. It's a popular place for a reason.

I release a relieved sigh. "That sounds good. What time?"

"Six?"

"Six, it is. How will I know it's you?"

It's not like he can drop trou and swing his massive length around until I see it and reveal myself. Though that image makes me chuckle softly.

He shifts his position, making all his hard muscles flex again. "I'll be in a blue button-down and jeans."

I need to wear something easy to spot, so we aren't wandering around looking for each other all night. "I'll be wearing a red shirt."

"Perfect. Then I'll see you tomorrow." He pauses for a moment. "Unless you want to go another round?"

His cock stirs to life almost instantly at the words, and I grin as I reach over to my nightstand for my B.O.B.

"I could definitely go another round or two."

"My kind of girl."

*My kind of guy.*

# 16

**RACHEL**

I can't believe I'm really doing this.

    With a shaky hand, I brush over my silky blouse and look down at myself.

*You look good, Rach. Relax.*

Actually, I look better than good. I look smoking hot. Hotter than any kindergarten teacher should. Black leather leggings hug my curves like they're painted on, and the deep V of my shirt shows more cleavage than I would normally allow. But tonight felt like a *going-all-out* night.

If I'm going to meet a total stranger who I've jerked off with, I might as well be the fun and flirty Rachel instead of the conservative teacher version I have to be during most of the time. Then again, maybe dressing like this will make him think I'm open to exploring what we did online in person. And I am nowhere *near* ready to say yes to that.

Yet.

*You're just having a drink.*

*It's not like you're gonna walk in and have sex right here at the restaurant.*

Although…if I really think about it, that might be kind of hot, actually. The whole public sex thing. I've never tried it, mostly because if I ever got caught, my job and career would go down the toilet so fast, it would make my head spin. But the idea of being *that* naughty. Of the possibility of someone seeing us. I can't deny it sends a shiver of anticipation and warmth through my body.

And, if anyone would be up for it, it's probably HRD4U.

*Jesus, I don't even know his real name.*

I'm walking in to meet with him—maybe…probably for sex, eventually—and I don't even know the guy's name.

I *am* crazy.

But it would be rude to turn back now and stand him up. And like I've told myself a thousand times since our "chat" last night, this is just a drink. Either of us can walk away with no hard feelings. Yet no matter how many times I remind myself of that, my heart won't stop racing, and the shaky breath I take doesn't do anything to calm my nerves.

*How do people do this?*

*Meet up for drinks or more with perfect strangers?*

I shove through the door into The Shed with that question still lingering. A cacophony surrounds me—the clang of silverware, the barrage of voices—people laughing, joking, having a good time.

My stomach churns.

*Ugh. I might throw up.*

I thought I had mentally prepared myself for this, but it's completely new territory. With another deep breath, I scan the small group of people waiting for a table but don't see anyone in a blue button-down.

*Maybe he's running late.*

My watch reads 5:55, so maybe I'm early. Or, he might have arrived even earlier and already gotten us a table. I guess we never talked about that.

This was a little ill-planned. A rushed idea neither of us really thought through. Spur of the moment. But if I had actually had time to sit and consider it, I may not have even agreed.

I might still be sitting at home on a Saturday night feeling sorry for myself instead of being here.

*Should I walk through and see if he's here?*

Typically, if I arrive somewhere early, I'll grab a drink at the bar, so that's the most logical place to start. I make my way toward the long, dark wooden bar, brushing past groups of people standing around with drinks and chatting, and freeze.

Someone with a very familiar profile sits on a stool at the end of the bar.

*Holy shit.*

*What the hell is Flynn doing here?*

He said he was busy tonight, but I didn't pry. Not after Monday and being unnecessarily mom-like by worrying about what he was doing. Not after the fight before that. I don't want to pry *anymore*.

But now he's here, and I can't let him see me with this guy. He'll want to know how we met, how we know each other...and we don't have a story for that. Plus, I'm supposed to be going on a date with Dan next week when he gets back into town. Meeting up with someone else now seems... odd...and Flynn might feel obligated to tell Dan about it. I don't want to hurt Dan by making it look like I immediately scheduled another date when I knew he wouldn't be around.

*Shit. Shit. Shit.*

*ABORT MISSION.*

I better get out of here before he sees me. If I duck around the backside of the bar and out through the patio, I have a better chance. I turn away and take two steps before his familiar voice stops me.

"Rachel?"

*Dammit.*

I twist back to Flynn and plaster a smile on my face. "What are you doing here?"

He rises to his feet and walks over to me, glancing around like he's looking for someone. His lips quirk into a half-smile, and he motions back toward the bar where a half-drunk pint of beer sits. "I am having a drink."

"By yourself?"

He grimaces a little. "Well, I'm supposed to be meeting someone, but I don't see her yet."

*Her? So, he does have a date.*

*That he didn't tell me about.*

That little twinge of what I refuse to admit is jealousy hits my chest. Plus, he didn't tell me his plans tonight were a date.

*Because he didn't want me to know or because he was waiting to see if it went anywhere before he told me?*

I force another smile. "Oh, I'm meeting someone, too."

While not exactly happy about him being here on a date and not telling me, at least that relieves a little of the pressure. Maybe his date will arrive first, and by the time HRD4U gets here, he'll already be engrossed in her and won't be able to give me the third degree.

One of his hands moves through his hair, and then he motions back toward the empty stool he just vacated. "Why don't you join me then. Until he gets here."

"Uh, okay."

It's so weird for Flynn to have a date and not tell me. Especially after we hung out all last night and had margaritas. He's typically pretty loose-lipped when the tequila hits. Then again, I guess I kind of have one and didn't tell him, either. So, I can't really be annoyed or say anything about it.

Or at least, I shouldn't be annoyed.

I think Alicia is starting to get into my head too much about my feelings for Flynn. That isn't why I'm troubled by it. It's because my best friend isn't telling me important things about his life.

Though, we've obviously *both* been keeping things to ourselves lately. That bothers me more than it should. Friends can have personal lives they don't share. That's normal. It's how *normal* friendships are. But it feels weird for Flynn and me.

I glance over at him. The dark splotches under his eyes tell me he didn't get much sleep. "You still recovering from last night?"

We did drink a *lot* of margaritas.

He chuckles and points to his beer. "Yes. I'm sticking with beer tonight. I'm never going to let you convince me to drink that much tequila again."

I slide onto the stool next to him and knock my shoulder against his. "You say that every time."

A smirk plays at his lips. "I know, but I mean it this time."

*Lies.*

Speaking of which...it seems like a good time to just come out and ask what I've been wondering. "So, who are you meeting?"

Maybe I shouldn't ask because questioning him is only going to open me up to the same line of inquiry, but Flynn almost never dates, and his behavior over the last couple of weeks is still so fresh in my mind.

He shrugs and takes a drink of his beer. "It's kind of a blind date."

I bark out a laugh. "You? A blind date?"

He nods and offers me a tiny grin. "You know it's probably my only chance right now."

I laugh and wave over the bartender to get a drink. I'm going to need alcohol because when my date arrives, we're going to have a whole lot of explaining to do to Flynn.

———

**FLYNN**

Of all the damn bars in the city, Rachel has to be at this one tonight...

*Just my fucking luck.*

The girl I love is going to see me with the girl I met online, jerking off.

*Sheesh.*

God is punishing me.

Father Lafayette would probably be pleased I'm now facing the repercussions of my actions. First, some crazed fan stalks me at work and destroys my car...twice...and now I have to meet up with INEEDSOMED with Rachel standing right here.

But there could be some way to salvage this, or at least make it look not quite so bad. My lie about the blind date seemed to work, and *she's* here on a date, too. If I turn the focus on her and away from me, I won't have to keep lying to the woman who holds my heart about the woman who watches me hold my dick.

I take another sip of my beer. "What about you? Who are you meeting?"

She pulls her lip between her teeth, and her eyes dart back toward the front door. "Just a friend."

I raise an eyebrow. "A friend? Really?"

"Uh-huh."

*No way.*

She's lying to me, too. I know all of Rachel's friends, so

180

she would tell me who it was if that's really who she's waiting for. It's a lot more than just a friend. Maybe someone else she's dating besides Dan.

*Why hide him from me?*

I've met every other guy she's ever dated pretty much right away, because we've always been so concerned that if they find out about our friendship later on, there would be all sorts of jealousy. It's better to get it out in the open right away. But maybe this is about Dan. A feeling of guilt about seeing someone else when they have a second date planned in only a week.

"Do I get to meet this mystery guy?"

She shrugs. "I guess, if he ever gets here."

"Think he's ditching you?"

Her eyes drift over the restaurant again. "Maybe. He's not here yet."

I nod and look down at my watch. "Actually, I may be getting stood up, too." I chuckle and raise my glass to her. "At least we're in good company."

She clinks her glass against mine and takes a sip of her martini. "We really are two giant losers when it comes to dating, huh?"

I laugh as I examine her—absolutely stunning tonight in a low-cut maroon top and skintight black leather pants.

The woman is a fucking bombshell. There's no way she should still be single. A fast I am reminded of every single time I look at her.

"Well, if your date never shows, you always have your second date with Dan lined up." The words sting a little bit coming out. "So..."

She nods and sucks down some of her drink. "Dan's really nice, but—"

*There* is *a but.*

I thought there was one coming the other night, yet she

agreed to the second date. Her *but* makes me pause with my glass halfway to my mouth. "But what? You don't want to go out with him again?"

She offers a non-committal shrug.

I turn on my stool to face her. "Uh, oh. I know that look." And frankly, now that I see it written all over her, I'm surprised she didn't say anything after their first date when I asked her about it. "No chemistry there?"

Her eyes flick up to meet mine. "I'm sorry. I know he's your friend, and I really did have a good time when we went out. But there just wasn't enough there for me to really feel a driving need to see him again."

"Then why did you say yes when he asked for a second date?"

She considers my question for a minute and twirls her martini glass on the bar top. "I was trying to give it another chance. You were so sure we would hit it off, and you were right. We did. But there's a huge difference between having things in common and getting along well, and being with someone romantically."

*Ouch.*

This woman couldn't have hurt me more if she had actually driven a stake through my heart. I know she's talking about Dan, but that felt pointed and directed straight at me.

We need to stop talking about this before I completely lose my shit in front of her. I down another gulp of my beer and swallow thickly to remove the lump her words formed in my throat. "Do you have any big plans tomorrow?"

She shakes her head and turns back to look at the door again. "Not really, you?"

I nod. "Church with Mom. Coffee after again."

A laugh bubbles from her lips, and the sound goes straight to my dick despite the fact I'm here to meet another woman. "You're such a mama's boy."

I laugh and nod because she's right; I totally am. I'd do anything for that woman. I *do* do everything for her, and I will continue to until the day I die. It's the least I can do for the woman who raised me. "I guess I am."

She twists the glass in her hand, her brow furrowing as if she's deep in contemplation over something. "You ever think about what it would be like just to say *fuck it* and stop being a good guy. Stop worrying about what your mom would think. Stop worrying about what's right and what's wrong and just start doing what feels good."

I practically choke on my beer.

*Where the hell did this come from?*

It's about as far from how Rachel thinks as possible.

I take another sip of beer and wipe the condensation off the side of the glass with my thumb. "Sure, doesn't everyone think about that at some point in time? Just letting go of everything, of society's strict standards and requirements of what's expected of us. But wanting to do it and doing it are two different things."

Of course, I'd love not to have to hide HRD4U or what I want. It would be so much easier to tell Rach and the rest of the world the truth if I didn't care what anyone thought about me. But how I view the world and the people in it has been shaped so much by my conservative upbringing that I'm not sure I can ever come out and say what's really going on in my life—with HRD4U or my feelings for Rachel— without feeling like I'm standing naked in front of my middle school class being laughed at and ridiculed...and judged.

She nods, the disappointment clear in her soft green eyes. "That's very true. Sad, though, isn't it?"

I nod because I couldn't agree more. If it were really possible to let go completely, I wouldn't have to hide HRD4U from anyone, especially her. "Definitely." I check my watch again. Almost 6:30. "I think we've been stood up."

She holds her drink up to me. "To being stood up in good company."

"To being stood up in the *best* company." I clink my glass against hers and down the rest of my beer. "Bartender, keep them coming. We're going to need them tonight."

# 17

FLYNN

Another Saturday night coming home drunk and alone. I should be used to it by now. It should be routine. I don't know what I was expecting, but I never thought INEEDSOMED would stand me up.

Yeah, it's kind of an awkward situation for everyone—to meet up with someone you masturbated with online—but she seemed so cool, so laidback. So interested. I don't know why she wouldn't at least tell me she wasn't coming. Then I wouldn't have sat there like an idiot. And I wouldn't have ended up spending the whole night with Rachel.

Karma must really want to fuck me. I finally try to move on in *some* way from this woman by meeting up for a drink with another, and Rachel walks in and sits down right next to me.

*Who would've thought that meeting a girl you jerked off with online would go south?*

I release a laugh at the absurdity of the situation and question, and it echoes into the empty house. It feels like so much bad is happening right now is a sign. A statement from up above that something in my life needs to be fixed.

Maybe I need to go back to Father LaFayette for some advice and penance.

I wander back to the bedroom and drop down onto the bed. My body sinks into the mattress, and I grab the pillow and pull it down over my face to release a scream without alerting Rachel and the other neighbors to my frustration.

But I guess I get it. Chatting with someone online or even jerking off with them is a lot different than meeting them in person. She was bound to be uneasy about it. Even though there was never any pressure or any statements made that it would be more than a drink.

Or...maybe she was there, saw me, and decided I wasn't what she was expecting in the first place. That's certainly possible...and a massive blow to my ego I hadn't considered before.

Having Rachel show up was a mixed blessing, I guess. At least it saved me from sitting there by myself, looking like a loser who got stood up, but it also just reminded me how she's the one I really want to be with. About how every single minute we spend together is so...right. Even sitting there, waiting for another woman, all I could think about was Rach and how beautiful she looked tonight. Much more risqué than she usually dresses. Sexy. Wild.

And how damn simple it is to fall into our regular routine and dynamic.

No one else will ever be like that. It can't be that easy with anyone else.

*So, where does that leave me?*

Home alone on a Saturday night again, screaming into a damn pillow while my life spins out of control around me.

I throw the pillow to the side and grab my laptop so I can log into the site to see what's going on. It's no surprise that hundreds of messages asking when I'm going to go live again flood my inbox, along with dozens of propositions and inappropriate photos.

But one message draws my attention.

*She has some balls, messaging me after she stood me up.*

*Don't look at it, Flynn. Just let it go. Ignore her.*

Any other night, I might have. I would have deleted it and moved on. But something forces me to click on the message from INEEDSOMED.

INEEDSOMED

> Where were you tonight? I can't believe I got stood up by a guy who jerks off online. I don't know why I thought you were a nice guy. I'm obviously a pretty shitty judge of character. I wish you all the success in the future with your website.

*Stood her up?*

HRD4U

> What are you talking about? I was there. You stood me up. I spent the whole night at the bar talking with my best friend, who happened to show up too and stayed after her date was a no-show.

I hit enter and stare at my message for a few seconds.

It's nothing but a jumble of letters at first. Then they slowly form into the words I typed. Then the sentences.

*Holy shit.*

The realization comes so fast, it's like a blinding-white light on the front of the train before it slams into you. My breath whooshes from my lungs. My heart slams against my ribs so hard, it actually hurts.

*Holy. Fucking. Shit.*

It was Rachel. It's *always* been Rachel.

And if I just figured it out, so did she.

*How could I have been so fucking stupid?*

I close my computer and scramble off the bed. Fast, heavy, determined steps rocket me down the hallway to the front door, but I can't get there fast enough. Not after how long I've waited for this. I turn the lock, yank open the door, and run out onto the front lawn.

The late-night silence of the neighborhood is only broken by a distant dog bark. It's almost like time stands still with me while I wait for some sort of reaction from her.

Her front door opens slowly, almost cautiously, and she walks out with her arms wrapped around her chest. The darkness of the night can't hide the worry and confusion on her beautiful face.

Or the shock.

I know how she feels.

It's like the rug was just pulled out from under both of us, and now, we're left lying prone and exposed, staring up at the sky over us like we've never seen it before.

Our slow steps bring her and me to opposite sides of the low hedge that runs between our yards, the same hedge we've been stepping over for five years to get to each other's houses rather than walk the extra couple of feet around it.

I stop and stare down at her, and she tilts her head up to meet my gaze. The same green eyes I've been looking into for five years suddenly appear totally different. Full of so much I never saw before. So much she never *let* me see.

Her eyes drop to my shirt and back up. "You're not wearing a blue shirt."

I look down at my favorite shirt. "It's midnight blue."

She shakes her head, and one corner of her mouth quirks up. "It's black, and I've told you that before."

*She has. Probably a dozen times.*

I snort and let my eyes rake over her, still dolled up in her sex-kitten outfit. "You're not wearing a red shirt."

188

She scoffs and grabs the fabric on one of her sleeves. "It's maroon. Maroon is in the red family."

There's no use fighting the grin pulling at my lips. Knowing what I do now, the world looks so different. *She* looks so different. "I have so many questions."

Her laughter floats through the chilly night air and across the space between us, and she waves her hand at me. "*You* have questions? I'm not HRD4U."

I lean forward slightly over the hedge, until our faces are mere inches apart. "No, but you sure were wet for me last night."

A flush spreads over her cheeks, the pastel pink practically glowing against her soft, pale skin, and she inhales a tiny little gasp.

*Bingo.*

She wasn't lying at all about what she likes, about what she wants, about what she's been looking for. I was just too stupid to make the connection and never thought to ask her. I've wasted so much time, lying to her and keeping this part of my life a secret because I didn't want to lose her, when all I had to do to have her was show her who I really was.

I reach across the hedge and grab her around the waist. She squeals slightly as I lift her over, but she easily wraps her legs around my hips, pressing her core against my raging hard-on.

*Fuck yes.*

She drops her forehead down against mine and shakes her head slightly. "What do we do now?"

There are so many ways to answer that. So many things I've dreamed about doing to her for so damn long.

But first things first.

I slam my lips against hers—hard. A commanding kiss designed to show her that she's everything to me, and I'm not letting her go again. Ever.

She moans and responds with a little whimper and by grinding her body against mine. The press of her leather-covered pussy against my aching cock almost makes me blow my load right out on my front lawn.

Our tongues tangle and twist together, and I finally taste the one thing I've wanted more than anything in my entire life—Rachel fucking Fury.

She tastes exactly like I always imagined she would—sweet and perfect. She tastes like *home*. Like forever. Like everything I've been waiting and praying for my entire fucking life.

I drag my mouth away from hers for a second. Too much time has already been wasted. I won't let another second go by before she knows what I want. I take her face in one hand and brush my thumb over her wet lips. "I'm going to take you inside, Rachel, and I'm going to fuck your beautiful cunt until you scream my name so loudly, you scare the damn neighbors."

She shudders and shifts against me with a raised eyebrow, the light blush from earlier darkening to a deeper shade of red. "And then?"

"And then, I'm going to do it all over again."

———

## RACHEL

Flynn's words send a rush of something through me unlike anything I've ever felt. It's not just attraction. It's not just lust. It's like what I imagine a shot of heroin or snort of coke feels like, roaring through my veins like a wildfire of pleasure.

Pure ecstasy.

This can't be real.

Can't be happening.

I must be dreaming. But having his hard cock pressed against my aching center and his lips molded to mine only solidifies the reality of everything happening.

When he typed those words, the truth hit me.

What had happened, who he was, what we had both been doing, and it was like a clash of worlds coming together—the real one where I hid what I wanted and lived in misery and the digital one where I was myself for brief moments in time.

Everything I ever wanted was right next door in the person who has been my best friend and my rock for so damn long, and I never even realized it.

*How could I have been so damn blind?*

It's Flynn. *My* Flynn.

He's been right here the entire time, hiding this from me while I've been struggling to conceal what I really want. The irony isn't lost on me, nor is the way my body responds to him so naturally as he turns toward his house and walks without taking his lips from mine.

Licking between exploring kisses.

Kissing between panting breaths.

Nipping between muttered filthy words.

He reaches the door, steps through it, and kicks it closed behind us. "I want to fuck you in every inch of this damn house, but there's one place in particular I've been dreaming about for a long time."

I jerk my head back and narrow my eyes at him. "A long time?"

*What does he mean, a long time?*

He presses his lips back to mine without an answer and walks straight over to the black leather chaise along the side of the wall near the fireplace.

I've always loved this chaise. And the sudden visions of Flynn drilling me bent over it has my pussy clenching and my clit throbbing. He stops next to it, and I release my legs and let my feet slide to the floor. He grips my chin and tilts my face up.

His eyes darken and swim with something I've never seen there before. Lust. And something much deeper that tears the breath from my lungs. "I never knew you wanted this."

"I never knew you could give it to me."

If I had, things would have been different. There's no doubt in my mind about that. I spent years ignoring my attraction to him, telling myself it could never happen because it would only end in disaster.

He leans down and stops his lips a mere hairsbreadth from mine. "Strip, then get on your hands and knees on the chaise. I want to see that beautiful ass in the air and that pussy spread wide open for me."

*Jesus. Where did he learn to talk like that?*

It certainly wasn't in Catholic school.

He takes a step back and watches as I grasp the hem of my blouse, tug it up over my head, and let it flutter to the floor, leaving me standing in my black leather pants and black lace bra.

Flynn has seen me in less than this before. Every time we hit the beach and I don a bikini. But a grin spreads across his face, one I haven't seen in the five years we've known each other. The look of seeing something he wants and knowing it's his.

And I *am* his.

I've been his the whole time; I just didn't know it.

I never *let* myself even consider acting on any attraction toward Flynn. I denied it when Alicia or Flynn's mother joked about us getting together. I cared about him, about *us* too much and knew it would only ruin things. But now, all those years spent pushing away the fact that I *was* attracted to him just feels stupid. Like such a waste of time and energy when we could have been doing this.

Flynn rubs his palm over the bulge at the front of his pants and licks his lips. "Lose the pants, babe."

I slide my fingers to the waistband and shimmy them down, taking it extra slow to ensure he has time to appreciate the goods. He unbuttons his fly and unzips his jeans while he watches. His huge cock swells at the top, begging to be freed, and the thought of it being so close, so in reach, has my mouth watering.

His tongue darts out across his lips, and his eyes roam over me, scorching my skin everywhere his gaze lands. "Damn, that's sexy, Rach. I can't wait to get in that ass."

*Damn.*

*He really is dirty.*

We'll deal with that later—the whole "going to no-man's land" idea. For right now, there's only one place I want him. I reach down and tug my pants off my feet before I unhook my bra and let it fall down my arms onto the floor.

Flynn's eyes glow with an appreciation I've never seen from another man. Because he *knows* me. He knows *all* of me now. "Christ, you're fucking perfect, Rach. I can't wait to taste every fucking inch of you."

My clit throbs, and I press my legs together against the heat building between them. It won't be long now. He's not going to draw this out any more than he has to. Neither one of us wants slow and sweet, and we both know it. My fingers find the strings of my thong, but his hand shoots out and grabs my right wrist.

"Stop. Let me take those off."

He slides his palm to my hip and across my stomach before his fingers slip down into my wet slit.

I shudder and grip his shoulders. "Oh, God, Flynn."

He presses a finger up inside me and flicks my engorged

clit with his thumb. A jolt of electric pleasure sizzles through me, and I grind against him, desperate for more friction. More everything.

*Why did we wait so long to do this?*

Because we were both blind and utterly stupid.

He pulls his hand away, and I release a frustrated groan. Deft fingers tug my thong down my legs, and I step out of it and kick it away.

Flynn swallows thickly, his lust-soaked gaze scanning every inch of my exposed body. "On your hands and knees."

The order sends another shudder down my spine. A good fucking shudder. One I wouldn't mind feeling every damn day of my life. Anticipation of finally getting what I *want*.

I turn around to face the chaise and climb on all fours as instructed with a glance over my shoulder at him. My entire body vibrates.

I've never seen Flynn like this. So hard. So on edge. So... almost feral.

This is a totally different side he keeps hidden far away from the world. A side I want to know.

He unbuttons his shirt and lets it slide off his shoulders before tugging off his pants and letting his dick spring totally free.

*Holy shit.*

It's even bigger than the videos and pictures made it look. Flynn steps up between my legs, and his hand connects with my ass in a sharp slap.

"Oww!" I rock forward, the sting of his smack still burning my skin.

He leans over me and grips my hair tightly to force my head back until our gazes lock. "You sure you're ready for this, babe?"

I try to nod but his grip in my hair keeps me prone.

"You want my cock inside you, don't you?" The fingers of his free hand play with the wetness between my legs, and I mewl and nod as much as I can in his firm grasp. He releases some of the tension on my hair, and I moan and shift my hips against his hand, urging him to find the exact spot I want him. His warm breath tickles at my ear. "Not as much as I want to bury myself in you. Do I need to grab a condom, or are we good?"

I manage to find enough breath to whisper an answer. "We're good."

He leans forward and turns my head to the side to kiss me brutally. A savage, soul-stealing, mind-melting kiss that almost makes me come on his hand still between his legs. My pussy clenches around his fingers, and when he tears his lips away from mine, he licks and kisses his way to my ear. "Good, because I want to feel your cunt squeezing my cock with nothing between us." He nips at the lobe, sending a bolt straight to where his hand holds me still. "You better hold on, Rach. This is going to be fast and rough."

*Thank fucking God.*

## 18

**RACHEL**

*God, yes.*

*Fast and rough.*

The words I've been dying to hear from every man I've been with for years. Ones that always eluded me. Because the men I was dating were just as gentlemanly in bed as they were out. They were perfect on paper, but when it came to fulfilling my needs, they never measured up. I've blamed them for the way our relationships always failed. For them never putting me first. For the distance that always grew there. But deep down, I know it was my fault. They sensed what I could never voice—that something was *missing*. They just never asked what it was or tried to solve the problem and figure out what I *wanted*.

But not Flynn.

He *knows*.

*Christ, how could I have been so wrong about him? So wrong about this?*

His fingers dig into my right hip possessively, and he grasps his cock and drags the head through my wetness.

Every fantasy I've ever had about exactly this moment rushes through my head at once, sending a full-body shudder rolling through me.

He leans down and nips at my ear. "This is what you want, Rach?" The head nudges inside me.

I instantly clamp around him, trying to draw him in deeper.

An approving growl rumbles in his chest, and he pushes inside me with one hard, determined thrust.

"Oh, God." I rock forward as his length spreads me open, and he bottoms out inside me.

"Fuck, Rach." He growls and leans forward to brush his lips along the back of my neck. His hips retreat. His arm wraps around my waist, and he slams back into me. If his strong arm weren't holding me in place, I'd face-plant against the chaise. As it is, I'm completely at his mercy. Held in place while he does to me what I've been craving for so damn long.

Warm breath flutters against my ear, and the low rumble of a groan in his chest vibrates against my back. "You were so ready for me, weren't you, babe? You needed my cock as badly as I needed this hot, wet cunt."

I clench around him, intensifying the drag of every inch of his flesh along mine.

He growls deep and low. "Yeah, like that. Squeeze my fucking cock while I make you mine."

Every retreat feels like I'm losing a part of me, a part I never realized I was missing until this very moment, but then he's right there again, filling me, completing me, and driving me to the brink of insanity with the need to find my release.

This is it.

What sex should be.

Out of control, unrestrained passion.

A need so strong, there's no denying it.

It might have taken us years, but once we knew what was possible, there was no stopping it. No pumping the brakes. No ignoring what was inevitable. No discounting what we need and who with.

Doing this with anyone else would have been good. It would have scratched an itch. But with Flynn, it's like coming home after being lost at sea and settling into a familiar, warm embrace. It's exactly where I'm supposed to be.

He pulls back slightly and smacks my ass, making me tighten around him again instinctively as the sharp sting radiates across my skin. "Come. I want you to come for me, Rach. I want to feel your cunt clenching and rippling around my cock. I want to hear you screaming my name. I want to feel you shaking under me. I want to see your head thrash and feel your entire fucking body quake." His hand wraps around the front of my throat, and he tugs my head back until I can see him—the feral glint in his darkened eyes. "I want to see you lose control, baby. Let go. For me."

*Haven't I already let go?*

This. Him. This *is* letting go and finding everything all at the same time.

But the tension in my shoulders and body tells me he's right. I'm still holding back, but I don't know why. Force of habit. The inability to truly let go of all the things that have weighed me down. My fear of rejection or exposure. The anxiety over potentially losing our friendship if we ever gave in to our attraction coming back. Any or all of it.

He pulls out his dick, until just the head rests inside me, leaving me trembling and clenching at it desperately. "Tell me, Rach. Tell me what you want. I want to hear it from those sweet lips before I fuck them, too."

I try to form words. Stringing together letters shouldn't

be so hard. But lust fogs my brain, making it impossible to think about anything but getting him back inside me. Right. Now. I open my mouth to tell Flynn what I want, what I *need* him to do, but all that comes out is a frustrated groan.

Twisting underneath him, struggling slightly against his hold, I finally manage to sputter something out. "Oh, God. P-please, Flynn. Please."

He smacks my ass again, harder this time, and the sound reverberates through the room as the sting floods across my sensitive skin. "That's not gonna cut it, babe. I want you to tell me, word for word, what you want me to do to you."

A minuscule roll of his hips inches him a tiny bit deeper into me. I clench around it, desperate for more, frantic to have him inside me again, filling all those empty spaces I didn't even know were there. Letting me feel whole for the first time in my life.

This is torture, the way he's toying with me. Like he's the hunter and I'm the prey stuck in a trap, and he's making me beg for my life.

I shake my head, but he only tightens his hand on my throat.

"I-I-"—I suck in a breath against his hold on my neck—"I don't think I can."

I love the dirty talking. It's the ultimate aphrodisiac. Listening to him on that screen was mind-bending, and now having him say it here, whispering it in my ear while he works me over, it's another level. But me doing it is something else. Something I'm definitely not ready for. Something I'm not even sure is possible.

He brushes his thumb across my throat slowly. Back and forth. Back and forth. Almost reverently. But Flynn doesn't move, his cock resting barely inside me. "Tell me all the things you dreamed of HRD4U doing. What you thought about when you touched this magnificent cunt and made yourself come."

*God, there were so many.*

But maybe that's the key. I'm getting hung up on this being Flynn—my best friend who I knelt next to at church. Who treats his mother like a fucking queen. Who holds doors open for people and always offers to help anyone in need. He needs to be HRD4U right now. Still Flynn. Just *also* HRD4U, the man on the screen willing to say and do anything and everything I've ever dreamt about.

He molds his chest against my back, so I can feel his heart thundering against his ribcage, but he doesn't give me what I really need. His hips stay still, frozen until I figure out a way to answer him.

I whimper, the words I want to say sitting on the tip of my tongue, waiting to fall off. "I-I want you to fuck me." It comes out in a rush. One sentence so fast, it's a garbled mess, but I know he hears it because his grip tightens, and he inches slightly farther inside me. "I want you to do it hard and fast and leave me a quivering mess."

"That's it, babe." He glides back in to the hilt, rocking my body forward against his firm grip around my waist and throat, and I clench around him with relief. "You want me to pound you so good you can't walk tomorrow, don't you?"

"God, yes."

His lips find that spot right behind my ear, and he sucks hard in rhythm with his thrusting hips. "You're going to feel every fucking inch of my cock between your legs for the next damn week when you try to move."

"Yes! Yes!" I dig my nails into the leather of the chaise, grasping for anything to keep me from flying away.

His thrusts get harder. Faster. More demanding. More frantic.

If his arm wasn't wrapped around me, I don't know that I

could stay up on my hands and knees anymore. The pound of flesh against flesh and slap of skin on skin echoes in the room, creating a goddamn symphony of our connection.

"God, Rach, you're so fucking perfect." His hand snakes down my stomach to where our bodies connect, and he finds my clit. "Now, come for me. I want to feel you clench around my cock and release everything you've been holding onto so tightly. Come on me, Rach."

I don't need the added contact of his fingers there because the heat of an impending orgasm is already spreading through my limbs. But as soon as his fingertips touch it and swirl, the explosion of release blasts through me like an atom bomb. I jerk forward, but Flynn holds me in place, hammering into me harder, brutally staking a claim on my body, demanding I take it and give him everything back in return.

———

**FLYNN**

Her tight, wet pussy clenches around my dick as she writhes under me, her head thrown back and eyes squeezed shut through her orgasm.

It's the single most beautiful thing I've seen in my entire life.

The only thing I've wanted since the moment she climbed out of her car next door over five years ago.

And now it's mine.

*She's* mine.

In every fucking way.

Every gasp and mewl. Each spasm of her body. The way her mouth falls open in ecstasy. All of it. *Mine.*

*Mine.*

*Mine.*

*Mine.*

My thrusts grow more erratic as Rach finally stops twitching under me, the hot walls of her cunt finally dragging out my orgasm. I grit my teeth and empty myself inside her with one more final slam of my hips.

"Fuck, Rachel..." The curse slips out in a rush of breath. "Fuuuuuck."

*When did I become so fucking inarticulate?*

Apparently, the moment my dick slipped inside Rachel Fury.

She collapses under me, but I hold her up and pull her against me until she's upright on her knees and my heaving chest presses against her bare back. I kiss along her sweat-slickened neck and push her soft caramel hair over her shoulder to get better access.

Fair skin touched by a pink blush glows in the moonlight filtering in from the window, begging for my touch. My kiss. My tongue. I want my mouth everywhere. All over her. All fucking night.

The scent of her shampoo and something that's all Rachel envelops me, and I inhale deeply and slowly drag a finger down her spine, sending her shuddering against me. "Dammit, Rachel." I kiss her neck. "Fucking perfect." I kiss her cheek. "Fucking beautiful."

She whimpers and sags back even more me. I plaster kisses along her hot skin again and let my cock slide from inside her. A whine slips from her lips, and I turn her slightly to scoop her up into my arms.

Her eyes flutter open but aren't quite able to focus yet, and she wraps her arms around my neck. "Where are we going?"

I flash her a grin. "To get you cleaned up."

She hums low, closes her eyes, and presses her cheek

against my chest, nuzzling tighter, like she can't get close enough—and neither can I.

*Is this a fucking dream?*

It sure feels like it.

The best dream I've ever had.

Literally the woman of my dreams in my arms, sated after I just gave her exactly what she's needed for so long. What no one else *could* ever give her.

I never thought this would happen. That we could be here like this. It was always a lost cause, and so far beyond my reach, it wasn't even worth thinking about unless I wanted to be miserable and punish myself.

For so fucking long, I convinced myself that any attraction Rachel might have toward me would and could never lead anywhere because what we wanted and needed were two different things, no matter how much we cared about each other.

It may have taken me being someone else to break down the wall between us and shatter both our misconceptions about each other, but that doesn't change who we are at this moment.

We're Flynn and Rachel, not HRD4U and INEEDSOMED.

And now...

My fantasy woman is in my arms...

With my cum inside her...

In my house...

And soon, she'll be in my bed.

All because of HRD4U.

The thing I let create so much guilt. The thing I hid from her. The thing I thought would be our doom is what brought us to this moment.

I carry her straight into the master bathroom and crank on the water in the shower. She lifts her head from my chest, tipping it back, and I kiss her. Deep. Slow. Unhurried. So unlike the kisses I gave her before. One that shows her the truth, that this is more than just wanting to fuck her. This is so much more than unreleased sexual tension that built between us over the years. Something that tells her how I really feel. How I've felt for a long fucking time.

She squeezes my neck and clings to me more tightly, kissing me languidly, like she wants to savor every second as much as I do. If I never had to let her go, I'd be able to die a happy man. But I'm not ready to do either, yet. Not when we've just started.

I step into the shower and turn her under the spray. She yelps at the harsh sting of the hot water then relaxes against me with a little sound of contentment.

Nuzzling against her, I issue a reluctant sigh. "I'm going to set you down."

Even though I want nothing more than to keep her in my arms forever...

She nods, and I slowly lower her onto shaky feet. Her arms cling to my neck, and those green eyes stare up at me from under the flow of the shower head. Droplets hang on to her impossibly long lashes, and rivulets of water ripple over her shoulders, across her breasts, and down her stomach to that beautiful place between her legs.

*My dream come true. Literally.*

I take her face in my palms and kiss her again, sliding my hand down between her thighs. The flowing water washes away some of the evidence of the mind-blowing sex we just had, but I wouldn't even care if it was still all there. I need to savor her. I need to know what she tastes like *everywhere*. Especially there.

A kiss isn't enough.

Not nearly enough.

I drop to my knees on the wet tile, and she buries her

hands in my hair. Water pours down over my head and shoulders, and I lean forward and run my tongue through her pussy.

A low, deep growl of satisfaction at the salty and sweet tang of our mixed releases sounds in my chest. "So fucking good, Rachel. I could eat nothing but your cunt every minute of every fucking day for the rest of my life and never starve or want anything else."

The flavor coating my tongue is one I never want to forget. One I want to savor and relish and enjoy. One I've been fantasizing about for five long years. And what I just said isn't some bullshit line. All I want to do is worship this woman for as long as she'll let me.

She's always brought me to my knees, only now, I can actually do it. I'm worshipping the true goddess in my life, and nothing could drag me away.

Rachel whimpers and shifts, bringing herself even closer to my face. It's an open invitation to continue, and I'm not going to turn it down. I grip her wet ass in my palms and drag her against my mouth harshly, driving my tongue into her as I throw one thigh over my shoulder to open her even more for me.

"Oh, God, Flynn." Her fingers twist my hair in a stranglehold, and she rolls her hips in time with my oral ministrations. "God…"

I moan and pull my mouth away from her flesh, staring up at her head tipped back, mouth open on a gasp. "Yeah, baby, fuck my mouth. Hard. Pull my hair and fuck me. Give it to me."

"Everything."

The word is merely a whisper. Barely audible over the flowing water, her gasps of pleasure, and my own blood rushing in my ears.

*Everything.*

She pushes up onto her toes to give me a better angle, and I shove two fingers up into her and refocus my attention on her clit. I suck the tiny pulsing bud between my lips and bite down.

Her nails claw at my head. "Jesus, Flynn."

I curl my fingers inside her to find that perfect spot and pump them in time with the sucks and nips and bites until she's squirming and gasping and begging me in a garbled language that isn't recognizable as English. Her pussy tightens around my fingers like a vise, and I hold her steady when she tries to pull away from the pleasure I'm giving her.

"Flynn, I ca-I can't..." She thrashes her head to side, fighting the impending orgasm and the attention to her over-sensitized clit. "I can't come again."

I tear my mouth from her and kiss across her inner thigh. "Yes, you can. You're not going anywhere, baby, until you and I are done. And I'm nowhere close to being through with you."

I'll never be finished with her. I never could be.

Rachel Fury is *it* for me, and now that she's here, at my mercy, I'm going to give her everything she's every dreamed of and more.

# 19

FLYNN

Rachel's soft, warm body in my arms and in my bed has to be the greatest feeling in the world. Actually, it's more like how I imagine Heaven. Peaceful. Calm. Absolute fucking bliss.

In a million years, I never could have imagined what happened over the last couple of hours. That it could even occur, let alone that it would end up here. With us. Like this.

I brush my fingers along her arm, soft goosebumps rising in their wake.

She stirs and shifts slightly but doesn't turn to look at me. "What did you mean before?"

*Shit.*

Rach doesn't have to elaborate. I know exactly what she's referring to. The statement I made without even thinking about it, without even considering what it would lead to.

I figured it was only a matter of time before she started asking questions I might not want to answer. A few more minutes of peaceful snuggling with the woman of my dreams would have been nice, but I guess there's no avoiding the inevitable. We're going to have to have some uncomfortable conversations, given what we just figured out and did. Conversations we maybe should have had before I fucked her brains out.

When I don't respond right away, she turns slightly to glance over her shoulder at me, but her gaze holds no real concern, only question.

I press a kiss to the back of her neck and squeeze her more tightly against me. Her ass rubs against my cock, bringing it back to life. Another round would be a welcome distraction from this talk, but something tells me she isn't going to be easily dissuaded from her line of questioning.

So instead of burying myself in her again, I'll play dumb. "What do you mean?"

"You said you've been dreaming about this for a long time. What did you mean?"

*Fuck, this is awkward.*

We've been friends for so long. Been through a lot together. Especially recently with her father's death. If she knew I was madly in love with her all the times I've comforted her or we've snuggled and watched movies, it might make her think differently about all of it. Like I had some ulterior motive for how I acted instead of trying to be compassionate and a real friend.

*How the hell do I tell her I've been in love with her for most of it without coming across as weird or creepy or a liar?*

I don't.

*Avoid.*

*Avoid.*

*Avoid.*

I brush my lips against her warm skin again. "Don't worry about it."

She shifts and rolls onto her back to look up at me. Her

small, soft hand cups my cheek, and she brushes her thumb across my lips. "Tell me the truth, Flynn. I want to know."

I sigh and run my hand over her exposed breast, then catch a taut nipple between my finger and thumb and tug.

She gasps a little, but a tiny smile plays at the corners of her lips. Her hand drops to my chest, and she pushes against it. "Don't try to distract me. Answer my question."

*Like it's so fucking easy.*

Confessing to Father Lafayette was easier than telling Rachel the truth.

"Fine."

*Fuck, this is hard.*

I press my palm against her cheek and meet her questioning gaze. "I've been in love with you for years."

Her eyes widen, and her hand stills against my chest. "What?"

I close my eyes and release a breath that comes from deep within my chest, a release of all the frustration that's built from not being able to say those words for so damn long. "I don't know when it happened. It just kind of *did*."

Every second. Every minute. Every hour. Every day we spent together just...made me love her. I can't even remember a time I didn't, though, in the beginning, it definitely wasn't so intense. It was more like an attraction I kept at bay. But it grew into something so much deeper.

"How come you never said anything?"

I open my eyes and meet hers. "Because I never thought you'd want anything like this. I thought you were a good girl who wanted a nice, wholesome guy who would make love to you every night, not someone who will brutally fuck your brains out and whisper filth into your ear."

She blushes even after everything we just did together.

*So fucking cute.*

"I do want that, too, Flynn."

"So do I." I want to spend *hours* making love to her and dragging it out. I want to worship her in every way imaginable. "There's a time and place for everything. But I was terrified if I told you how I felt, I would lose you as a best friend, and I wasn't going to risk that. I care too much about you, even if we could never be together. Plus, I never thought you were attracted to me like that."

A grin tugs at her lips, and she lightly traces her nails across my pecs. "I would have to be blind not to notice you and think you are attractive, Flynn. That was never the issue."

"Then what was?"

She chews on her lip for a second, considering her answer. "Honestly? I thought you were a mama's boy who would be just as boring in bed as the rest of the guys I have dated lately."

I bark out a laugh and drop my forehead against hers. "Do you still think I'm a boring mama's boy?"

Her lips press to mine in answer. "Definitely not boring, but you *are* kind of a mama's boy. That's not necessarily a bad thing, though. I love the relationship you have with your mother. It shows what a truly good guy you really are."

The fact that she doesn't think it's weird and isn't jealous about the time I spend with Mom only makes me love her more.

A frown tugs at her lips. "But I guess there are a lot of things I don't know about you."

The distress in her voice has me pulling away and taking her face in my hands. "Why do you think that?"

"Because how could we have been best friends for five years and I not know about this...about the website... about...I don't know...all of this?"

"Rachel, you know me better than anyone on this planet. Like I said, I only kept this from you because I never thought you'd understand. I thought it would send you running for the hills as my friend, let alone if I tried to pursue you for more. And this hasn't been going on the whole time. Only the last year or so. It was something that just kind of happened when the market crashed. It was never planned. Never something I thought about doing before."

She shakes her head. "We were so stupid and maybe a little blind."

"Maybe."

"Alicia kept insisting I was secretly in love with you and that was the reason all my relationships were failing."

I chuckle and shake my head as I move over her. She drapes her arms around my neck, and I press her legs open with my knees and settle between them, bracing myself on my elbows over her. "Was that why?"

She worries her bottom lip between her teeth. "Honestly, I don't know. It wasn't conscious. But looking back, I was comparing them to you. Which was part of the problem."

"What do you mean?"

"I think I was looking for another you. Someone I would have the same rapport and easy laughter with, someone I would feel the same around—relaxed and happy and carefree. Someone who can always make me feel better when I am upset about something..." She trails off before her eyes widen. "Jesus, I *was* looking for you."

"I've been right here all the time."

She flashes me a grin, and her hand slips down between us to wrap around my cock. "I know, I just never thought you would be so...*dirty*."

———

## RACHEL

Flynn lets out a laugh that sends his entire body shaking against mine. His hard dick in my hand brushes against my overly sensitive clit.

My body twitches at the contact, and I scowl at him. "I'm glad you think my revelation is funny."

He shakes his head and gives me a smoldering look. "It's not that, Rach. It's just, I can't believe this entire time, I never told you how I felt because I thought my dirty side would scare you off while the whole time you were just looking for a dirty version of me."

*Well, when he puts it like that.*

I chuckle at the sheer absurdity of it all. "You're right."

With a grin, I release his cock and wrap my arms around his neck to drag him down for a kiss. Our warm breaths mingle as his tongue languidly explores my mouth. Every kiss we share opens my heart further and makes my soul sing in a way I didn't even know existed.

He pulls away, breathless, and I brush my thumb over his kiss-swollen lips.

It's impossible to imagine not kissing him now that I have. The thought of *not* having this makes my chest ache. "It is pretty funny, and we were pretty stupid. But, what now?"

His lips return to mine, and he shifts until his hard length is pressing along my wet core and into my clit with every slight movement of his body. Our tongues tangle, and our chests heave with the effort to take more from each other. The drag of his cock against me reignites my need for him, my pussy clenching, and my skin heating rapidly.

This is it. What I've been looking for—the *filthy* version of Flynn.

It's *always* been Flynn.

And we wasted five years dancing around each other instead of being like this. Lying to each other and keeping things hidden that would have changed everything a long time ago.

But he didn't answer my question.

I pull away from him...reluctantly. "That's not really an answer, Flynn. You can't just try to distract me with your dick every time I ask you something you don't want to talk about."

He leans back and raises an eyebrow at me. "I can't?" He rolls his hips, pressing his erection against my wet core and clit again, eliciting a groan as I dig my nails into his back. "I think I *can*."

"That's not fair."

A smug grin tilts his lips. "Who says I have to play fair?" He shifts even closer. "I thought you like it when I play dirty."

I do.

I have to grant him that.

*And didn't Bash tell me that sometimes you have to play dirty to get what you want?*

Digging my fingers into his ass, I grin at him. "I very much do, but I want to make sure we're on the same page here."

"What page is that?"

Acids turns in my stomach as I stare up into his warm blue eyes. For the first time since I saw his message and realized the truth, fear grips me. We rushed into this physical thing so fast, gave in to what we both wanted in the blink of an eye, and I didn't even think that we might not ultimately want the same things.

*My God, what if we aren't on the same page?*

*What if what we just did ends our entire friendship?*

He captures my face between his palms, concern

furrowing his brow. "What page, Rachel? The one where this is actually something and neither one of us wants to do anything that will jeopardize our friendship? The one where this isn't just fucking?" He drops his forehead against mine again, sucking in a sharp breath. "I just got done telling you I've been in love with you for years. Of course, we're on the same page. If that wasn't clear enough, let me tell you now."

His lips capture mine, hard, possessing me and devouring me at the same time before he pulls back.

"I love you. I am *in love* with you. You are my other half, my best friend, and now, my lover. This is everything I've ever dreamed of and everything I never thought I could have. I want to spend the rest of my life with you. I want to make my mother happy by telling her we're going to get married and have beautiful babies together. Maybe not six, but you know, some."

My heart swells as tears well in my eyes.

But it appears he isn't even done. "I want to come home every day to you in my house and in my bed, and I need you in my arms as I fall asleep every night. I want that now and forever. So, are we on the same page?"

The tears finally trickle down the sides of my cheeks and onto the pillow.

He brushes them away. "Don't cry, Rach. Please don't cry."

I sniffle. "It's okay. They're happy tears. We are most definitely on the same page, but..."

This is a deal-breaker, and I have no idea how he will react. It's the thing that's been weighing on me since the first moment I figured out who he is but that I managed to push aside in favor of giving in to my baser needs first. I can't ignore it anymore, though.

He raises an eyebrow. "But what?"

"But there's one more thing I want to make sure you understand. You're going to be giving up HRD4U."

He flashes me a breathtaking, devious grin and leans down, stopping with his lips a hairsbreadth from mine. "Why is that, love?"

I glower at him and push at his chest to get him to move away. He can't be serious. "Did you really think I'd be okay with you continuing that now that we're together?"

A low chuckle vibrates in his chest, and he shakes his head. "I was thinking more like a change in programming."

"A change in programming? I don't follow."

His hand snakes down between my legs. I shudder under him as he lines up his cock at my entrance and brushes his lips against my ear. "Think about it, babe. You and me on camera. Doesn't the thought of knowing somebody's watching you turn you on?"

Heat floods between my thighs at his words.

*Shit.*

Flynn pushes up into me slowly. His dick spreads me open and drags against all the right places inside me. It's like we were always meant to be like this. Two puzzle pieces that fit together perfectly.

Public sex could be hot.

The thought of strangers watching us ignites a fire inside me, making me bow up to meet him and urge him to move faster.

*So maybe?*

He rolls his hips, pulls out, and then pushes back into me.

It's so hard to remember to think when he's doing this to me.

"Our own sex site?"

He nods and thrusts up into me again slowly. "Yeah, babe. Does that make you hot? The thought of all those people getting off, seeing us get off? Letting people watch while I fuck you all over the house. Bending you over the chaise. Up on the counter. Plowing you on the couch. Against the wall in the shower. Making you scream while I pound into you over and over again as many times as you can take it? Having my cum all over you for everyone to see? People watching me claim you like a fucking feral animal."

His fingers find my throbbing clit as his dick glides in and out of me, and another orgasm starts to build, heat spreading through my limbs and up my spine.

He pumps into me and lightly drags his lips over mine. "You know that turns you on, Rach. To know people are watching us. I can feel how fucking wet it makes you. You're practically dripping. So, let's do it. Let's be dirty. Together."

## 20

FLYNN

A pink flush spreads across Rachel's cheeks, and she gives me a reproachful look from next to me in the booth. "Stop looking at me like that."

I grin at her as she tries not to smile while she peeks at me out of the corner of her eye. "Like what?"

She sighs and finally turns to lean toward me, like someone at a surrounding booth might hear whatever she's about to say. "Like you want to *fuck* me on this table."

I slide my hand onto her thigh and trail my fingers up the inside toward the spot where I want to be so badly, relishing the way she shivers under my light touch. "But I *do* want to fuck you on this table. Or duck under the tablecloth and eat your pussy until you come all over my face."

She turns beet red and bats my hand away, then slaps my bicep. "Behave."

"Ouch!" I rub at the stinging skin and shift across the leather booth seat until I can brush my lips against her ear and feel the heat radiating off her. The thought of really crawling under the table and doing what I just threatened crosses my mind, and I quickly scan the restaurant to see who has a line of sight to our table. "You don't like it when I *behave*."

A tiny, resigned breath slips from her lips, and she pushes away her almost-empty plate and shoves our copy of the receipt into her purse. "I do when we're in *public*."

That makes me flinch, but I don't move away from her, just slide my hand back onto her thigh and squeeze it gently.

"So, is that a no to the video?"

Her body goes rigid against mine, and she averts her gaze, suddenly very interested in the drink menu on the table even though we're done and already paid for our dinner.

She's been avoiding answering my question for the past two days while we lived in our own little private world. Barely leaving my bedroom except to eat—and that only led to kitchen-counter sex. Twice.

I even feigned illness to get out of church with Mom this morning. Lying to my own mother to stay in bed, fucking my girl...

Father Lafayette would have a field day with that in the confessional booth.

Aside from the family engagement I avoided, there wasn't even any reason for her to go home to get clothes since she hasn't been wearing any.

It's been two days of sheer bliss that left her walking on shaky, weak legs when she finally forced me out for dinner tonight. Our first real "date" now that we aren't simply best friends anymore.

Though, what we *are* is still a little in the air.

It isn't lost on me that she hasn't told me she loves me. At least, not in the same way I told her I love her. She agreed we were on the same page with what this would be, but she hasn't said the *words*. And I think HRD4U may be the sticking point and might be holding back what she really wants to say, what I've been longing to hear since the moment I realized I loved her.

Even though he's what brought us together, my alter-ego is looming over us like a dark cloud. And now, instead of answering my question about making the video, she slides out from the booth and waits for me to do the same.

I've tried not to push it, not to push *her* where my suggestion is concerned even though I've definitely been pushing her in other ways—to tell me what she wants, what she likes, what she *needs*. But her repeated dodging is making something abundantly clear.

I reluctantly climb to my feet, and when she moves for the door, I grab her hand and tug her back to me, wrapping my arms around her and holding her close so I can lean down and ensure no one else hears me. "Don't think I haven't noticed you running away every time I bring it up, Rach." I feather my lips against her ea. "You can just say 'no' and be done with it. I would let it go. But the fact that you *haven't* dismissed the idea out of hand leads me to believe that a part of you, probably deep down, hiding under all the kindergarten-teacher uptightness and repressed by what you worry people will *think*, really *wants* to try it."

She sags back against me slightly and squeezes my hand in hers. "I'm thinking about it. That's all I'm giving you right now."

It's more than she's said on the subject in two days.

I grin and kiss her cheek lightly. "I'll take that. Now, let's get home and into bed. I plan on keeping you up for a few hours, and we both have work early in the morning."

As much as I'd love to stay up all night and spend every foreseeable day in the future lost in her, we both know that's not feasible. We need to leave the bubble. It's time to stop being INEEDSOMED and HRD4U versions of ourselves and become the "presentable" Flynn McAllister and Rachel Fury again.

It's time for the bubble to burst.

She pulls me toward the front door of the restaurant and out into the cool evening air. The lamps in the parking lot cast long shadows across the half-full spots. But even the dark of night can't hide the damage to my car.

I stop dead in my tracks and put an arm out to stop Rachel. "What the fuck?"

"Oh, my God." Rachel bumps into my arm, staring at the smashed windshield and dented hood. "What happened?"

I wrap my arm around her, jerk her against me, and scan the parking lot for any sign of who might have done this and to ensure we aren't in any danger. We were inside for over an hour, so it could have happened when we first arrived or only a few moments ago. Either way, it's not safe to be out here. Not when we don't know.

*Not when this isn't the first time something like this has happened...*

Rachel shivers in my hold. "Flynn, what's going on? Who would do this to your car?"

*Shit. Shit. Shit.*

After the paint incident, I told myself I was going to be more vigilant. Everything checked out on my site in regard to the security measures, so there wasn't any obvious way someone could have identified me. But with as busy as I was all week, and then being tied up with Rachel all weekend, I hadn't given the apparent threats much more thought.

Until now.

Because this is *different*.

Not only is it more violent, but it proves whoever is doing this is following me. When it was only at the office, in a parking structure where my name was plastered on the cement wall right over my car, it would be easy to find me. But coming here. Doing this *here* is a statement.

*I just don't know what the fuck it's saying or who is saying it.*

And as much as I would love to keep Rachel from having to worry about any of this, now she's right at the center of it as much as I am. By being with me, she's put herself in the crosshairs of a danger she never knew was there...because I kept it from her.

I pull her away from my chest and glance down at her. "We need to call the cops."

Fear darkens her green eyes. "What's going on?"

"I don't know." I grab my phone from my pocket and usher her back toward the restaurant. "But we're not safe standing out here. Let's wait inside."

I dial 9-1-1 as we make it to the front door.

She turns back toward the car and stares at it for a moment. "It has to be a mistake, right? Someone got the wrong car?"

*Christ.*

I wish I could tell her that's what happened. Revealing that there have been other incidents I kept her in the dark about isn't going to go over well.

———

**RACHEL**

The police officer glances down at his notebook and then back up at Flynn and me, where we stand near the car, Flynn's arm wrapped around my shoulders and mine around his waist. "So...you didn't see anything, didn't notice anything suspicious or unusual, and just came out here and found this. Am I right?"

Flynn's jaw tightens, and he nods. "Yeah. But..." He rubs

the back of his neck with his free hand—one of the little tics he has when he's nervous or thinking about something.

I squeeze my arms wrapped around his waist in support, but I honestly don't know what he's about to say. Since we walked out here and saw this, he's seemed off.

The officer raises his dark eyebrows at him. "But what, sir?"

Flynn's gaze meets mine, and the trepidation there makes the delicious dinner we just had churn in my stomach.

*What's he so afraid of saying?*

Even in the shadowy, half-lit parking lot, Flynn's unease matches mine. "Well, officer, there have been other incidents recently."

"What?" I jerk my head around and look up at him. "What are you talking about?"

The officer narrows his eyes on Flynn. "I think you better give me the whole story here, son. If you have any idea who did this, we need to know."

Flynn nods. "That's just it...I don't know who did it. Or who slashed my tires or put paint on my car."

I step in front of him to face him and plant my hands on his chest. "Jesus, Flynn, when did this happen? Where?"

*And how the hell didn't I know about it?*

The now obviously annoyed officer clears his throat. "Ma'am, if I can do the questioning, please."

*Shit.*

I step back to Flynn's side and offer a contrite smile. "I'm sorry, officer. I just wasn't aware any of this was going on."

It seems I was right when I said Flynn has been keeping things from me. And more than just being HRD4U, apparently.

The man I thought I knew better than anyone casts an apologetic look at me. "The first incident was two weeks ago.

Monday. I went to leave for the day and found all four of my tires slashed in the parking structure at my office."

The officer scowls. "And you didn't report this to the police?"

I should keep my shock and annoyance silent since the officer doesn't want me involved right now, but the words fall out before I can stop them. "Or tell me about it?"

Flynn casts a guilty look toward me and then turns to the officer. "I couldn't be sure it wasn't just a random, stupid-punk kid, or somebody who hates BMWs." He shrugs. "I honestly wasn't that worried at that point."

"But you said there was another incident?" The officer doesn't even look up from scribbling on his notepad. "When was that?"

"The next Monday. I went out into the garage with a friend to leave for lunch and found red paint on my car."

*A second incident he didn't think to tell me about.*

My anger simmers beneath the surface of my skin, tightening it until I have to take deep breaths to keep from breaking out of it and completely losing my shit in front of this poor cop.

Officer Higgins—as his name badge indicates—peeks up at Flynn with a furrowed brow. "Okay, and you're sure it was intentional and not just somebody accidentally spilling some paint?"

Flynn lets out a mirthless laugh and shakes his head. "Oh, it was definitely intentional." He swallows thickly and glances at me. "The word '*whore*' was written across my windshield."

*Whore?*

The images of Flynn on the HRD4U site flash before my eyes. The photos. The live feeds. The thousands of comments he gets every performance from viewers. The private messages he told INEEDSOMED about that he says come frequently.

Higgins raises his eyebrows. "Whore?"

Flynn nods slowly but doesn't look my way. Probably because he knows he won't like what he sees if he does.

Higgins jots something down in his notebook. "Sounds to me like you might have a disgruntled ex out there."

"No." Flynn shakes his head. "No, officer, that's just it…I don't. I haven't really dated anyone in a couple of years, and all those relationships ended amicable, anyway. This isn't an ex."

As much as I would like to believe that's all it is, an uneasy feeling slithers up my spine, and I can't shake what HRD4U does from my mind. "I have to agree with him, officer. Flynn and I have known each other for years, and I've never seen any of the women he dated mad or even remotely violent. Definitely not enough to do anything like this."

Higgins releases a sigh. "So, you have no idea what could've brought this on?"

Flynn steps away and paces. The loss of his body heat against me makes me shiver, but it's the fact that he wants to put physical space between us that worries me more.

He motions for the officer to move a little bit closer as a couple walks past us on the way into the restaurant. "If I tell you something, do you have to put it in the report?"

Higgins scowls at him and hardens his stance. "You called us for help with this, to report a crime. We need to know all the facts if you want us to try to figure out who did it or we'll never be able to prosecute anyone."

Flynn's entire body tenses. He's going to have to come clean, and he knows it. "It's possible someone may have discovered my real identity."

"I'm not sure I follow, son."

Poor Higgins is clueless about what's coming, but I brace myself for it.

"Shit." Flynn squeezes his eyes closed and swallows thickly. "I have a webcam business. I do it under a performance name."

Higgins' dark eyebrows rise at him. "Webcam? Like a porn site?"

Both Flynn and I flinch, but he nods.

"Kind of. But I double-checked all my encryption software and security measures on the site, and I couldn't find any way anyone could have discovered my real name." He sighs and scrubs his hands over his face. "But the word '*whore*' does make me question if it has something to do with that."

*Jesus...how could he not have told me about this?*

It has to be one of his viewers.

It *has* to be.

*Who else would call him a whore or be obsessed enough to do these things?*

Higgins releases an uncomfortable chuckle. "Well, this is certainly a first. I'm not trying to make light of the situation, son. I'm just not entirely sure how we could go about checking everyone who might've viewed your website. It's not very realistic."

Flynn nods and offers an understanding half-smile. "I know. And there's no real definitive evidence it *is* one of my viewers, anyway."

The door to the restaurant opens, and a large party tumbles out, laughing and talking loudly until they see the cop and his cruiser. Their revelry dies as they quietly make their way to their vehicles, eyes never leaving our little group huddled by Flynn's damaged car.

Higgins motions toward the restaurant. "The manager

told me your car is parked in an area of the lot that isn't covered by the cameras."

I roll my eyes and cross my arms over my chest.

*Of course, it isn't.*

It would never be that easy. And since Flynn doesn't have any info about what happened at his office garage, my guess is their cameras didn't catch anything, either.

"But"—Higgins flips his notebook closed—"he said he will send them to us to review to see if any suspicious vehicles are leaving or entering around the time that this would've happened. I gotta tell you, though, I don't have much confidence we're going to be able to find who did this."

Flynn sighs and drops his head back to stare at the night sky. "Me, either."

Higgins offers me a sympathetic look, but whether it's because of the damage and a culprit who will never be caught or because my boyfriend—or whatever the hell he is —is an online porn star, I can't tell. "I suggest you be a little bit more vigilant about your surroundings and maybe reconsider your profession. It's inviting people like this into your life."

"It isn't my profession. I have a real job—" Flynn starts to argue then waves a hand at the officer. "Never mind. It's not important."

And I'm starting to wonder if I really am.

His tires were slashed, and *whore* was written on his car. Both very real, very imminent threats he has kept from me for weeks.

*What else is he hiding besides HRD4U and this?*

I thought I knew Flynn inside and out, especially after the last few days we've spent together, but now, it's like I'm staring at a complete stranger.

## 21

FLYNN

The door clicks closed behind me, and I follow Rachel into her living room. The fact that she came straight to her house instead of mine when the cab dropped us off outside didn't go unnoticed.

She's pissed, and I can't say I blame her.

If the shoe were on the other foot and she kept something like this from me, I wouldn't be very happy. I would probably be furious. And her absolute silence after Officer Higgins left and during our uncomfortable ride home has only served to build the tension between us.

She drops her purse on the end table and stands with her back to me, her shoulders tense and her body practically vibrating. I approach her slowly, cautiously, the way I would a wounded animal that might snap at me because it's in pain.

I reach out but almost like she can sense it, she glances over her shoulder at me.

"Don't touch me."

"Rach"—I let my hand fall—"I'm sorry."

"Sorry for what?" She whirls to face me, her green eyes flashing with something I don't think I've ever seen focused on me before. Anger. But there's something else there, something even worse. "Are you sorry for keeping what was going on from me? Sorry you lied? Or just sorry you got caught? Because I'm kind of at a loss here."

I close the distance between us and grab her shoulders before she can back away. She gives a halfhearted protest and attempts to try to get out from under my hold, but I tighten my grip.

She sighs, and her body sags slightly in resignation. "This is serious, Flynn. Someone is obsessed with you and is pissed enough to do violent stuff like that. And it's only escalating."

*Like I don't know that.*

*Like I haven't felt like someone put a target on my back since the moment we saw my car.*

She's no doubt already worked out what I did earlier. Whoever this is followed us tonight. A true stalker capable of God only knows what.

I squeeze her shoulders gently. "I know, Rach." I shift one hand to tilt up her chin, forcing her to look at me. "And I need you to understand. I wasn't trying to lie to you. With the tires, I honestly didn't know what was going on. Like I told the officer, I thought maybe it was stupid kids or a mistake even, and there was no reason to get you upset about it."

Her bottom lip quivers. "Except I'm your best friend. Or...I thought I was. I thought we told each other everything."

*Fuck.*

I knew she would read too much into this. Things were too easy. Too happy. There's no way that could last. Not even through an entire damn weekend, apparently.

"I know, Rach. And I'm sorry. When I found the paint on my car, I realized it might be connected to the site. And then I *really* couldn't tell you because…" I trail off and let her fill in the blanks because she knows exactly what I mean without me having to say the words.

Tears shimmer in her eyes, the pooling liquid like acid eating away at my heart. "Because you didn't think I would understand and thought I would judge you."

I nod slowly, admitting what I now know was stupid. "I did everything I could to make sure the site was secure. I still don't know how anyone could possibly have figured out who I am, especially if *you* couldn't."

The tiniest grin pulls at her lips even though she tries to fight it. "Because I was intentionally trying not to notice certain things about you. Certain things I was attracted to."

"I know."

"But this is my point, Flynn. The site…I understand it might have been fun and you enjoy doing it, but it's dangerous. Not only might you have obsessed fans like this, but what if, God forbid, your mother found out."

I release her and step back to run a hand through my hair. "You think I haven't considered that? That's why I went through so many steps to make sure I was anonymous."

She fists her hands at her sides, the tension working its way up to her shoulders. "You don't need to do it anymore, Flynn."

The other night when she told me I needed to stop being HRD4U, I kind of laughed it off as her being jealous that other women—and men—would be watching me now that we are together. I wasn't mad because I thought it was kind of cute. Endearing, really. But now, it feels more like she's trying to dictate how I live my life, and I'm not sure how I feel about that.

It's not cheating on her. I don't engage in any conversations or webcam sex with anyone...INEEDSOMED being the *only* time it has *ever* happened. She can't blame me for that when it was *her*. And the viewers on my site have become friends—as weird as that may sound, especially since they pay me. I don't know that it's something I want to stop even if I financially can.

I was serious when I said I wanted her on camera with me, that I thought she would find it hot to know people watch us together. It's hot knowing people watch me solo, knowing they were watching me fuck the woman I love would be beyond incredible.

But it seems I'm not getting any consideration.

All I'm going to get is Rachel's anger and demands.

"Rach, I don't want to fight with you about HRD4U. If it weren't for that damn site, we might never have gotten together."

She crosses her arms over her chest. "I don't want to fight, either, but I'm more than just mad, Flynn. I'm hurt."

And everyone knows that's ten times worse. Like your parents saying they're not angry, just disappointed when you fuck up.

I never thought I would hurt Rachel. Never in a million lifetimes. But I already have so much in the last couple of weeks.

She squeezes her eyes shut for a moment and takes a deep breath before opening them and meeting my gaze again. "Even if I didn't have a problem with you keeping the site active—"

I open my mouth to interject, but she holds up a hand.

"And I'm not saying I do. I'm just..."—she closes her eyes again and shakes her head,—"I don't know how I feel about it right now. But even if I didn't have an issue with it, doesn't this prove to you that this is a bad idea to continue?"

Maybe it should. Maybe I ought to be racing over to my

house to shut down the site right now. But something won't let me do it. HRD4U has become a part of me. A way to be who I can't be in public. Even with the guilt I've recently been feeling about it, and even though I have Rachel now—hopefully *still* have her after tonight—I don't know that I can let the other me go so easily.

I rub the back of my neck and sigh. "I don't know, Rach."

"Honestly, Flynn, it's not even about the site, really. Ultimately, it's about the fact that all this was going on, you were *threatened,* and you felt like you couldn't tell me about any of it."

A vise tightens around my chest. It's like I can feel her falling away from me, distancing herself and shutting down her heart right in front of me, even though I only just managed to get it open to me.

I close the distance between us again and grab her shoulders again. "How could I without telling you about the site?"

Tears flow down her cheeks now, tiny streams leaving wet lines across her flawless skin. "I guess I thought you had more faith in me. As your friend. That I would love you no matter what you were doing in private or anywhere in your life."

I snort and shake my head. "That's hardly fair, Rachel, when you've been hiding a big part of you from me, too."

Her eyes darken. "That's different."

My hands fall away from her, annoyance starting to build. "How so?"

"Because I'm not the one jerking off for strangers."

I recoil and step back from her slowly.

*Fucking wow!*

Each retreating step I take puts more distance between us, physically and emotionally, but it doesn't matter.

*I can't believe she said that.*

My back collides with the front door, and I sigh. "And here I thought you didn't judge me for it. I guess I was wrong."

She bites her lip but doesn't deny it.

"I guess we were both wrong about a lot of things." I twist the knob, step out the door, and slam it closed behind me.

I don't even bother to point out that she jerked off online with a total stranger, too, and then agreed to go meet him in person. Just because she broke my heart doesn't mean I have to be a complete douchebag and throw that back in her face.

The best weekend of my life has turned into the worst.

And I don't know if there's any way to fix this.

———

## RACHEL

The words on the page in front of me blur together. These damn tears keep welling in my eyes despite my best efforts to keep them at bay.

*Thank God I don't need to see the words to finish this one.*

I've read this story to the kids a thousand times over the years and know it by heart. In retrospect, I should have picked a different book. One with less love and soul mates BS that might bring on the waterworks today.

"And they all lived happily ever after. The end."

I close the book and peer down at the back cover for a moment. The smiling princess staring up at her prince, the one who used to be something else—a beast.

They somehow managed to find true happiness in the end, even with all the things that stood between them, yet Flynn and I fell apart after only two days together.

*What does that say about us?*

Maybe it's a part of the harsh reality that happily ever after only exists in fairy tales. And this isn't one.

What happened this weekend just complicated things too much. If we had continued on as merely friends, we would've been blissfully unaware that we were lying to each other. Because that's what we were *both* doing. Flynn was lying to me about being HRD4U, about all the threats he received, about his feelings for me, and I was lying to him about why all my relationships fail and why I can't find anyone to settle down with. I was also lying to myself when I tried to deny my attraction for Flynn and convince myself there wasn't anything more there.

But we could've faked it.

We could've gone on like things were.

It might not have been perfect, but at least we had each other. At least we had our friendship. Now, it feels like we have nothing. Except maybe a whole lot of pain.

"Miss Rachel? Are you okay?" Connor stares up at me from his spot in the front row of the colorful rug. His wide eyes, so much like his father's, look up at me with concern.

I plaster on my best reassuring smile and nod. "I'm fine. I just really love this story."

He grins. "Me, too.

Next to him, Jessica bobs her little blonde head. "It's my favorite."

The other dozen kids on the rug chatter and nod their agreement.

I glance up at the clock hanging above the classroom door. "Can anyone tell me what time it is?"

Abigail raises her hand. "Ooh, ooh, me! Me!"

"Yes, Abby?"

She checks out the clock again before turning back to face me. "It's eleven-thirty."

"And what do we do at eleven-thirty?"

Connor bounces up and down, barely able to contain his excitement. "We go to lunch."

"Yes. You'll go to lunch as soon as Michaela comes."

And I'll get half an hour that I normally take to catch up and check in on social media and texts to bury my face in my arms on my desk and try to nap. I barely slept at all last night after Flynn left, and we barely slept at all the two nights before. Every bone and muscle in my body reminds me of that fact with extreme vengeance. I'm just exhausted —emotionally and physically—and a few minutes of uninterrupted quiet time is what I need right now.

The door in the classroom opens, and Michaela pops her head in. I wish I had her in the room with me all day today, but I needed her to organize some projects for this afternoon, so I've been flying solo most of the morning.

She waves to the kids. "Come on, guys. Time to head down to the cafeteria."

They all climb to their feet and race toward the door.

Michaela holds up her hands. "No running!"

Their little feet slow down, barely, and they form a single-file line. Michaela does the headcount and waves to me. "Have a great lunch!"

I wave her off. "At least I'll try."

Though I have no confidence in my ability to keep myself together once the only thing I have to think about is what happened.

I shove the offending children's book back onto the bookshelf and release a heavy sigh. Only a few more hours 'til I can head home. Although home might not much be much better. Not when I know Flynn is right next door.

Living so close used to be such a major benefit, but now, it feels more like a curse.

I push myself off the stool and trudge over to my desk. Trepidation tightens around my heart as I slide open the top drawer and lower myself into my seat. My phone sits exactly where I left it. But there aren't any new messages.

*Was I hoping he would text or call or that he wouldn't?*

It seems I don't know *what* the hell I want anymore.

I grab it and slide open my emails. Junk. Junk. Junk. Junk. A text message pops up on the screen.

*Bash.*

**I hope I'm catching you at lunch.**

Maybe talking to big brother is exactly what I need to keep my mind occupied. His timing couldn't be better. I press the button to call him right away.

"Hey, Rach. Everything Okay? I wasn't expecting you to call."

I lean into my chair and let my head fall back so I can stare at the white popcorn ceiling.

*How much should I tell Bash?*

Just enough to get some advice but not enough to reveal all of mine and Flynn's secrets.

"I'm really not doing okay."

"What's wrong?"

*Literally everything.*

Sunlight from the window filters through the students' tissue-paper stained-glass projects taped to the glass, sending multicolored beams across the ceiling. I wish I could appreciate the beauty of it right now. "Well, Flynn and I..."

No need to actually say the words. Bash will get where I'm going.

"Holy shit. Did you two finally hook up?"

I rub a hand over my face. "Finally? Jesus, was everybody in the world just waiting for it?"

He chuckles. "Pretty much. So, was it bad?"

I bolt upright, the rickety old chair creaking awfully with the abrupt movement. "Bad? No, why?"

"Just wondering why you'd be upset. The only reason I can think of is he's terrible in bed."

That brings a smile to my face despite how unhappy I am at this moment. "Definitely not the problem."

My body heats, remembering how incredibly *not bad* he really is.

"Then what's the problem, Rach?"

I twist a strand of my hair around my finger and sigh. "We had a great weekend and then ended up having a huge fight last night."

"A fight? About what?"

*How do I explain this?*

It's almost impossible without revealing the things that kept us together in the first place. "I guess about our expectations going forward."

"You lost me, Rach. Are you saying you and Flynn don't want the same thing? That this was just a one-time or friends-with-benefits thing for him? Because if you need me to come kill him, I will."

I laugh, rest my elbow on the desktop, and drop my forehead into my palm. "No. We were in agreement about that. There are just some things he never told me about that seem like they want to come between us."

A car door slams in the background behind Bash, and he mumbles something to someone. "Sorry about that. Greer says, hi. I was just dropping her off at the arena."

"Tell her, hi."

"Look, Rach, I know you're the smart one in the family, so taking advice from me probably seems pretty stupid, but here's how I see it. You and Flynn have been best friends for a long time. And I've seen the way he looks at you. I don't think he would ever do anything to hurt you intentionally, no matter how much you might believe that he did right now. Having said that, if you need me to come to give him a beat down, I totally will."

"I know you will." One of the perks of having Bash as a brother.

"So, don't be stupid. You both might be mad about it now but think about the long-term here. Is whatever you fought about really so important that you'll give up what you two might have together and not only end your friendship but any chance at anything else? Is that the road you really want to go down?"

"It's the furthest thing from what I want."

"So, carve out a new path."

"I'll think about it."

"While you're thinking about that, the reason I sent you a text is Greer reserved the box for the game on March 8th. I'm inviting Caleb and Tara and their kids and was going to invite Jameson, you, and Flynn, too, if you think you two will be talking by then."

"Smartass."

"Do you think you'll be able to come?"

It's a short, cheap flight to Vegas, so it shouldn't be a problem, assuming we *are* talking by then. Though even if we aren't, I would likely still go to see Jameson and Bash and everyone else. It would probably ease some of that lingering homesickness that's been plaguing me. "I'll let you know as soon as I can."

"Okay. Don't forget that sometimes you need to play dirty to win."

"This isn't a hockey game, Bash. It's my life."

"I know that. But there are a lot of ways to play dirty while keeping yourself clean. Figure it out and see if it helps you fix things with Flynn."

At this point, it feels like nothing can fix us.

# 22

## FLYNN

I pull the rental car into the familiar parking lot and turn off the engine, but I don't get out right away. Not just because of the light drizzle falling, but because I don't know what the fuck I'm doing here. I don't know what answers I think I'm going to find or what help I think I might get.

But after I woke up this morning, got the rental car, and went to work, all I could think about—besides how badly I fucked things up with Rachel—was coming here to talk to the man who was never around to see me become one.

It's crazy to talk to a headstone. To act like Dad's here and can understand me and actually offer advice. But the few times in my life I have desperately needed solace, this is where I've always wound up.

Mom tends to go to church when she's feeling lost. She seeks peace in the house of the Lord. On her knees praying for help from Him. It gives her what she needs, but that building and praying to the Heavenly Father has always been her thing.

I come to Dad.

It's been years since I've been here, though. Things have been good, mostly because I had Rachel next door to be my sounding board. And though my return was inevitable at some point, I just hadn't anticipated it being because of Rachel.

*She* has become my solace. My safe place. The one person in the world I thought I would never lose.

*How quickly things can change.*

For those two days, it felt like everything had finally come together. That life was finally giving me the things I've hoped and prayed for. Then it was ripped away in an instant when we both said words we can't take back.

I pull the hood of my raincoat up over my head and step out of the car. The cool drops send a shiver through me, but I push past it and make my way across the wet, green lawn, weaving through headstones until coming to a stop in front of a familiar one.

*Niall William McAllister*
*Beloved Husband and Father.*

I can't even look at the date, and I don't need to. The exact minute Mom told me he was dead is etched into my memory so deeply, I could never forget it. I had known something was wrong when she showed up in the middle of the day at my school, but I never imagined that Dad was gone. It was an inconceivable as losing Rachel.

An icy cold gust of frigid air hits me, and I pull the jacket tighter against my body.

My eyes water and burn, but not because of the wind.

*God, I fucking hate to cry.*

For so many years after he died, I refused to. Fought it tooth and nail. Acted tough, like it didn't get to me that he wasn't there at every basketball game, graduation, birthday. I fought acknowledging his absence as much as Mom couldn't stop thinking about it. It broke her, and I wouldn't let his death break me, too. But now a woman might do it.

Not just a woman.

*The woman.*

The only one I'll ever want or love.

I stand staring down at his final resting place, letting the water drip off the plastic raincoat and down my exposed hands. "Hey, Dad. Sorry it's been a while. I wasn't sure where else to go."

With a sigh, I scan the deserted cemetery. Today's finicky weather is keeping away anyone who might usually be here. And I'm fine with that. I don't need an audience for this.

"You remember me telling you about Rachel a couple of years ago? Well"—I run a hand over the scruff covering my jaw because I didn't even bother to shave this morning —"I've fucked things up with her royally. I thought I had been doing such a good job living my life and hiding how I felt about her, but things eventually came to a head. And Christ, Dad, they were good so fucking good for a minute. But it all crashed down just as fast as we found it."

I swallow through the knot in my throat.

"I've been doing something. Something I've kept from Mom and everyone else because I think deep down, I am ashamed of it even though I logically know I'm not doing anything wrong. It's actually how Rachel and I finally got together. But now, it's the thing that is breaking us apart."

*Shattering us, actually.*

When something breaks, you can put it back together. It might take a lot of glue and patience, but you *can* salvage it. But when something *shatters*, there are too many tiny shards to ever put things back into the proper place again. Even if you try, give it your best efforts, it will always be *off*—a warped, ugly version of what you once had.

I look up into the rain, letting the drops hit my face with a cool splash.

"She's mad because I lied. By omission. But I guess it was a lie all the same. I didn't tell her about something because it would have meant revealing other things." I return my focus to the headstone and swipe my hand over my face to remove as much water as I can. "Christ, it's such a mess. You and Mom were never this intense, were you? I know you guys met when you were pretty young, but I never remember you arguing or there really being anything overly dramatic happening in the house. I wish my life were more like that because I'm not really sure where to go from here. I can apologize to her, hell, I *did* apologize, but she thinks that this means I don't love her. She thinks that this means I don't trust her or care. But she couldn't be more wrong."

*About so many damn things.*

"I kept it from her *because* I care. *Because* I love her, and I didn't want to worry her or upset her or drag her into something that she is too good to touch. I don't want the dirt and filth of my life and what I am doing with it to mar her. Because she's fucking perfect and pure. But now, I think I've lost her."

Water trickles down the front of the granite monument, washing it and cleaning away all the dirt and grime that's accumulated.

I wish the rain could do the same for me. Wash away everything that happened between Rachel and me that was bad and only leave what was good.

But life isn't that simple.

"I'll give it up, Dad. I will. It's not even about that. It's about the fact that she judges me, even though she says she doesn't. I don't know if she'll ever be able to look at me the same, knowing what I've done. As much as she says it's okay, she made it clear that it's not."

*And what she said was like a knife to my fucking heart.*

Even now, almost twenty-four hours later, my chest still aches and burns with the wound. I still physically feel it every time I take a breath. Those words leaving her lips...

"I need a sign, Dad. Some way to know which way to go and what to do."

I squeeze my eyes shut against the sting of the tears and suck in a deep breath to keep the sob that's climbing up my throat from escaping.

The wind picks up out of the north and swirls around me almost violently. A whirlwind spinning up dirt and debris from the cemetery.

Something hits my hand, and I glance down and freeze.

White petals.

Yellow centers.

An all too familiar flower now stuck to my wet skin.

I pull it off and whirl around to look at the grave next to Dad's.

*Daisies.*

*Fucking daisies.*

Wind whips more from the planter in front of the headstone up into the air. The flowers twirl around me for a moment and move across the grass toward my car in the parking lot.

I run my hands over my damp face and rub my eyes.

*This has to be a hallucination.*

Maybe the sheer lack of sleep and stress has finally gotten to me. It's making me see things that aren't even there. But maybe, just maybe, the hallucination is telling me where I need to go.

It just doesn't help me get there.

Not when there are so many roadblocks between here and there.

Between Rachel and me.

## RACHEL

The warm water of the bubble bath swirls around me, soothing some of my tense, aching muscles but doing nothing to help the pain slicing at my heart. It's only been twenty-four hours since our fight, but it already feels like an eternity.

Our other little tiff was a mere millisecond compared to this one, even though that lasted far longer. Maybe because last night felt more final. Like losing something in a way that you can never get it back instead of a little nothing that I knew we'd eventually get over.

As soon as I get out of this bath, I'm climbing into bed and praying I can actually get some sleep. The kids don't deserve to have me a practical zombie in class tomorrow. I feel worse than the undead from the movie I made Flynn watch with me.

The sound of the front door opening and closing tenses every muscle in my body. Through the cracked door in the bathroom, the sound of footsteps making their way down the hallway toward me has me searching the bathroom for some sort of a weapon.

*Did I lock the front door when I came in?*

I don't even remember. Everything since last night has been such a blur, and I can hardly remember driving home from work today, let alone what I did once I got here.

My razor sits on the edge of the tub, and I clutch it in my hand and hold it out toward the door.

It swings open slowly, and Alicia bursts out laughing. "What the hell were you gonna do with that thing if I was a real intruder? Give me a damn shave?"

I sag back into the water. "Ha, ha. Very funny." With the

razor firmly back in its place, I glance down to ensure the goods are all covered by the bubbles. "What are you doing here?"

She steps into the bathroom and pulls herself up to sit on the counter with her legs dangling. "Connor came home from school and said you were sad all day. I came over after the kids went to bed to see what made you such a sad sack."

"Oh, Christ." I duck deeper into the water until my chin is below it, and I am hiding behind a wall of bubbles. "I guess I did a pretty crappy job controlling my emotions in front of the kids. Teacher of the year, I am not."

She chuckles and shakes her head. "They're five. They probably won't even remember tomorrow. I wouldn't worry too much about it. But now, I *am* worried about you. Cade and I haven't seen you and Flynn for days, and now, you're upset enough that my kid noticed. What's going on?"

*Shit.*

I hadn't thought about how to explain any of this to our mutual friends. And I really should have. Of course, they're going to notice something's different. But I think Flynn and I were so wrapped up in each other over the weekend that we didn't think about telling anyone. Plus, it was so new...it never got a chance to get old.

"Do you promise not to say anything to Cade?"

Alicia raises her eyebrows at me. "I can't make that promise until I know what it is."

I blow on the bubbles in the water to give myself a chance to think. Other than Flynn, Alicia's my best friend. My *only* close friend here in California, actually. And if this thing with him never gets sorted out, I'm going to need her more than ever. She can't help me if she doesn't understand.

"We slept together."

"What?" She practically falls off the counter. "You're joking."

I squeeze my eyes shut and shake my head. "No."

"What the hell happened?" She grins and waggles her eyebrows. "Was it good?"

I roll my eyes at her. "Yes, it was good. In fact, it was beyond great. We spent the whole weekend wrapped up in each other and barely left the bedroom."

A grin splits her face, and she practically vibrates with excitement. "Rach, that's awesome! Why are you so upset?"

*Here we go.*

"I swear to God if you tell Cade—"

She holds up her hands. "Okay, okay, I won't, but how do you know Flynn isn't gonna tell him the exact same thing you're telling me?"

"Good point. But still, I don't want it to have come from me if he doesn't."

With mock importance, she crosses over her chest. "Scout's honor."

I chuckle. "You were a Boy Scout?"

She shrugs. "Brownie. Same difference. So, what happened?"

Swallowing thickly, I shift in the water. "Do you remember the HRD4U website?"

Alicia nods and leans back against the counter. "Yeah"— her eyes widen—"did Flynn find out you were talking to that guy? Did you ever message him back?"

I hold up a hand to stop her inquisition. "It's more complicated than that."

"How so?"

*Christ, I can't believe I'm saying this.*

"Flynn *is* HRD4U."

Her jaw drops to the floor, and she opens and closes her mouth a few times before she manages to find some words. "You are fucking *kidding* me."

I shake my head. "I wish I were."

"So that giant dick I saw on the website was Flynn's?"

I nod slowly as her jaw drops even farther than I thought possible.

"Holy...wow." She grins. "Good for you, girl."

I smirk at her and move around the bubbles with my hand. "Trust me, sex isn't the problem."

"Then what is?"

"The fact that it looks like one of his viewers has been stalking him and he never told me."

She stiffens. "What do you mean by stalking him?"

"Someone slashed his tires and wrote the word '*whore*' in paint on his car, and then last night, when we were at dinner, someone smashed the windshield."

"*While* you were at dinner?"

I nod slowly.

"So, the person had to have been following you."

"That, or by some miracle, they happened to be at the same restaurant as us at the same time, but I highly doubt that."

She shakes her head slowly. "Yeah, I don't, either. So, this is one of his viewers?"

"It appears that way."

"But there's no way to know for sure?"

I shrug. "Apparently not."

"And what? You're worried that you'll be a target now that you two are together?"

The bathwater suddenly drops in temperature.

"Well, hell, I hadn't been until you just said that, but no. I'm pissed because he didn't tell me that any of this has been happening over the last couple of weeks. And he didn't tell me about HRD4U."

"Why would he?"

I raise an eyebrow at her. "Excuse me?"

"Why would he tell you about HRD4U?"

I shift up in the bath, straightening my spine and squaring my shoulders for a fight. "Oh, I don't know. Maybe because I'm his best friend."

"Well, yeah, but I mean, look at Flynn. Look at his mom and his family and his upbringing. Don't you think there's gotta be some struggle somewhere in there with what he's been doing?"

I hadn't thought about it that way. But now that she put that in my head, the way he was acting at church a couple of weeks ago suddenly starts to make a little bit more sense. "You think he didn't tell me because he felt *guilty*?"

"Or maybe he thought you would judge him."

I wince.

"Oh no, Rach. What's that wince for?"

"I *may* have made a comment last night that sounded a little bit judgmental."

Alicia drops her head back and closes her eyes. "Shit."

"Yeah."

She opens her eyes and refocuses on me. "What happened after that?"

"He left."

"Double shit."

I drop my face into my wet palms. "Yeah."

"Well...do you?"

I glance up at her. "Do I what?"

"Do you judge him because of it? Do you look down on him because of what he was doing?"

I consider her question. One that has always been at the back of my mind, yet I never really fully contemplated. But instead of needing time to come to an answer, it's so obvious. "No. I don't."

"Then why did you say it?"

"Because I was hurt that he had kept things from me. Because I wanted to hurt him back."

250

She raises an eyebrow. "So...revenge?"

*God that sounds petty and spiteful.*

I nod slowly. "I guess so."

She swings her feet lazily, like we're not talking about the single most important thing in my life right now, maybe ever. "Did you feel better after you said it?"

"No, of course not." I'm not some heartless bitch who says something that hurts someone and cackles about it later. "I felt like shit."

"Does it make you feel better *now*?"

I glower at her. "What the hell do you think?"

She sighs and slides off the counter to kneel next to the tub. "I think you and Flynn are both being stupid. I think there's nothing keeping you two from being together, and yet, you're both coming up with reasons not to make it happen. I have never seen two people more perfect for each other than you two. Probably not even Cade and me. So, stop fighting it and stop creating problems that aren't there."

"You make it sound so simple. When I talked to Bash earlier today, he did, too."

She shrugs. "Maybe that's because it *is* that simple."

## 23

**FLYNN**

Trying to drown myself in bourbon doesn't seem to be working. Even my third glass of the warm, spicy alcohol can't help me forget what went down last night. I don't know that anything can.

Nor do I know what to make of what happened at the cemetery. I asked for a sign, and the damn flower literally hit me. One would think there isn't anything clearer than that, yet I don't know what it's telling me to do.

*Apologize?*

I already *did* apologize for not telling her what was going on, but the fact that she can't understand *why* I couldn't tell her and that I was protecting her still eats away at me.

*Forgive her for what she said? How she judges me?*

Her words won't leave my head. They've been echoing around in there so loudly that I wasn't able to concentrate on anything today and blew off all my phone calls from clients before I left early to head to the cemetery.

Any capacity to interact with other humans left me when I walked out of Rachel's door last night.

I can't keep going like this, but I'm not ready to face her yet. Not when I don't know what to do or say. I can't be with her if she's pissed about something I did before we were together and can't move past it.

We're at a stalemate. And I'm not sure how to break it.

The sound of the key in the lock sends a shiver of panic through me. I freeze and watch the door with my glass raised to my lips. I'm not ready to see her. To confront what was said and all the feelings swirling through me.

Only when it pushes open, the green eyes and flowing caramel hair I'm hoping to see despite my reservations aren't there. Instead, Cade offers me a cocky grin.

"You fucker." I down a gulp of my drink. "When I gave you and Alicia a key, it was for an emergency."

He closes the door and makes his way toward me on the couch. "This is an emergency."

*Oh, shit!*

I push myself up. "Are the kids okay?"

"They're fine, mate. But Alicia just came from Rachel's and told me in no uncertain terms that I needed to come to talk to you, yet she wouldn't tell me why."

*Fuck.*

That means Rachel spilled.

*But was it everything or only the tamer bits and pieces of what went down?*

I push myself off the couch and wander over to the bar. "Want a drink?"

He waves off my offer and sits in the chair across from the couch. "You want to tell me what's going on?"

At this point, if Alicia knows, it's only a matter of time before Cade does.

I lower myself back onto the couch with a sigh. "Well, somehow, in the span of forty-eight hours, I told Rachel I loved her, we had sex, and then had a massive fight and basically aren't talking to each other now."

Cade's dark eyebrows shoot up. "Wow, when you go for it, you really go for it. Though, I can't say I'm surprised about the hooking up and undying love thing, I am a bit shocked you guys got into an argument. Aside from your recent little tiff, I don't think I've ever seen you argue."

"Yeah, well, that little tiff was about how I felt about her. She just didn't know it back then."

"But she does now, and yet, you two aren't together?"

I nod slowly and take a sip of my bourbon. "There's something you don't know about."

He sits for a moment, waiting for me to continue before he throws up his hands. "Are you going to tell me, mate?"

My laptop sits on the coffee table where I left it the night I figured out who INEEDSOMED was. I haven't even *thought* about opening it, doing a video, nothing. I nod toward the thing that brought us together and broke us apart. "Open it up."

He eyes me cautiously as he grabs it and pulls it onto his knees. "What am I looking at?"

"Open up the web browser and type *H-R-D* the number four and the letter *U* dot com."

He peeks at me over the top of the laptop. "And just why would I want to do that?"

"Just fucking do it already."

He nods, types on the keyboard, then releases a laugh that fills the room. "Have you been watching this guy, mate? Is there something I don't know? Are you gay?" He holds up a hand. "Not that there's anything wrong with that if you are."

I shake my head and take another sip. "Not gay. And no, I haven't been watching the site. I've been producing it."

255

Cade's eyes widen and then return to the screen. "Shit, so that's *you*?"

I rub my hand over my face and nod.

His jaw drops. "Why the hell are you doing a site like this?"

Releasing a sigh, I ponder the question I've asked myself a thousand times. "That's kind of irrelevant. Suffice it to say, I needed the money and had the goods."

"I should say you do." He grins at me. "Impressive."

I smirk a little. "Thanks. But it turns out that despite the fact that Rachel and I connected through the site"—he opens his mouth, I hold up a hand to stop him—"and I'm not going into more detail about that. That's her business. She doesn't want me doing it, nor does she seem to be able to get over the fact that I *was* doing it."

"I'm lost." He shakes his head. "If she was on the site, then how is that any different?"

"Fuck if I know. But apparently, it is. That and the fact that one of my viewers might be stalking me."

Which actually has a lot to do with it.

He motions toward the garage. "Is that why you have a rental car? I noticed it when you came home earlier."

"Someone slashed my tires, painted *whore* on my car, and smashed my windshield."

"Wow. Somebody's pissed. A jealous husband?"

"It's a possibility. I talked to the officer investigating this afternoon, but he said they have nothing—no leads, so unless something else happens and I catch the person in the act, I may never know."

He leans back in the chair. "Well, shit. Maybe you should just shut down the site."

I down my drink and hiss through the burn. "That's what she suggested."

"But you don't want to?"

"I don't know what I want to do. But I know I don't want to be told what I *have* to do. Nor do I like the way she judged me for it."

"I don't think Rachel is judging you, mate."

Easy for him to say. He wasn't here last night. He didn't hear the way she shot those words at me like arrows.

I rub at my aching temple. "Why do you say that?"

"Because I know her. I know you two. Are you sure she wasn't just upset and saying something because she was mad, not because of how she really felt? I've done that a time or two in my life."

*Was she?*

I hadn't really considered that. "It's not like Rachel to try to get back at someone like that."

Especially not me.

He shrugs. "Doesn't mean it didn't happen."

A pinging sound comes from the computer, and Cade narrows his eyes on the screen. "Hey, what's this little red icon in the upper right-hand corner?"

"Private messages."

"It says you just got one and have a total of twenty-three."

I snort and shake my head. "A lot less than I thought I would since I haven't been on since last week."

"Are they all from viewers?"

"Yeah, mostly propositions."

He chuckles. "Now, *this* I have to see."

I don't give a shit if he reads the private messages. I barely glance at them most of the time, other than what's necessary to open and delete them.

He clicks on the screen and then freezes. "Flynn, mate? I think you need to take a look at this one."

I squeeze my eyes closed. "I can't deal with the horny viewers right now."

"You need to see this one." He flips the computer around and points the screen toward me. "Really."

"Who is it from?" Between the multiple glasses of booze and our positions, I can't make anything out.

"Someone named INEEDSOMED."

"Rachel?" I lurch from the couch, grab the computer from him, then settle it on my lap.

My hand shakes as I roll the cursor down the message. The timestamp says it was sent two minutes ago.

INEEDSOMED

I hate fighting with you.

That's it. Her entire message is one sentence. But it comforts my heart and threatens to break me open all at the same time.

"What did she say, mate?"

"That she hates fighting."

"It sounds like an invitation to fix whatever is wrong." He pushes up from the chair. "I wish you the best of luck."

"You're leaving?"

He points in the direction of his house. "I have a wife I'm not fighting with that I would love to go spend some quality time with." He waggles his eyebrows. "Good luck."

The latch clicks into place behind him, and I return my focus to the message in front of me. Without even realizing it, I click on the reply box.

My cursor sits there, blinking at me. "What the hell do I say?"

———

## RACHEL

The light drizzle that's steadily fallen all day has become a deluge. Yet, even through the driving rain, I can still see the front door of Flynn's house open.

My breath catches in my chest.

I should move away from the window. If he caught me standing here, staring at his house like a stalker, I'd feel like an idiot. Even more so than I already do over all of this.

Only the figure who emerges isn't Flynn. Even through the rain, I recognize Cade before he darts across the street toward his house. I should've known he would go over as soon as Alicia went home, and it probably means Flynn hasn't seen my message yet.

He might never see it.

*What if he never logs back on to the HRD4U site?*

I bite my nail and continue to watch Flynn's house like a lovesick puppy, waiting for its owner to return home, only what I'm waiting for is a sign.

Sending a message was probably the coward's way out rather than crossing the lawn, climbing over the low hedge, and talking to him in person, but I couldn't face him. Not when I still don't know how I feel about the whole situation. Not when my heart is being pulled in two directions—one toward hurt and resentment that he kept so much from me; the other toward the only man I can say I've ever really loved, regardless of what's happened the last few weeks.

I had to tell him how much I hate the situation, how much I hate any tension between us, even if I am still hurt and angry.

We're in the unknown now. We've never had a fight of this magnitude. When we had our little disagreement the other week, I knew it wouldn't last long. I knew Flynn would come to his senses, eventually. But our entire relationship changed so fast, and now, I'm not sure about how any of this plays out.

I thought I felt alone before. Losing Mom and then Dad left me lost and out of sorts, but what I was feeling then is nothing compared to now, staring at his house, willing him to open that front door, step out into the rain, and meet me at that damn hedge.

But wishing something to come true doesn't make it happen. That's another falsehood created by the fairy tales we grew up with. The ones like I read to the kids that promise happily ever afters and nothing but hearts and flowers even if you come from two different worlds.

The blinds on his living room window facing my house shift and part.

My heart stalls, and I hold my breath.

He stands there, staring back at me, nothing more than thirty yards separating us, yet it feels like an entire ocean filled with deadly waves threatening to drag me under to fierce predators waiting to strike. And even worse, I can't fucking swim. I'm drowning. There's no way to keep my head above the water.

I'm going down.

Fast.

My tears, combined with the torrent outside, warp Flynn until I can't even see him anymore. I swipe them away and lean closer to the glass. He hasn't moved.

Several long minutes pass.

It could be hours.

I don't have any sense of time anymore while we stare at each other. Then finally, his hand drops, and the blinds close.

There's no point in my standing here, hoping he's going to return. I let the blinds close and wander back to the bedroom to my computer where the message I sent HRD4U still sits open on the screen.

INEEDSOMED

I hate fighting with you.

*So damn lame. Lame. Lame. Lame.*

But it's all I could think to say without getting into the reasons why we are fighting in the first place. The reasons that seem so stupid now.

I was the one who pushed Bash and Jameson so hard to forgive Dad and to make peace with him before he died. Forgiving that man for what he did to us, for what he did to Mom, so he wouldn't have to die alone was far easier than I even thought it could be. Because I saw the end coming. He was going to die. And what would my hostility and anger do for me then? Nothing.

This thing with Flynn has no end in sight, no logical conclusion. I don't know how this is supposed to end or what I need to do to work toward it. We didn't make any decisions. He just walked away.

The stupid message was an olive branch of sorts, I guess. My *super* lame attempt at telling him I still care and hate where we are. But I don't even know if he read it.

Maybe it was my fault for not chasing him down, for not apologizing immediately and telling him I didn't mean it. Because looking back, I know I didn't.

I was hurt he didn't trust me enough to tell me about HRD4U. That, I can understand, given that I was hiding my own predilections from him, but the fact that he didn't tell me about the tires or the paint is another thing altogether. That was where he crossed the line from hiding the secret he might've been embarrassed about to not having faith in me at all. That's why it feels like my heart is in pieces right now.

The cursor moves in the open chat window, and his response pops up.

HRD4U

I do, too.

His simple reply brings tears to my eyes for what feels like the thousandth time.

I hover my hands over the keyboard, but my brain can't seem to process what I need to say. There are so many things I *want* to say, so many things that *should* be said, and probably to Flynn's face, but the thought of looking into his blue-gray eyes while having to say them is just too much.

*Get your head together, Rachel.*

This is it. This is my chance to hopefully turn the tide.

*Don't blow it.*

Finally, my fingers move, almost of their own accord.

INEEDSOMED

I'm so sorry about what I said. I didn't mean it. I was hurt. Really fucking hurt. I felt if my best friend can't trust me with something this huge, then really, how strong is our friendship? Knowing that I might not know you like I thought I did destroyed me. Because I love the you that I know. I love the Flynn who makes pancakes with me and kicks my ass at miniature golf. The one who has sat here and held me while I cried over every stupid guy I've dated in the last five years without complaining once.

When you said you didn't tell me to protect me, that wasn't totally true. You did it to protect yourself from having to reveal HRD4U to me. I never want you to keep something that big from me again. I would rather you not keep anything from me again, but I know that's not realistic.

> I know that HRD4U is just another part of the Flynn I already know. He's always been there, just under the surface, and I caught glimpses of him at times, but now that I've really seen him, I love that Flynn, too. And there's nothing wrong with what you do on the site. Don't let yourself believe you're doing anything wrong.

> If you want to continue doing it, I can't say I won't be jealous that other women get to watch you, but it's as much a part of you as anything else. It's not my place to tell you to stop. It's not my place to tell you to do anything. So, I'm sorry.

> And please, forgive me, even if nothing else happens, even if we can't get back our friendship after all this, please, just forgive me so I know you won't go on with your life believing I think anything negative about you. It couldn't be further from the truth.

I sit and stare at the literal word vomit I typed through a flood of tears and hit send before I can second-guess myself and delete every letter of it.

Acid churns in my stomach, and I press my hand over my chest in a vain attempt to stop my racing heart.

*Is he going to respond?*

Every second waiting is like an hour. Every minute like a day.

And still...

Nothing.

The tears well again, and I swipe them away and reach for the top of the laptop to close the screen. His words pop up just before it clicks shut.

> HRD4U
>
> Meet me outside.

# 24

FLYNN

I wasn't going to keep messaging her after my simple reply. Not when I didn't know what I wanted to say. I was going to have another drink, pass out, and hope that in the morning, I'd have some clarity I currently lack.

So, I wasn't going to respond to anything else she might have to say tonight.

But then, when I poured my drink, instead of heading back to the bedroom, I found myself drifting to the window. Just to glance over at Rachel's house, as if staring at some inanimate object was going to somehow change the situation.

And through the pouring rain...she was there. Staring right back at me. Like we've done so many other times over the years when we would happen to catch a glimpse of each other.

Only this wasn't a glance. This was the kind of connection that you feel in your soul when you're looking into somebody else's eyes, and even with our side yards between us, I felt it in every fiber of my being. Every part of me was screaming at me to run over there. But I didn't know if that's what she wanted or not.

Then I checked my computer instead of going to bed. I read her words. How she really feels. The confession that went straight to all the parts of me that hurt and have longed for her so badly.

There was only one thing I could do—tell her to meet me outside.

I tug open the door and step out into the cold rain. This isn't the mere drizzle it was before; this is God angry at the world, flood of biblical proportions type of rain. But it can't stop me now.

I don't even know if she responded. All I know is that even being struck by lightning at this moment wouldn't keep me from going over there even if she *doesn't* come out.

But her front door opens, and she steps out into the rain. The white T-shirt she's wearing over tiny sleep shorts soaks through almost instantly, perfectly molding to her body, accentuating every valley and curve I love so much.

I fight against the desire to sweep her up into my arms and ravage her right here and right now.

We meet at the hedge. The same place we discovered what we should've known all along. Where we truly *saw* each other for the first time.

She stares at me, her perfect black eyelashes clinging together, from rain or tears. Her soft, pink lips part, and a gentle rush of breath flows out, visible in the freezing air.

*Christ, she's beautiful.*

All I want to do is take her into my arms, but there's too much to say, too much that can't be skipped over.

I swallow thickly, remembering the words she wrote. "You love me."

She said it in her message, the three words she couldn't say all weekend, the words I kept saying to her, but she

266

couldn't repeat. Even when I pounded into her and made her orgasm more times and harder than she has in her life, they didn't leave her mouth. She just couldn't say it, but for some reason, with the keyboard and internet between us, when she was INEEDSOMED and I was HRD4U, she was finally able to.

That's not good enough, though. I want to hear it from Rachel—from her lips. I want to know it's true and not something she said to try to smooth over the situation. I want *Rachel* to tell *Flynn she loves him.*

She shakes her head. "Of course, I love you. Was that ever in question?"

"I don't mean as your best friend, Rachel. I mean, in the 'I would die for you and forgive you anything because you're the most important thing in my entire fucking world' kind of love—the way I love you."

Tears visible in her eyes trickle out and mix with the falling rain. "Of course, I love you like that, you idiot. Do you think I'd be such a wreck over someone who didn't own my heart and soul?" She fights back a sob and holds out her hands. "I'm so sorry."

"I am, too."

We reach for each other at the same time, her arms wrapping around my neck and mine around her waist to lift her up and over the hedge. Just like the last time, she wraps her legs around me and squeezes as I capture her mouth with mine.

The icy-cold rain cascades around us, but neither of us cares. It may have only been twenty-four hours, yet it feels like an eternity since I held her, since I touched her, since I kissed her. And now that she's finally said the words that I wanted to hear so badly, I'm not ever going to let her go.

It's like every prayer I've ever prayed has been answered in the form of this woman. And she's *mine.*

Time to bring her inside and show her how much I love her properly.

Headlights flash over us from a vehicle that turns onto the street. At this time of night, with the vast majority of the exterior house lights off, it's so dark that I doubt the driver will even see us, but I still freeze in place and pull my mouth away from hers for a second until they pass.

An older Lexus sedan drives slowly down the road, and I turn back to the house to bring Rachel inside. Two steps later, the headlights fall on us again, and I crane my neck around to find the vehicle pulling into my driveway.

*What the hell? Who the fuck is that?*

With the lights directly in my eyes, I can't see the driver.

I set Rachel down reluctantly and cup my hand over my eyes to squint into the windshield. All I manage to make out is an amorphous shape in the driver seat. I glance back over at Rachel. "Maybe someone's lost?"

She shrugs and huddles closer to me, shivering in the cold rain. She has to be freezing by now. Whoever this is needs to get on his way so I can bring her inside and warm her up.

I take a step toward the car.

The door opens, and the driver steps out and to the front of the car. "Flynn McAllister, I've been waiting a long fucking time for this."

Even in the dark, the glint of the headlights off the gun aimed at me blazes like the sun, but I force myself to look away from it into the face of the man pointing it at me. The *familiar* face.

*Oh, fuck!*

I shift to make sure I'm completely covering Rachel. "Mr. Kelly? What are you—"

He waves the gun around while always keeping it pointed in my direction. "You ruined my life, McAllister."

I raise my hands. "Dustin, we can talk about this."

*That's what you're supposed to do, right?*

If somebody threatens you, you use their first name, talk to them calmly, and tell them whatever you need to in order to save your life. At least, that's what every show I've ever seen about these situations says.

"The time for talking is over, McAllister. I tried to tell you. I tried to tell you how my life was falling the fuck apart because of what you did."

The multiple calls. The messages. So many damn messages.

I ignored them, because every time we talked, it was the same damn thing. We had the same conversation over and over, and there was nothing I could change. "Now, Dustin. You knew that investing that much in those stocks was risky. We went over it several times before you made the call to dump into them instead of something more stable. You knew there was a chance this could happen."

He wipes water from his face with one hand while keeping the gun pointed at me with the other. Rachel vibrates behind me, her teeth chattering while she clings to the back of my soaked shirt.

Dustin growls. "Don't try to blame this on me, McAllister. You're the one who convinced me. You're the one who pushed me to put in my money. You're the one who did it all."

*He's fucking nuts.*

I bite my tongue. There's no point in arguing with somebody who's this crazy. Someone who is so delusional they can't even remember what *actually* happened.

He *insisted* on risky investments. He wanted big money *fast*. That only comes with big risks. I never hid anything from him or misrepresented what we were doing. That's not the kind of business I run.

The gun wavers slightly, but he re-centers it on me. "I lost it all because of you. My money. My business. My house and then my fucking wife." He chuckles mirthlessly. The dead hollow sound sends ice through my body. "She took the kids. She said it wasn't safe to be around me anymore." He steps forward and points the gun at me. "And it's all your fucking fault. You're nothing but a whore, seducing people with promises and then fucking them blind."

His anger only appears to be growing as his hold on sanity seems to be slipping further away. It's a recipe for disaster and I'm in the line of fire.

I reach back, unclasp Rachel's hands from my shirt, and step forward toward him. If I'm ever going to get that gun out of his hands, I'm going to have to get closer. "We can fix this, Dustin. You can come to my office, and we'll figure it out."

"There's no fixing it, McAllister. What's done is done. Once I kill you, I'm leaving this fucking world, too."

*Christ. He's suicidal.*

That's never a good sign.

All he can see is his current pain.

I take advance toward him, and he steps into the middle of my driveway, only a few feet away from me. If he fires at this range, even if he isn't a good shot, he'll easily hit me and do some major damage or kill me. "Please, Dustin, we can talk about this."

He snarls at me and strengthens his stance. "Save your talking for the big man upstairs. You're gonna have to answer to Him." He aims the gun squarely at my chest. "Goodbye, Flynn McAllister. May you rot in fucking Hell!"

———

# RACHEL

"You first, asshole."

I swing my makeshift weapon and smash it against the side of his head as hard as I can, channeling everything Bash ever taught me about inflicting the most damage.

It cracks and shatters, sending pieces of plaster across Flynn's driveway. The man with the gun crumples to the ground, and the gun clatters against the cement away from his outstretched hand and toward where Flynn stands stock still with his hands still raised.

Flynn's eyes dart to the weapon, and he kicks it away and closes the few feet between us, pulling me into his arms. "What the fuck, Rachel? What the hell were you thinking? He could have killed you."

He holds me tightly, and I cling to him as he keeps his eyes on the man sprawled out on the driveway with blood trickling from his head. It mixes with the rain and slowly runs down the concrete toward the street.

So much blood.

My vision turns red as I watch it, and my stomach turns violently, bile crawling up my throat.

"Rach?"

I shake my head to clear away the image, swallow thickly, and pull away from Flynn slightly so I can look up at him. "I was thinking that psycho was going to shoot you and that I wasn't going to lose you when I literally *just* got you."

Flynn's hands capture my face, and he kisses me harshly. There's nothing slow or romantic about it. It's desperate and hard, filled with all his panic and passion. He tears his mouth from mine gasping for breath. "Don't *ever* do something so damn stupid again."

Here I just saved his life and he's making demands. "Or what?"

Something sparks in his eyes, a heat I wouldn't expect in a moment like this. "Or I'll bend you over my fucking knee and spank you."

A low heat flares between my legs at his words. "I'm not so sure that's a threat, Flynn."

"Christ, I love you."

He kisses me again, another frantic and needy molding of his mouth to mine, and I fall into him, letting him drag me away from where my mind *wants* to go—to what I just did.

But we can't ignore that reality for long.

Flynn pulls away and bends down to check on the man in the driveway.

I peer over his shoulder. "Who is he?"

Flynn touches the side of the man's neck as the rain picks up even more and thunder rolls through the night air. "A former client of mine. Dustin Kelly. Put a whole lot of money on some very risky stocks and wasn't too happy with the outcome when the market crashed."

"Jesus, so he's the one who has been doing all this?" All the incidents that have happened over the last few weeks, the attacks on Flynn's car, race through my head. "It had nothing to do with the site?"

Flynn shrugs and pushes to his feet. "Apparently not." He turns back to me and rubs his hands on my arms as I shiver in the rain. "Run inside and call 9-1-1. My phone is on the coffee table. He has a weak pulse."

I nod and race past them into his house, my bare feet slapping on the wet wood floor. His laptop sits open next to this phone with our messages on the screen. It's so hard to believe that the site is what brought us together—not once, but twice. We were so stupid to ever let it get between us, even for a moment.

My hands shake, and water drips from my soaked

clothes and pools at my feet. I dial 9-1-1 and make my way back outside.

*"9-1-1, what is your emergency?"*

Flynn rises from his squat over the man and approaches. He urges me back into the foyer of the house and out of the rain. "There's no reason to stand outside and freeze to death. I can't find a pulse anymore."

*What?*

His words replay in my head. *I can't find a pulse anymore...*

"Y-you mean...I k-k-killed him?"

*No.*

*That can't be.*

I hit him, but I was just trying to knock him out. Stop what he was about to do. I didn't think it was going to kill him.

*He can't be dead.*

*He can't be.*

*"Ma'am, what did you say? Do you need police and rescue?"*

Flynn snatches the phone from my hand as I stare out at the body on the driveway, the rain falling around it. So still. No movement.

*Oh, my God.*

*Did I just kill someone?*

"Ma'am, a man just came and threatened me at gunpoint. My girlfriend smashed something over his head to prevent him from shooting me, and now, I think he might be dead on my driveway."

I vaguely hear Flynn's side of the conversation over the rushing of blood in my ears, and I stagger slightly. Flynn wraps an arm around me to steady me, tugging me against his side and pressing his lips to the top of my head.

Flynn listens to the operator and rattles off his address. He shifts me until I'm leaning against the doorjamb for support and steps away, mumbling lowly into the phone, clearly not wanting me to hear whatever he's saying.

Alicia and Cade's door opens across the street, and they both come rushing out.

Cade grabs Alicia by the arm to hold her back halfway across the road. "Rach, what the hell is going on?

"I..." My mouth won't work. I can't even form the words. "I..."

They make their way across the yard and into the foyer, and Alicia pulls me into her arms. The heat of her warm body wrapped around mine doesn't help with the bone-deep chill making me tremble.

Cade rushes past us toward Flynn, but their voices blend together in the background.

Alicia squeezes me. "Are you okay, Rach?"

"I think I just killed that guy...th-that shouldn't have killed him. I-I don't understand..."

She pulls back and glances out the door toward the driveway. "What happened?"

"He-he-he was going to shoot Flynn. I-I didn't have a ch-ch-choice."

Alicia pulls me back into her arms and squeezes me tightly. "Oh, my God. It sounds like you didn't."

I don't know how long she holds me, but eventually, her embrace falls away and another set of warm, familiar arms engulf me. Flynn's soothing scent, mingled with that of fresh rain, fills my lungs, and I inhale deeply and press my face against his soaked chest.

He buries his face against my neck and holds me tightly, lightly pressing his lips to my damp skin. "You saved my life, Rach. You had to do it. Don't feel guilty about doing what you had to do."

*Don't feel guilty...*

It's a strange statement coming from him, someone who

274

seemingly carries it around like an old friend. But somehow, his words calm me, allow me to release some of the panic and tension gripping my body.

I cling to him because I don't think my legs would hold me up right now if I tried to stand on my own, and because he's always been my *rock*. The loss of Mom, then Dad, being out here in California on my own...through *all* of it, he's stood by my side and ensured I always had what I needed. And he's giving me the same now.

Reassurance that I did the right thing.

Confidence that there wasn't any other choice.

Strength to hold it together when I want to completely fall apart.

He pulls back slightly and takes my face between his palms. "What did you hit him with, anyway?"

I swallow through my dry throat. "My garden gnome."

His brow furrows. "What?"

I nod slowly as the events of only a few minutes ago return in a flood of vivid memories. "When you pulled my hands off your shirt and started to walk away from me, I saw where things were going. He was crazed. He wasn't going to stop until you were dead." Tears flow freely down my cheeks. "I backed up slowly, hoping he wouldn't notice because he was so focused on you. And I reached over the hedge and grabbed my gnome, then ran around the back of your house and came up behind him."

"Jesus, Rach." The corner of his mouth twitches. "You fucking MacGyvered that shit."

A laugh that feels totally inappropriate given the situation bubbles between my lips, and I bury my face against his wet shirt again. I don't know how the hell I'm laughing at a time like this, after what I just did. I'm probably in shock and totally losing it, but somehow, standing here in Flynn's arms, I know everything is going to be okay. Eventually.

Somehow, we'll get through this, just like we've made it through everything else over the last five years—together.

Sirens sound in the distance, and Alicia dashes across the street and waits a step inside her front door, watching what's happening. She needs to stay there in case the kids wake with all the commotion, while Cade waves down the approaching squad car.

Flynn walks me to the door to peer out into the rain. The headlights of his attacker's still-running car illuminate his body on the driveway, and I have to turn away and squeeze my eyes closed.

*I did that...*

*You had to. He would have killed Flynn.*

Flynn's arm around my shoulder tightens. "Everything is going to be okay, Rach. You didn't do anything wrong. We'll just tell them our story. It will be all right."

I glance up at him. "You're not going to leave me, are you?"

He presses a kiss to my temple and squeezes me to him. "Never. You're stuck with me for life."

The words we've said to each other so many times before in jest, in reference to our friendship, mean something else now. Something deeper.

For me. For Flynn.

For INEEDSOMED and for HRD4U.

For us together.

Whatever comes in the future, my filthy friend will be by my side, walking the same path, carrying me when I need it, because that's what we do for each other and aways will.

# EPILOGUE
## ONE MONTH LATER

**RACHEL**

Flynn kisses his way up my neck, his hand slowly inching its way across my stomach toward my breasts, raising goosebumps everywhere he touches. "You're sure you want to do this?"

I arch into him and turn my head to press my lips to his. The familiar sweet taste of his favorite bourbon coats my tongue, and I groan and bury my hands in his hair to hold him in place.

He returns my kiss, pressing his hard cock against my hip and pinching my nipple before giving it a sharp twist.

*Just the way I like it.*

In the last month, he's spent countless hours learning every inch of my body, exploring what I like and what I *love*, what makes me go absolutely feral for him. And it doesn't take much. Once I was completely at his mercy, it became abundantly clear that he could give me everything I need—and more.

But his playful hands are fogging my brain and making it impossible to formulate a verbal response to his important question. With a groan, I drag myself away from his reach, and I can't fight the grin pulling at my lips for what we're about to do.

"I'm sure."

It's been a long time coming.

At least, it feels that way.

In the grand scheme of life, four weeks is just a blink of an eye, but so much has happened, so much has changed, that it's impossible to believe so little time has passed.

Each day has been a whirlwind and not always in a good way. Between dealing with the police in the aftermath of that night, explaining everything to Flynn's mother—minus the HRD4U information—and Dan—who was thankfully very understanding—and my having to tell Jameson and Bash that I killed someone, there hasn't been a lot of relaxation or peace happening in my life. Save for my time alone with Flynn like this.

It's the only thing that's got me through.

Taking someone's life is something I may never fully get over, but the fact that he was trying to kill Flynn and that an underlying medical issue led to the blow killing him so easily has helped me live with the guilt easier than I had anticipated. And having Flynn to come home to every night and wake up with every day is the soothing balm my soul needs.

Flynn is, without a doubt, my other half. The fact that I could've been so blind still makes me question my own sanity sometimes. But in the end, we found each other and we found something neither of us thought existed—our own happily ever after.

Which is why I said "*yes*" when I never thought I could.

It's why there's a camera focused on the bed right now.

It's why we're about to make a damn sex tape.

I never fathomed this being a possibility, that I would

ever *want* to do it, but Flynn was right. The idea of people watching us *does* turn me on. And once Flynn assured me of all the safeguards we would take to protect our identities, I knew it was what we needed to start fresh.

To release all the things that held us back and pushed us down over the last few weeks.

To say goodbye to all the doubts and insecurities.

To really find *us*.

We aren't HRD4U and INEEDSOMED, but we aren't the same Flynn and Rachel we were before, either. Things have morphed and changed in ways we never could have anticipated. It's a whole new world, and we're whole new people.

Now that the investigation into Dustin Kelly's death is over and everything has finally started settling down, this is what we both need desperately. And the way Flynn's been working over my body for the last half an hour, prepping me and toying with me as only he can, has me practically vibrating with need underneath him.

He kisses his way down my neck, across my breasts, stopping to lick my nipples and blow lightly over them, making me twitch. His lips continue their descent of my body, each press against my heated skin ratchets me tighter and tighter. This kind of long, drawn-out foreplay isn't really the norm. Flynn and I both prefer things hard and fast, but when we slow everything down, when we really put off the main event until we can't take it anymore, the result is the most mind-bending sex I've ever had. And that's saying a lot, considering the things Flynn has done to me in the last month.

His lips hover just above the apex of my thighs, his warm breath fluttering against my skin, sending a shiver of anticipation through me. He raises an eyebrow. "You're one hundred percent sure?"

I bury my fingers in his thick hair and tug. "If you don't

fuck me hard and good in the next five minutes, you're going to be in real trouble."

Flynn smirks at me, the lecherous grin I've learned over the last several weeks means he's about to do something really fucking filthy to me.

Heat floods my core, and I shift under him, pressing my body against his in a way that tells him I'm more than ready to go.

He shifts back up over me and kisses me deeply, his tongue tangling with mine greedily. "Then, let's do this thing, babe." He grabs the small remote control for the video camera from the nightstand and hits record. "Here we go."

With the voice distortion software he uses for the website, we won't have to worry about anyone recognizing us. And with the camera angled to avoid our faces, we'll remain completely anonymous. Even if we lose control and flash something we shouldn't, we can also put blurs over anything we don't want seen. Recording it rather than doing it live provides numerous levels of protection, and if we watch the video and I don't want it played after seeing it, we'll toss it into the trash.

Though, I think it's more likely to end up in his private stash.

Flynn shifts slightly to give the camera a better view of his hard-on—the *star* of the show. "Good evening to all my viewers. It's been a while. You probably thought I had permanently abandoned you or that something bad happened to me, but I assure you, it's quite the opposite. Tonight's going to be a very special, one-time only farewell show. I wasn't sick or out of town or anything like that. Why haven't I been online?" One of his hands slips under my chin to tilt my face up so he can press a light kiss to my lips. "Because I fell in love. Actually, I've been in love with

280

her for years, but it turns out she loves me, too. Which is even better. So, as a final farewell, I wanted to let you see how much I love her. And I want to remind you that you can have anything you want in life if you believe in it enough. Tonight's show won't be live just in case our camera positioning slips or one of us accidentally says a real name, but I promise when I post this, both of us will be online to chat with you as you watch." He pauses for a moment and stares deeply into my eyes, the blue of his darkening. "You have no idea how much I've enjoyed being HRD4U, but once this video has posted, I won't be him anymore..."

He grins at me.

The viewers won't be able to see it.

It's mine and *only* mine.

Forever.

He feathers his fingers across my wet core, then strokes his cock. "Because I'm no longer hard for *you*. I'm hard for *her* and her only. Enjoy the show."

Even though I knew what he was going to say—at least the first part—his words still bring tears to my eyes. It wasn't even anything we talked about again, him giving up the site, and I genuinely would've been okay if he wanted to continue it.

But this is the best possible resolution.

I get to selfishly keep Flynn all to myself, and he gets what he wants—the two of us on video with the world watching. Given how hard his cock is pressing against me right now, he's more than ready to go.

We haven't exactly discussed the plan. I figured we'd just start the way we normally do, with him jamming his dick into me so deeply that I lose my breath, but instead of settling over me like I'm expecting or ordering me to my hands and knees or to the edge of the bed to bend over, he rolls onto his back and brings me with him to straddle his lap.

His cock stands straight up and rubs against my clit. I grind against it and roll my hips, shooting little zings of electric need through me.

His hands tighten on my hips. "That's it, babe. I want you to fuck me hard. Take whatever you need because it sure looks like you could use some *D*."

———

## FLYNN

*And I can't wait to be buried inside her.*

After kissing, sucking, licking, and touching every inch of Rachel leading up to the start of this video, I'm already hovering on the brink of a very embarrassing early eruption. Something I've never done on camera, let alone with a woman.

But she's different.

Rachel is everything warm, good, and right in this world. She blazes so brightly, there are times I fear she'll burn me. And a huge part of me believes I don't deserve her. But that's mostly the Catholic guilt I can't seem to shake eating away at me. Though, it's been a lot easier to attend church with Mom now that Rach and I are together and she comes with me.

It's almost like finding Rachel and having her love absolved me of my sins.

Christ on the crucifix doesn't stare down in judgment anymore. He sees us and has an almost sly smile on his painted-on lips. Like he's been waiting for this. And Father Lafayette's sermons have steered away from topics that seemed to be directed at me since he started seeing Rachel by my side.

There's absolutely no reason to feel guilty about what we're doing tonight.

And I don't.

It's the culmination of everything it took to get us here. It's a goodbye to HRD4U and INEEDSOMED and a formal hello to the *new* and far improved Flynn and Rachel, the couple being dirty together—forever.

Rachel wraps her hand around the base of my dick and strokes it slowly as she rubs the head against her wet clit.

"Christ, babe." I dig my fingers into the flesh of her hips. "Don't toy with me. Sit down on my fucking cock right now."

Her green eyes flare at my command, and she eases herself up and positions me at her wet core. After the way I've been working her over, she's practically dripping down my length, so fucking ready for me. With her eyes locked on mine, a little grin curling her perfect pink lips, she lowers herself down in one smooth movement, burying me to the hilt.

"Fuck, babe." I grit my jaw to keep from blowing my load inside her on the spot. "Your cunt is so hot, so fucking tight..."

She clenches around me like a vise, eliciting a groan from somewhere deep inside my chest. Rachel on top is better than any other position. Watching her take control and what she wants from me makes me hotter than fucking her any other way.

Her breasts swaying with her movement.

Her head tipped back slightly.

The way she pulls her bottom lip between her teeth as she rides me frantically.

I smack her ass, the sharp sound of my palm striking her

ass filling the room for a second. "Do that again! Squeeze my damn cock as you fuck me."

She clamps down hard again, and a jolt of pleasure shoots up my spine and tingles through my arms. Like this, fully seated inside her, I can't even imagine a time when we weren't together. Everything *before* is a black void where life wasn't truly living.

*This* is living.

Rachel leans forward and pushes her lips to mine hungrily while she grinds down and around on me, keeping me deeply imbedded in her hot cunt.

*Fuck. Fuck. Fuck.*

My body screams for her to rise up, to move, to glide along my length so the head of my cock can catch on that perfect spot inside her that drives both of us crazy. But she's in control tonight.

I force myself to take the torture of her gyrating hips and the grind of her pelvis against mine. Tipping my head back, I groan and tighten my grip on her hips.

Instead of continuing to toy with me, like she can so easily do in this position, where she has almost complete control, the woman takes mercy on me and raises herself up to slam back down on me hard.

"Fuck, yes!" I squeeze my eyes closed because as much as I want to watch her fucking me, the sheer pleasure of knowing she's finally all mine and is willingly doing this with me is almost too much to contain. I'm fucking terrified I'm going to cry if I have to look at her while she does this.

It wouldn't be the first time she's brought me to tears, and it certainly won't be the last...

The roll and flex of her hips in perfect rhythm steals my breath, and she presses her hands against my chest and digs her nails into my flesh.

*Fuck!*

A tiny sting. The bite of her scraping away at my skin. It's enough to almost have me shoot off inside her. I open my eyes and meet her wild gaze. "Dig your fucking nails into me, babe. Make me fucking hurt."

She groans and redoubles her efforts, her long caramel hair swirling around her with every movement, her fingernails biting into me hard enough to probably draw blood.

But I don't give a fucking damn.

Rachel could brand me with her name for everyone in the fucking world to see, and I'd be happy.

All I care about is her getting off.

I trail a hand off her hip and down between us, and my thumb finds her clit. She jerks, and I roll and press against it as she rides me, her head dropped back, mouth falling open with her gasp. I dig my heels into the mattress to give myself more leverage and thrust up into her at the new angle as she comes down.

Her eyes fly open. "Oh, yeah, baby. Right there! Harder!"

I drive into her, trying to give her exactly what she needs. The head of my cock drags against her G-spot, and she groans, her rhythm faltering. I pinch her clit, and she gasps, her body jerking, pussy clutching at me with her release.

Rachel during orgasm is the most fucking beautiful thing I've ever seen. And watching her come undone is the ultimate push over the edge.

"I'm so fucking close to coming. I'm ready to shoot my load inside you, babe."

The quivering pulses of her pussy slow, and she sags down for a second as I continue to brace my feet and pump up into her. But she pushes down with her knees to halt my movements and plants her palms flat against my chest.

Something wicked gleams in her eyes, and she shifts back, letting my hard, straining cock slide out of her. "You're not coming inside me tonight."

*What the hell?*

This is some time for her to suddenly become dominant. She's been getting better about voicing what she wants without embarrassment, but the way her eyes are shimmering with mischief and lust right now, she's definitely up to something.

She swallows thickly and scoots back between my legs.

*What is she doing?*

The camera sits to our left, angled to cover the bed but not too high. I can blur out anything we may not want it to catch, a fact Rachel must remember because she drops her head and flips her hair to the side, completely exposing her face—and giving the best view of what she's about to do—before she lowers herself down. "I want to taste myself on your cock and drink your cum tonight."

*Oh, sweet mother of God.*

*And here I thought I was the filthy one.*

I may have created a monster, but one of the best kind.

"That's the sexiest thing I've heard come out that sweet fucking mouth of yours, babe."

In response, she sucks me into her warm mouth in one smooth motion and moans around me.

*Sweet fucking hell!*

If I thought her pussy felt good tonight, it has nothing on what she's doing now. Sucking, licking, flicking her tongue over the head of my cock.

She's a woman on a mission. One I can definitely get behind.

And the tingle at the base of my spine tells me things have reached that critical stage. "Fuck, babe. I'm gonna come." Her groan of approval around my flesh unleashes my orgasm like a tidal wave. "Yeah...fuck...suck it all down. Swallow every fucking drop of my cum."

She sucks me so deep, the head of my dick brushes

against the back of her throat with the last spurt, and she swallows, the muscles massaging the aching flesh.

I sag onto the bed.

*Jesus fucking Christ.*

Rachel hums around me, sending another little jolt through me, and she gazes at me with pure fire in her eyes.

Seeing her with my cock shoved down her throat after she just did that to me is the single hottest thing I've ever experienced in my life.

I push myself up, slip my hands under her arms, and drag her up across my trembling body. Her lips, swollen from the fucking magic she just performed on my cock, are too incredible to resist. I capture her mouth with mine, devouring every fucking ounce of her, the taste of my release still dancing on her tongue.

When she finally pulls away and rests her forehead against mine, our rapidly beating hearts pressed against each other, there isn't any doubt it's the perfect time.

I stretch to reach into the side table drawer and grab the box I've been hiding from her for the last week. Her eyes widen, and her hand flies to cover her mouth. I grab her wrist and pull it away, but tears well in her eyes.

"Don't cry." I brush the tears away with my free hand and press under her chin to tilt her face up to mine. "I don't want to waste any more time. We've wasted too much as it is." I flip open the box, and the solitaire diamond ring glitters in the overhead lights. "Will you marry me?"

Her tears fall in earnest now. There's no way to stop them. Her lips tremble, and for one brief second, she opens her mouth and nothing comes out.

She swallows and nods. "Yes, you're stuck with me forever."

"Fuck, yes, I am!" I seize her mouth in a soul-searing

kiss, giving her my breath and taking hers all at once. When I finally force myself to pull away, we're both panting.

I pull the ring from the box and slide it onto her shaking hand. "By the way, this isn't going on the site. This is just for *us*. I think I'll cut the video right after that cataclysmic orgasm you just gave me."

She chuckles and presses her forehead to mine again. "I'm sorry I didn't let you come inside me."

I jerk back. "Holy hell! You think I'm *mad* about that? That was the single hottest thing that's ever happened in my fucking life. Besides"—I shift under her, pressing my hard cock against her hip—"I'm already hard for you again."

---

I HOPE you enjoyed *Fabulous Filthy Friend.* The Fury Family Series continues in *Sinfully Shameless Chef,* Jameson Fury's steamy rivals to lovers story!

Get your copy: books2read.com/ SinfullyShamelessChef

To stay up to date on news, sales, and releases from Gwyn, join her newsletter here: www.gwynmcnamee. com/newsletter

# ABOUT THE AUTHOR

Gwyn McNamee is an attorney, writer, wife, and mother (to one human baby and two fur babies). Originally from the Midwest, Gwyn relocated to her husband's home town of Las Vegas in 2015 and is enjoying her respite from the cold and snow. Gwyn loves to write stories with a bit of suspense and action mingled with romance and heat. When she isn't either writing or voraciously devouring any books she can get her hands on, Gwyn is busy adding to her tattoo collection, golfing, and stirring up trouble with her perfect mix of sweetness and sarcasm (usually while wearing heels).

Website: http://www.gwynmcnamee.com/

Facebook: https://www.facebook.com/AuthorGwynMcNamee/

FB Reader Group: https://www.facebook.com/groups/1667380963540655/

Tiktok: https://www.tiktok.com/@authorgwynmcnamee

Newsletter: www.gwynmcnamee.com/newsletter

Instagram: https://www.instagram.com/gwynmcnamee

Bookbub: https://www.bookbub.com/authors/gwynmcnamee

Made in the USA
Monee, IL
15 September 2023

42745084R00164